She Stopped for Death

She Stopped for Death

A Little Library Mystery

Elizabeth Kane Buzzelli

CROOKED
LANE

NEW YORK

Published in the United States by Crooked Lane Books, an imprint of The Quick Brown Fox & Company LLC.

Crooked Lane Books and its logo are trademarks of The Quick Brown Fox & Company LLC.

Library of Congress Catalog-in-Publication data available upon request.

ISBN (hardcover): 978-1-68331-013-6
ISBN (ePub): 978-1-68331-014-3
ISBN (Kindle): 978-1-68331-015-0
ISBN (ePDF): 978-1-68331-016-7

Cover design by Matthew Kalamidas/StoneHouse Creative.
Book design by Jennifer Canzone.

Printed in the United States.

www.crookedlanebooks.com

Crooked Lane Books
34 West 27th St., 10th Floor
New York, NY 10001

First Edition: January 2017

10 9 8 7 6 5 4 3 2 1

Sweet is the swamp with its secrets,
Until we meet a snake;
'Tis then we sigh for houses,
And our departure take
At that enthralling gallop
That only childhood knows.
A snake is summer's treason,
And guile is where it goes.

Emily Dickinson

Chapter 1

In Bear Falls, Michigan, summer lay like hot lead over the shops along Oak Street. It was August, and it was a Saturday night. The stores had emptied out a while ago. The heavy air smudged the neon *Closed* signs of Harrington's Drugstore, Trixie's House of Beauty, Laymen Brothers Hardware, the US post office, Suzy Q's Bakery, Sally's Florist, and Townsend's Antiques and dimmed the running marquee of the Falls movie house, where the last show had already let out. Even the mysterious Myrtle Lambert had locked the door to her restaurant by now and, holding onto her ever-present, floppy green hat, started off down Oak toward her home on Pine Street, muttering as she walked about something terrible in the hot air. "Something awful, for sure," she whispered to herself, then wondered, as she loped along, if she had enough vanilla for the French toast in the morning.

The summer tourists who came in flocks to see the waterfall in Cane Park were gone for the day. The dark shadow of the park's lone statue fell over beds of roses and petunias. The statue seemed taller and more ominous at night than during the day, when it looked like what it was: the likeness of a slightly dumpy town father.

Down Oak Street, north of the shops, the imposing dowager Abigail Cane bid her dinner guests good-bye and shut the massive doors of her Victorian mansion against the growing wind. She leaned toward her new secretary, the pretty and highly capable Elizabeth Wheatley, and said she thought the dinner with the town council went very well.

The objective of her late-dinner parties was to convince the town politicians that it was time to pull the bronze commemorative statue of her father, Joshua Cane, from Cane Park, melt it down, and turn it into something of more value: a pile of cannonballs, sewer grates, or maybe ornate restroom signs with bronze branches and flowers outlining *Men* and *Women*.

She smiled as she pictured his statue coming down, its bronze head rolling, the arms coming off with soul-tearing cracks. She lived the imagined moment again and again as she sat through those endless dinners, persuading council members to give up the man's ugly gift. And she lived for the day that she would proudly point to the ladies' room sign as all that was left of Joshua Cane—or perhaps it would be the sewer grates, or the stack of cannonballs, whatever it took to get rid of the man.

"One more dinner party," Abigail said to Elizabeth as she sighed, then unclasped her diamond necklace and let it slither down to her open hand. She yawned. "And then we'll throw a party for the entire town. We'll sing and dance. How my father hated parties."

Elizabeth, already a friend to Abigail after only two months, nodded. "I'll take care of everything if you'll tell me what you would like."

Abigail clapped her hands softly. "A celebration for the people of Bear Falls. And a celebration of art, because he hated art the way he hated every expression of the human spirit."

She clapped her hands again. "And I know just the thing. Our own hometown poet, Emily Sutton. Her first book of poetry was praised. And then she came home and never left that house over on Pewee Swamp. But, of course, she's been forgotten now by all but a few of us." Abigail thought hard. "As Joshua falls, so Emily Sutton shall be raised. We'll have a continuous reading. Everyone doing their share. Her poetry will fill the air!"

Elizabeth gave her usually controlled employer an odd look. "Don't you want work by a more famous poet? I mean, work that resonates today? We could read Carl Sandburg: 'I tell you the past is a bucket of ashes, / so live not in your yesterdays, nor just for tomorrow, but in the here and now. / Keep moving and forget the post mortems.'" Elizabeth smiled broadly at the line—it could save a person's life. "From what you've told me of your father, it seems somehow fitting."

Abigail shook her head. She didn't want the obvious. She wanted Emily Sutton, whose poetry had stayed with her through the worst of Joshua's cruelties.

"You don't know," she almost whispered. "Emily knew who we were. I was in my twenties when her book came out. I was shy. Father made fun of my height, of my full figure, of my nose that was too large. He had a comment for every part of my body and expressed them all in front of everyone. Through most of my twenties, I wanted to die. And then I read her book, and this line that stayed in my head: 'Down to dark phantasms, entailing trespass in the brave. / In boots and stick, sent flying by the slither of a snake.'

"Father was that snake. I was the one sent flying, though I was brave inside. In her words I found hope for myself. I wasn't alone."

"Then we will read the work of your wonderful Emily Sutton." Elizabeth smiled and dipped her head, bringing her well-cut blonde hair down over her eyes. "Would she attend, do you think?"

Abigail thought awhile. "How I wish. But I doubt it. Too many years spent in that house with her sister, Lorna. The mother's tragically gone. An accident so terrible . . ."

"Then we'll read her poems anyway. We'll read them again and again. A marathon of Emily Sutton's poetry to chase evil from the park."

And their plan was set in motion, though neither woman could have imagined the long, dark path ahead of them.

* * *

Out in his woodworking shop, Tony Ralenti stretched, then bent to rub his knee where a bullet had entered a few years back, when he was a detective on the Detroit police force. He yawned, looked down at his watch, and found it was almost eleven. Too late to call Jenny and wish her good-night—it might disturb Dora, her mother. He missed Jenny's voice, something he felt more and more often. He needed to see her, talk to her, be with her. It wasn't what he'd expected, moving here to Bear Falls. He didn't expect to meet anyone like Jenny Weston and was afraid to hope, even now, that his life could turn out to be different from what it was.

He snapped off the light in the shop, leaving the new Little Library house he was building behind him. The house was a replica of one of Dora Weston's Little Libraries, which were set on posts in front of her house on Elderberry Street. Her curbside libraries were a huge success in town, and the rules were simple: take a book, leave a book. Now the idea was spreading across Michigan, from small town to small town, bringing books to everybody who lived where there were no municipal libraries. Due to the high demand, Tony had started building the houses. Many people wanted a replica of their house and sent him photographs. Others only asked for a receptacle that was strong and kept out rain and snow. For those, he used the plans for Dora's two Little Libraries: Adults and Children.

He shut the door to the workshop and took his time walking across the grass through the humid August night. He swatted moths hanging around his porch light then heard the faint ringing of the phone inside. He hurried, nursing his bad leg up the porch steps, all the while hoping it was Jenny.

It wasn't.

It wasn't anyone he wanted to hear from.

* * *

In the dark, a shadowy figure stood in front of the old field-stone house on Thimbleberry Street. She bent to open the crooked gate, held still, and listened to the noises coming

5

from Pewee Swamp. Night birds gave strange cries before settling into nests built in tangled trees. Animals the woman never could put names to gave soft grunts, then screams, as they fought off predators. Everything went quiet as she waited until the wind, blowing in from Lake Michigan, stirred the hemlocks into making an odd sighing sound. The wind got stronger. A dead limb crashed into the swamp.

Satisfied that all was well with her familiar world, the dark figure arranged the bonnet atop her head and, with a flashlight in hand, looked anxiously over her shoulder at the draped windows of the old house.

She stepped through the gate, clicking it closed behind her, and breathlessly began her unaccustomed walk in the warm night air.

* * *

Miles away, in another town, a woman sat in the front seat of her car in a closed garage. She stared straight ahead, out the car's front window, though she saw nothing. Flies buzzed around her head. She didn't see them, didn't hear them, and didn't mind them. She never had, not in all the days of the weeks she'd been sitting there, watching nothing.

Chapter 2

The wind from the swamp didn't reach Elderberry Street, where Dora Weston, her daughter, Jenny, and their neighbor, Zoe Zola, along with Zoe's small, one-eyed dog, Fida, rocked and fanned themselves in the thickening dark of the Westons' screened porch. From time to time the women remarked how there were fewer moths tonight, then talked about the heat and how they hoped a breeze would find them and the mosquitoes wouldn't. They wiped sweat from their faces, drank tall glasses of iced tea, and spoke in whispers while waiting for something to happen.

By ten thirty, the scratching, piercing calls of mating cicadas had quieted. Fireflies, pinpricks in the darkness, slowed their circles and disappeared. Families up and down Elderberry shut their doors, and soon only a single child's dream-cry broke the quiet.

Dora Weston sighed and slowed her rocking. "I swear she's been here the last two Saturdays in a row. I hope she comes tonight."

The other two yawned and continued waiting with her.

There'd been an orange moon. Truly big and round and deeply orange. The kind of moon that gives you a feeling of something strange going on around you. But then the breeze died, a mist moved in from the lake, and the orange moon disappeared. That had been something to talk about while it lasted, but now there was little left to say. A starless sky. Thickening air that predicted rain during the night. Zoe briefly fell asleep with Fida snoring on her lap. Jenny thought about her childhood bed at the back of the house. Dora hummed softly to herself.

At first, when the women came out to sit and wait, there'd been talk of what could happen if the figure appeared, then talk of whether it was the right night or if rain might stop her.

"Saturday," Dora said in a voice she reserved for dark places, where awkward things came out when one spoke too loudly.

"It could be anybody." Jenny yawned and thought fondly of her bed again. What bothered her most about waiting wasn't that some odd poet might or might not show up but that she hadn't heard from Tony.

"No." Dora's whisper was emphatic. "I thought about that. I even worried it was somebody fooling around out there that first night. You know how bad it was when Johnny Arlen broke my library box, and we had to start over. New books. *Two* new boxes. But then I just knew—it was Emily Sutton. Don't ask me how. Who else would sneak over here at night? I'm positive. Probably coming after poetry books and, wouldn't you know it, I've got nothing of any real value in the box. No Emily Dickinson. No Sylvia Plath."

Zoe moved in her big chair. Her short legs, sticking straight out in front of her, were cramped. "Maybe you should have called to her," she suggested, stretching her legs and arms and yawning. "Could be she just wants company."

Zoe Zola, a little person with a huge personality and an even larger talent as a writer of books on fairy tales and famous writers, lived next door to the Westons in a pretty white bungalow with a red door and many gardens. The garden beds were big and passionate, with brightly colored flowers. Nested in among the daisies and the roses were fairy houses of all sizes—castles to caves. In or near each house, a fairy peeked from behind mullioned windows or danced down a pebbled lane. One hid behind an old mill. A golden-haired fairy sat at a castle window, looking out. Others gathered around a cold fire pit, while still others peeked from a rocky cave.

"Emily Sutton? Heavens no. I would have scared her, and myself, too, if I'd hollered."

"But Mom, how can you be so sure it's her?" Jenny Weston rocked and thought she'd be better off looking over a Little Library house plan Tony Ralenti had dropped off that morning, wanting her opinion. She was beginning to imagine it wasn't her opinion he wanted as much as to see her and talk to her. For the most part, she refused to think about that, or hope for anything. She wasn't good at love. She'd had enough strikeouts now to know better than to hope she had a place in the game.

"I watched her walk away," Dora said. "I didn't have a clue who it was that first night. I knew it wasn't a teenager though. It was a woman. Small statured, you know. She had a skirt on, ankle-length. I thought that was funny for

August. And there was something draped over her head."
Dora stopped rocking, waking Fida, who stretched, jumped
down, then made her way to Dora, then to Jenny, sniff-
ing them to make sure things hadn't changed while she
slept. "Can you think of anybody else in Bear Falls who
would dress like that? I'm sure it's Emily Sutton. How
I would love to meet her. She was quite a famous poet for a
while, you know. Had a well-reviewed book of poems out
and traveled the country giving readings. That was before
we moved here—at least twenty-five years or more ago, I'd
say. Abigail Cane told me the story. Said one day Emily
came back to town and disappeared into that house down
on Pewee Swamp with her sister, Lorna, and her mother
and almost never came out again. As if she fell off the face
of the earth, it was. Then there was that awful fire."

"Humph, never heard of her." Zoe Zola pushed to
the front of her rocker. "And I would say that I, of all people, would know the poets."

"Only if they wrote ages ago," Jenny teased, because she
knew Zoe's love for Lewis Carroll, L. Frank Baum, Emily
Dickinson, and P. L. Travers.

"That's not true. I'm very much up to date."

"Name one modern poet," Jenny challenged her, as
much out of boredom as from interest.

"Robert Creeley. 'He wants to be a brutal old man . . .' I
met him at the Vermont Studio Center when I was just out
of high school. A writers' retreat in Johnson, Vermont. He
seemed very sad. I remember, at the end of our workshop,
he said he enjoyed my company." She sniffed and waited a
minute for a response to her bit of name-dropping. When
Dora and Jenny gave her silence back, she slipped from her

chair to the floor with a thump, reached down to scoop up Fida, and said she was going home since nothing was going to happen there that night.

"You can't leave," Dora protested.

"I'm tired, Dora, and I've got the manuscript of my *Two Alices: Adventures in Madness and Murder* to e-mail off tomorrow. I promised Christopher Morley. He'll be tapping that watch of his at a great rate if the day goes on and he gets nothing from me. I know you don't like fantasy, Jenny, but I would swear my editor is the White Rabbit himself."

"Just a while longer, Zoe," Dora begged. "I don't want her frightened away. I'd like to walk down and speak to her. I hope she won't mind if I say a quiet hello."

"All right." Zoe leaned back against the rocker. "I just don't see the reason for excitement. She's probably not the one you think she is anyway. And Dora, you know I'm not one to throw cold water on anybody's thrills, but I've been smelling a foul odor all day. And you know what that means."

"Garbage day," Jenny said, enjoying bursting Zoe's fanciful bubble. "Bob was late picking up."

"Humph," was all Zoe answered, not used to having her uncanny nose for trouble brushed aside.

* * *

The first inkling that something was happening came with flashes of dim light along the street. Flashlight flashes, mostly pointed at the sidewalk, but from time to time sent out to the street, or to the bushes and trees lining front lawns, as if the person behind the light was nervous, keeping an eye out for dogs or cats or rabid raccoons.

"Mom," Jenny was the first to notice. "Look!"

"I see her," Dora whispered back.

Zoe, holding still, mumbled, "So! We get to meet the Dodo Bird."

Dora hushed her and they watched silently as the light came up the street, stopping at Dora's Little Libraries. They could hear the hinged top of one house open, saw the light flash inside, and then minutes went by without another sound.

Dora got up quietly from her chair. She pushed the screen door open and stepped out to the top of the steps.

Jenny and Zoe watched her in shadow as she stood still a moment, then moved down to the walk. Dora's sturdy body—black against the night—went stealthily toward the light still moving at the library box.

They heard Dora's voice say simply, "Good evening, Miss Sutton."

That was all.

The top of the box clapped shut. The flashlight turned away. The odd woman ran off up the street.

Chapter 3

The next day at 403 Elderberry Street began as Sundays there always began. Dora was off to church while Jenny lolled in her single bed, back in her childhood room, a room filled with childish things in childish sizes she hadn't gotten around to throwing out. She meant to, if she stayed at home much longer and didn't get her butt moving and find a job and a new place to live. If she didn't quit acting like a coward, staying here with her mom after the awful divorce from Ronald Korman. She mumbled something under her breath about a thirty-something woman who didn't have the backbone of a jellyfish and let a rotten, two-timing husband knock the stuffing out of her.

She kicked the teddy bear sheet off the bed and thought about taking her Bon Jovi poster down. She would replace the thin, matching teddy bear quilt and sheets. Paint the walls and buy pretty linens. But that was like saying she would stay at home for the rest of her life. Get herself a couple of cats she'd dress in matching outfits. Buy a gardening hat and ten boxes of tea she would steep in a delicate silver tea ball.

Anyway, she didn't like shopping. Except for that one time. Back in Chicago.

She and Ronald were newly married. A new apartment. She'd shopped for days, picking out fluffy towels and flowered sheets and basket-weave blankets and wildly colorful rugs and gold-edged dishes and on and on and on until she'd worn herself out and her last purchase had been a cheese grater shaped like a lady in a paisley skirt.

Ronald hated all of it. He made a snide remark the first night in the new apartment about being married to a hick from northern Michigan, which dimmed the joy she'd taken in their new things and dimmed the joy she'd taken in her new home. And maybe started to dim the joy she'd taken in her Chicago-lawyer husband.

The apartment had been too spare, not one damned floral teapot in the whole place. The furniture he ordered was all big, chunky pieces, cheaply made. And reproductions of modern sculptures were set on faux marble pedestals in every corner of the living room. Ronald trained bright ceiling lights down on his choices, masking every quality the work might have had with terrible shadows. A blank, modern painting hung—always a little crooked—over the huge sofa. The side chairs were all sticks—and not the Stickley kind of sticks. The apartment embarrassed her, although she wasn't sure why she had the right to be embarrassed. It was just that something was missing. When she walked in it was never like walking into her own home. She saw it on people's faces when Ronald showed them through the five rooms, then poured mediocre wines as the guests, mostly his employees, were made to *ooh* and *aah* over everything but her cheese grater lady—though two women did, proclaiming the grater "darling."

It was never a matter of money, his penuriousness. It was more a matter of his needs. He explained again and again that he had to dress well. And "After all, Jenny," he'd said more than once, eventually setting her teeth on edge, "I'm not only your husband. I'm your boss. I have larger needs than you." Which made her bite her lip hard enough to hurt. Maybe it wasn't the apartment that bothered her at all but that she had become another one of his inexpensive possessions, one that needed to be told how to dress and act and stick her nose in the air. And by the way, "take care of me in bed," he would have added if he'd dared.

She shuddered and rolled over. Her feet fell off the end of the bed. Her arm hit the wall beside her, making one corner of the yellowed Bon Jovi poster come loose. The poster flapped and dropped dust balls on her head.

What she didn't want to think about too deeply was how upset her mother had been last night. Poor Mom. Standing there watching as that woman went flying up the street. Then walking up the steps with a hand over her mouth, tears running down her face.

"What did I do?" Dora'd whispered as she hurried past Jenny and Zoe, into the house and into her bedroom, where she closed the door and wouldn't answer when Jenny knocked.

Jenny pulled clothes out of drawers and hunted under the bed for her sneakers. She was mad at herself for not getting up before Mom left for church. She should have been in the kitchen, saying things to make Mom feel better, instead of cowering in bed with a teddy bear sheet over her head.

She always ran from trouble now, wanting life as smooth as a pane of glass. No cracks to fall into. Nothing threatening to blow her fragile ego into pieces.

Her robe lay on the floor of the closet and had warped into a ball of terrycloth that required a good shake and a check for spiders before she could put it on. *Drudge*, she thought and tightened the belt tighter than necessary around her waist. Who could she blame for how she'd turned out?

"I don't run from trouble," she assured her reflection in the dressing table mirror. "Just . . . just . . . I don't go looking for it." Which made her think of Lisa the Good, her younger sister, a filmmaker in Montana now, who always knew the right thing to say and do and made the people— all people—around her feel better about themselves.

There was one good thing in Jenny's interim life. Tony Ralenti. Well, not really in her life, but hovering at the edges the way a man does before zeroing in—if a woman lets him. If a woman could get over a lot of the things she had to get over first. Before she could trust again.

She heard the back door open and close. Mom coming back from church. Or Zoe Zola climbing up on a chair to sit with Fida, her feminist dog, at her feet. Zoe, with a hundred and one things to say about everything that existed in this world and also in that odd imaginary world where Zoe lived all by herself.

Jenny smelled the coffee. She had to get out there and face whatever the day was going to bring. First the bathroom, then back to dress—clean underwear, even if the bra was old and the underpants holey; a pair of white shorts; a yellow T-shirt with *Save the Planet* on it, faded but serviceable; those way-off-white sneakers—then down the hall to cheer up Dora's day.

Poor Mom. She'd once been a librarian until she married Jim Weston and moved to this small Michigan town without a library. How she loved literature and people who read books. Her greatest joy was the Little Library Jim surprised her with on their twenty-first anniversary. That was six months before he was killed in an accident out on the highway between Traverse City and Charlevoix, out where the pot-holed side road that led to Bear Falls ended.

Jim was a traveling salesman with a line of farm equipment. He'd brought Dora to Bear Falls to live because the town was at the center of his territory, which stretched from Grand Rapids to the Mackinac Bridge. He had promised Dora that he would do something about the no-library situation. And he did on that last anniversary, with the Little Library box that he'd built to look exactly like their green-and-white house with the brick chimney at one end, two dormers, and a screened porch running across the front.

When she got to the kitchen, it was quiet except for the ticking of the wall clock. No Zoe. Morning sun poured through the thin white curtains at the wide windows. Mom, coffee cup in front of her on the table, had obviously not gone to church at all. She wasn't dressed and sat with one hand holding her cotton robe closed at the neck, as if she were cold. Her brittle, ash-colored hair was uncombed. An open book lay in front of her. When she looked up, her eyes were puffy and sad.

Jenny planted a kiss on her mother's head, then reached down to hug her, holding her close as much for her own need as for her mother's.

"Everything will turn out all right." She said words people always said when they didn't have a clue how things would really turn out. "Emily Sutton's a frightened bird. She'll come around."

Jenny, not into coffee at any time of day, made herself a cup of tea and then took her cup to settle across the table from Dora.

She nodded to the book in front of Dora and asked what she was reading.

Dora looked down at the cover of the gray book, dropping her hand gently to it as if something in there could be jarred. "Emily Sutton's poems. Beautiful work. Such a shame."

She put her hand up to stop Jenny when she began to protest. "I don't mean about me and what happened last night, scaring the poor soul the way I did. I mean such a shame she stopped writing. I wonder what happened. How does a person stop doing something they were meant to do? How did she stop taking up a pen and letting words come out?

"I found a poem that broke my heart. Listen," she said. "It's like she's talking straight to me: 'Escape is a place of vision, / where others cannot go. / It hides from darkness monsters, / and daylight tedium.'"

She looked up, eyes gleaming. "I'm the darkness monster. She had to escape from me. I'm so ashamed of accosting the poor thing the way I did."

"Oh, Mom. Don't torture yourself. Obviously there's something wrong with her. All those years shut up in that dreary house on Pewee Swamp. Anybody would get a little screwy."

Dora's eyes flew open. "*Wrong! Screwy?* Would you have said there was something *wrong* or *screwy* with Emily Dickinson?"

Jenny thought a while. "Probably."

"Well, let me tell you, Jenny Weston, Emily Dickinson was a woman dropped into the wrong century and made to deal with Amherst matrons who spent their days gossiping and paying afternoon calls. Can you imagine Emily Dickinson in that world? All piety and jealousy? I'll bet anything you would have hidden in your house, too. So much better to write poetry, bake black cakes for your family, and hide from tiny souls."

She ran her finger down the middle of the book lying open in front of her.

"That's what happened to Emily Sutton. Far ahead of her time. Ahead of a world of readers who can't begin to understand her work. How much safer, I suppose, to be home with her sister these last twenty-five years or so. Imagine the quiet in that house. Quiet to write, without critics and sour poets snapping at her heels. I understand both Emilys completely." She closed the book and took a deep breath.

Jenny made an unhappy face. "Mom, think about that poem. She's obviously talking about the mind, not a physical monster with a pretty face and curly whitish hair, like you. Come on. It's Sunday. Let's call Lisa. She'll cheer you up. She always does."

Dora brightened at the idea of calling her daughter, who had just finished filming a documentary about children on an American Indian reservation.

Just as it was every time she called Lisa, Dora's first question was when could Lisa come home. Today Dora quickly used Jenny as bait.

"I don't know how long she'll stay, Lisa," Dora was saying into the phone while Jenny thought about the day ahead. If she was right, how things were going to come between her and Tony, he should be calling soon. At first it had been with excuses to come over: a Little Library house plan to show them, a new siding he'd found. But now it was almost like dating. They'd have breakfast at Myrtle's Restaurant, where the French toast was always good. One day he had suggested a swim over at a beach on Lake Michigan. Another day she went into Traverse City with him, doing a paint run to Home Depot. And on the days in between, he was in their house more and more often, always looking for an excuse to stay a little longer, linger over a beer, talking and laughing the way people getting to know each other talked and laughed.

"You should come as soon as you can," Dora was saying. "Yes, I understand. But I'd so love to have the two of you here, together at the same time."

After Dora hung up, she smiled at Jenny and nodded, satisfied. "She's going to try."

The next diversion was a knock at the back door.

Zoe walked in with Fida in her arms. She set Fida on the floor, where the little dog ran under a chair to curl up and fall back to sleep. Zoe headed straight for the coffeepot.

"Wouldn't you know it?" Zoe scrunched her small face into disgust as she climbed on a chair by way of the rungs and settled at the table, placing the mug in front of her. "My printer won't print and I have to go over the manuscript page by page before I e-mail it to Christopher. I require black words on paper, not only on a screen. That's the way I work. I need the manuscript in front of me. Then a few days for editing. I'll call Christopher and tell him. I refuse to send him anything less than my very best. He won't take this too well, such a stickler for deadlines. He'll talk about editorial and covers and time for blurbs and things only he cares about. But he'll end by telling me to take all the time I need and to let him know when the book is finished. He wants me to come to New York sometime soon. I don't know why, but I think Christopher likes me. He certainly seems to cheer up when he hears my voice. Starts laughing when I say hello. But, oh dear, first I need to get into Traverse City and buy a new printer. A new printer is of maximum importance. It is the finger in the dike. It is the dam in the stream." She turned her alarmed face from Dora to Jenny.

"I must have it today. Would you go with me, Jenny? A printer will be heavy and I could use some muscle."

"It's Sunday, Zoe. I think Tony and I have plans for later . . ."

"Oh." Zoe's face fell. "I suppose you're not the muscle type anyway. But could you call Tony and check? I can't do it alone. Maybe at the store. Someone there will help me, but when I get back . . ." She narrowed her round blue eyes. "Lunch will be on me. If a bribe can convince you. We could go to the Brew and sit among the clackers—the people on their computers. We can talk about anything we like and the people around us won't hear a word. It's refreshing to me, you know, not to be surrounded by eavesdroppers and interlopers."

Jenny smiled at Zoe's exaggerated picture of the Traverse City coffee shop. Then she smiled wider at Zoe's pursed red lips, naturally red cheeks, and bright-blue eyes. She melted. After all, some things were owed. Zoe was the first to offer Dora help when she was sick and needed to get into Traverse City to a doctor. She was the first to come over to welcome Jenny back to her hometown.

"You just bought yourself some muscle." Jenny got up to go call Tony and break their date—if they had one.

* * *

Zoe watched Jenny leave the room. She scratched at the end of her nose and shook her head. "Are you any better today?" she asked Dora.

Dora shrugged. "I'm still mad at myself, if that's what you mean. The woman's got a right to walk around at night without being pounced on. I don't know what I was thinking, accosting her like that. I acted like a star-struck teenager."

"That wasn't accosting." Zoe waved away the thought. "You were being friendly, wanting to let her know what her poetry meant to you. She'll be back. Where else can she get poetry books? In fact, I was thinking—you know what might be nice?"

Dora shook her head.

"What if Jenny and I stop at Horizon Books when we go in to get the printer? That is, if Jenny can go. There, Jill or

Amy will give us ideas for books Emily Sutton might like. You know, maybe find her some great modern poetry. Just imagine all those years closed up in that house. She must be thirsting to know what's been happening in literature."

Dora thought a moment before her face lit up. "What a great idea! But don't buy her any Emily Dickinson. I'll do that later."

"Great!" Zoe thumped her hands on the table. "On our way back we'll drop the books off at her house. No knocking or anything. I promise." She threw her hands up at the look Dora gave her. "Maybe just a single knock and off we'll go."

"And don't hide in the bushes spying on her."

"Why, Dora! I'm crushed." Zoe sat back, looking more amused than crushed.

"I want to pay you, of course."

Zoe opened her mouth to nix that proposal since they were all involved in last night's fiasco, but Jenny was back, looking oddly confused.

"I can go with you." She shrugged in Zoe's direction. "Tony said we didn't have plans to do anything today. Too busy in his workshop, he said. He sounded funny. You know, odd. I have no clue. Anyway, let's go."

Zoe slid from her chair as a great knocking came from the front of the house, and soon their neighbor, Minnie Moon, was standing in the kitchen with one fist in the air, waving slips of paper at them.

"Found these in your library box, Dora," Minnie said, setting the papers on the table. Minnie was dressed for the day in a purple muumuu and tennis shoes with rolled-down white anklets. She stood next to the refrigerator, chest heaving. "I've been collecting them the last couple a weeks but it came to me maybe you didn't know anything about 'em."

Dora offered coffee but Minnie shook her head and moved to take a seat at the table.

"Coffee makes me sweat," she said over her shoulder as she fanned at her flushed face. "Love a glass of ice tea though, Dora. Lots of ice, if you don't mind. I see you didn't make it to church." She watched Dora pop ice cubes from the trays. "Didn't miss anything. The sermon was on venal sin or something like that. Lost my interest after the first five minutes." She accepted the tall glass from Dora then sat back to spread out the strips of paper on the table. "Came down to get a book for Candace. She just turned fourteen, and I figured it's time to teach her about sex and stuff, and I don't have a clue myself what to say."

"You must have had sex at some time in your life." The squeak in Zoe's voice hid laughter.

Minnie leaned back, giving Zoe a wide-eyed look. "Of course I have. Where the hell you think I got those babies from?"

"What'd you tell Deanna when she turned fourteen?" Jenny asked.

Minnie thought hard. "Deanna? Told her to keep her legs closed. And you see what good that did me."

Dora leaned over Minnie's shoulder, reading the wrinkled scraps of paper in front of her.

"Found 'em in your library box, Dora. Thought it had to be some kid thinking it was funny to stick papers in there. But when I looked close, seems somebody wrote something on each one of 'em. Look for yourself. There's a poem on every one of these papers." She counted. "Six poems. Seems funny, somebody putting things like that in one of your library boxes." She leaned back in the chair and grinned at the women around her. "Coals to Newcastle? Ice cubes to Eskimos. Poems to a little library."

Dora picked up the first of the papers, then the next, the next, and finally the last of them. When she looked around the table, her mouth hung open.

"This is what Emily was doing down here last night," she said. "She didn't come to take a book. She wanted to share her poems with us. Oh, my, listen to this:

Echoes in the house
Predict the universe.
Simple sounds that
Only death can share.

A gong, as time hangs waiting.
The rasp of her winter's cough.
A crack marks temperature descending,
From silence to divinity."

"Huh?" Minnie sipped her iced tea. "It doesn't rhyme. I like poems that rhyme myself. You know: 'There was a young girl from Paducah, who—'"

Dora interrupted, "But this is a *wonderful* poem. And we might be the first to ever read it."

Not to be quieted, Minnie jumped back in. "Who are you talking about? That Emily Sutton down by the swamp?"

"She was here last night." Dora nodded.

"What do you know? Nobody's seen that one since before I can remember. Supposed to be getting famous and instead came home here and doesn't leave that old house."

Minnie leaned back and sniffed. "I don't like to speak ill of anybody, as you well know, but talk about nose in the air! Saw one of them out on the street—the poet or her sister. That was a long time ago. Hair was a mess, kind of brown and gray even then. Like a refugee from some old country. Tried to be friendly to her but she wouldn't give me the time of day." Minnie nodded twice to make sure they understood what she was saying, then picked up her napkin and tapped gently at her lips, drying them. "You know they got a cousin does the shopping and such for them. Used to live here. Lives in Traverse now. Talked to her a couple of times over at Draper's market. Althea Sutton's her name. She sure wouldn't say much about the two sisters. I asked a couple of times. Not meaning to be nosy or anything. I just wondered if the girls were sick or something."

"There must be a reason she's reaching out like this now." Dora turned to Zoe and Jenny, but they couldn't get their mouths open before Minnie jumped back in, not about to give up center stage.

"And then there was that business with the mother. Died the way she did. Went down there with my brothers to watch the back of the house burn. House is made of stone but that back ell was all old wood. My dad said it was a disaster waiting to happen. Nobody knew the mother was even in there until later, when the police went through the ashes and found her bones."

"Terrible!" Zoe was shocked. This was a piece of town history she hadn't heard before.

"Someone told me when we first moved to town," Dora said. She got up to get more tea and ice for Minnie. "I have to admit, I've been by there many times. So sad about those two sisters. Both of them friendless and alone."

Minnie was thinking hard. "So that's Emily putting poems in the box? Well, what do you know? Abigail Cane will be tickled to death to hear it. You know she's been wanting to have some kind of celebration of Emily's poetry. Readings and such. Wouldn't it be great to have her there to read her own work? We could have a kind of Glad-You-Are-Out party."

Dora ignored Minnie and turned to Zoe, patting the slips of paper. "Oh, please go to Horizon. Get her something wonderful. We have to say thank you somehow—for these."

She picked up the slips of poetry, one after another, and hugged them gently to her breast.

Chapter 4

Traverse City was as it always was in late summer. Front Street was swamped with slow-walking, ice-cream-licking vacationers enjoying the best that a small city on a large lake can offer. Souvenir shops vied for attention with fine dress shops and galleries and coffee shops and restaurants and bars down the whole of Front. The other shops sold cherry products like jellies and jams and ice cream and fudge and T-shirts and calendars and any apron you could ever desire with a cherry on it.

Jenny, hunting for a parking place along the curb, liked driving slow and watching people, especially happy people on vacation. It made her miss Chicago a little—not enough to go back yet, but Bear Falls was a sleepy town and sleepy towns get dull if you don't have much to do. And Jenny didn't have much to do. Not at the moment. Maybe something would come up. Maybe she'd find a job. Or maybe something would work out with Tony—this "thing" growing between two damaged people.

Thirty-six years old. Two failures behind her. Johnny Arlen, her first love, whose complicated mistakes and allegiances had destroyed not just the two of them but so many others. Then two-timing Ronald, whom she felt no love for anymore.

Everything in her past made her not just skittish with Tony but downright wary. She found she parsed every word he said, watched his body language, and counted kisses and hugs while passing her own out like candy on Halloween— one at a time.

There was a lot to think about. A woman her age couldn't just slink back home and hide for the rest of her life. Well, unless you were a weird poet like Emily Sutton. But that wasn't who Jenny was. The time would come when she'd get antsy and nervous and want to return to the working world. How and if that would include a carpenter from Bear Falls was still a long way beyond her.

She and Zoe had sandwiches at the Brew, then strolled down to Horizon Books, stopping to give directions to a perturbed family, the father with his sunglasses flipped up to his forehead and a finger on a downtown map.

The employees at Horizon greeted Zoe and Jenny and asked about Dora. Did she need any more books for her libraries? How was she doing now, with her library back in service after the vandalism earlier in the summer?

And then both Jill and Amy, true book women, offered to find poetry for Emily, both amazed she had been out in public. "She is still loved in poetry enclaves everywhere. Any time she wants to come in and give a reading, we'd be happy to have her," Amy offered.

"People would be lined up." Jill smiled a pretty smile at them.

"Does she have new work?" Amy asked. "How exciting!"

They headed to the poetry section, looking for contemporary female poets. Jill found Claudia Emerson's *Secure the Shadows* and put the book carefully into Zoe's hands.

"You sure this is something Emily Sutton would like?" Zoe asked, looking skeptically at the cover photos and bits of writing. She skimmed through the poems, stopping at "Late April House Fire along Interstate 81." Zoe closed the book thoughtfully. Maybe it wasn't the best choice—would the poem bring up memories of her mother's death? Still, Zoe believed in signs from the universe, and she had a creeping feeling that this was one poet talking to another.

Jill nodded, her head tipped to Zoe. "She's a real poet. Emily will love her work."

Amy put a finger into the air. "And I've got just the thing." Her sweet face was eager. "It's in my office. My copy, but I want her to have it."

When Amy came back she delicately put a copy of Hannah Weiner's *Code Poems* into Zoe's outstretched hand. Zoe stared at the cover. A wheel, with words embedded in it: "When does it or you begin?" The message swirled at the very center of the wheel.

"What do you think?" Amy asked, her eyes lighting up.

Since Jenny knew nothing about poetry, she relied on the experts. *Code Poems* would be fine.

Leaving, they thanked Amy and Jill for their help, Zoe giving a special smile to the book women who'd made magic for them that day.

With the books for Emily purchased, they were on to Boomer's Electronics to buy a printer. Zoe found one on sale and bought it. The salesman carried the printer to the car, then helped Jenny stow it in her trunk.

On the way out of town, driving up 31, they argued about stopping at a resale shop in Elk Rapids. Zoe loved resale shops. Jenny won, so they didn't stop. They argued about hunting for puffball mushrooms in the woods they drove past. Nothing suited both of them but going back to Bear Falls and setting the books on Emily Sutton's porch.

"What we should do," Zoe said, scrunching her face into a kid's devilish grin, "is drop the books on the porch, ring the bell, and run."

Jenny didn't enter into Zoe's game. She had her mind on that house by the swamp. It was a place that always scared her. On every Halloween, she'd run past there just to be frightened, never to stop and cry out, "Help the poor!" None of the other kids did even that much; they went blocks out of their way to be spared. Her mom had told her the Sutton house was like the house in *To Kill a Mockingbird*, where strange things happened and strange people lived, but it wasn't right to be afraid just because the women who lived there were different.

"We will put the books on the porch, ring the bell, and walk away like two grown women." She was firm with Zoe.

"Maybe you will, but if that door opens, I'm running like hell."

Jenny shrugged. "Your legs are short. If she catches somebody, it's going to be you."

31

Zoe frowned, thinking about her fate and wondering how she could work up better traction, maybe find a pair of magic shoes. What she imagined was flying right by Jenny and sticking her tongue out as she got to the car and sped away.

"Soon as we leave the books we'll go tell Mom," Jenny said. "She'll be eager to hear what we did and what we bought for Emily."

"We'll put Dora's name on the bag so she'll know who brought the books."

"You're just afraid she'll blame you if she doesn't like what we bought."

Jenny sped up, excited now about the book delivery, and maybe later seeing Tony—if he found the time. *No*, she told herself. *If we both find the time and really want to see each other.* She wasn't going to get trapped into that sitting-by-the-phone crap she'd done with Johnny. Waiting for hours. Hoping. Then acting mean as a snake to Mom when he didn't call.

She was thinking ahead and didn't take much notice of a white truck coming the other way, heading back toward Traverse City.

"Isn't that Tony?" Zoe watched the truck approach, then frowned over at Jenny. "I thought he was working all day."

"That's what he said."

They watched as the truck drove by, *Ralenti's Carpentry* emblazoned on the side. Jenny was about to wave and honk, but thought better of it. He was staring over the wheel, deep in thought. He didn't notice them as their vehicles passed.

For some reason, Jenny's face burned. An old, empty feeling rolled over her. Nothing she could name. Not surprise. Not even anger. Something deeper in her gut, closer to hopelessness, a leftover of curdled bad memories. It felt like the first time Johnny Arlen had lied to her, then told bigger lies, and then dumped her. Or the first time Ronald Korman lied about working late, and she'd been nervous but told herself not to be silly. And the other times when he lied about where he'd been. Lame lies, as if it didn't really matter anymore, even though she worked in his law office and people talked.

And then that last betrayal, when he and a young female client ran off to Guatemala to meet the girl's wealthy parents, and he called to ask Jenny for a divorce.

"Maybe he's picking up wood or something." Zoe flounced back around in her seat.

"All the way to Traverse?"

"Hey, if you've got questions, call him, Jenny. Don't get mad for nothing."

Jenny nodded. Zoe was right. She was heaping Tony with the sins of past loves. She fished her cell from her pocket and hit his number in her favorites.

"Hey!" she said when he answered. "What are you doing?"

She turned and made a face at Zoe as she listened to the deep voice on the other end.

"Really?" she said. "All day, huh? I'm at home, too. Just thought you might like to take a break and come over. Oh, of course. All those house plans to work on. Yup. Sure. I can tell you're busy . . ."

She hung up and stared straight out the window without a word until Zoe piped up. "Why'd you lie about being home?"

"Same reason he did."

"What'd he say?"

"Working."

"Oh." Zoe chewed at a thumbnail as if that's all she had to think about.

They said nothing more about Tony. Jenny turned at the long side road toward Lake Michigan and back to Bear Falls.

In town she took Oak, then went over to Thimbleberry Street and Emily Sutton's house. She was no longer excited about the possibility of meeting the famous poet, but only wanted to get home where she could stomp and swear about perfidious men in the privacy of her childhood room.

* * *

Jenny drove down the narrow road that ran beside Pewee Swamp, a dark, buggy place where thickly twined cedar and hemlock trees grew up to the side of the road, their dark trunks reflecting in standing water. Tangles of upended trees with clawlike roots and twisted, bare limbs blocked all ways into the swamp, giving it a forbidding look that kept most people away.

Into the curve of the road, where it narrowed, the swamp opened to wider spaces of water dotted with hillocks of vegetation, small islands in the black, filmy water. The swamp was a mass of moving shadows. The few kids who'd braved the swamp here at its widest—never Jenny—bragged about seeing dammed beaver pools and water so deep they couldn't say how long a big rock took to settle to the bottom. Some kids trekked farther in during a dry year and still came out soaked from shoes to caps, bitten viciously by mosquitoes, telling high tales of strange things watching them from dark places. The best way to know the Pewee, it was said, was in winter when the waters froze and you could get to the interior, though you'd have to be careful if you wished to make it back, testing every step you took on the ice, marking your trail along the way.

Jenny had no plans to go into that dank place. Too many sudden bursts of flapping wings even as she drove past.

"I went into the swamp a little way once," Zoe said. "Down by Freddy's Bait Shop. Freddy cleared a path. Still, just a little way in, the path got squishy. I thought I'd sink for sure. Lots of birds. Pewees nesting. Cute little things. Herons standing in the water. Talk about prehistoric—watching one of those herons take off is like some *Jurassic Park* thing. There was a lizard sunbathing in the middle of the path. A big lizard. I could've sworn it was an alligator. Scared myself right out of there. Haven't been back since. You ought to go in at least once, Jenny. Different world from the rest of Bear Falls."

Jenny shuddered. "No thanks," she said.

"There're probably Indian Pipes in there right now. Emily Dickinson's favorite flower. Up on dry places. Strange to see them growing in the swamp, or anywhere. White pipes on leafless stalks. I was struck dumb the first time I found one."

"Don't doubt that," Jenny said as she rounded another curve. The Sutton house was just ahead.

Both women fell silent.

The two-story house, built of stone—stones of many shades of gray, black, and white and of many textures, from polished rock to angular, rough stone—grew out of its boggy acreage, one of those aged farmhouses found at the edge of many small northern Michigan towns. This one didn't sag, as if tired, the way most old houses did. The stone walls were straight and solid. It was only the wooden pillars across the front that were giving way, the porch roof swaying slightly to one side.

Zoe held the books, fumbled in her purse for a pencil, then wrote "From Dora Weston" on the Horizon bag.

They stood outside the gate looking up the slight rise to the house.

A set of narrow, tall steps led to the wide porch and then to an old screened door hanging from its hinges. Beyond the screen was an unpainted door with a large window covered by a thick lace curtain.

Nothing moved around the house or beyond the unpainted picket fence. The small crooked gate opened into a bare dirt yard with patches of tall weeds and a few wild daisies. A large oak to the side of the yard had grown to an ungainly width and height. Dead branches littered the roof of the porch and the ground around the tree. Piles of last year's leaves, windblown, lay caked against the fence.

Jenny couldn't see into the swamp from where they stood. Too many weeping trees and thick bushes hid it, but she heard jungle-like screeches from birds, a croak from a bullfrog, and a sudden rush of wings as herons flew off, over the trees, toward Lake Michigan.

The two women stared at the silent house as it seemed to move oddly in all the swaying shadows. It looked like a place where nothing could possibly be alive. Where nobody could ever live. If there were human beings in there, they only sat in chairs in corners and never spoke. If they moved, it would have to be in a crouch, darting quickly, heading toward another corner and another chair so as not to break the glass-like quiet that would shatter at any decibel above a whisper.

Jenny couldn't help but shudder. Beside her, Zoe put her hands on her bare arms and rubbed hard as she looked at the windows across the front. Four of them. Narrow and tall, all covered with heavy lace drapery. Zoe straightened her shoulders, then cleared her throat.

They were in no hurry, now that they were standing in front of the house.

"I saw a movie when I was a kid," Jenny said as she looked again at the windows on the second floor, then down. Nothing moved. If a curtain did move or the door opened, she decided she would turn and run after all. Normal people just didn't live the way these two women lived. "In the movie, a man went into a swamp and got stuck in quicksand." She leaned over to half-whisper to Zoe. "He went down slowly until there was only the top of his head showing and then nothing. I never forgot it. I don't want that to be me."

"Where'd you get that?"

"In that movie."

"You see monsters everywhere," Zoe said. "That's nothing but fiction. I'm afraid of the real thing."

Jenny had a comeback, but a curtain twitched in an upper window. She caught her breath.

"I saw it, too," Zoe whispered, her round eyes growing huge. "Let's get this over with."

Zoe pushed the gate, stepping through it to a flagstone path, half buried by years of moving dirt.

"She can't bite us," Jenny mumbled to make them braver.

"Can't come out with an axe and chase us into the swamp," Zoe whispered back, eyes glued to the front door.

They stopped, side-by-side, at the bottom of the steps, checking the narrow windows on either side of the door.

"Not exactly welcoming," Jenny said.

"She's a poet," Zoe whispered back. "Never knew one with fangs."

"Really? Not even one?"

They climbed the steps, ignoring creaking boards. Zoe carried the bag of books, holding them tight against her chest.

"I think I'll run after all," Jenny muttered as she set her foot down and the old wood boards sagged under her.

"I'll ring the bell and be right behind you."

Zoe pushed the doorbell.

Nothing happened. No sound of a ringing bell came from beyond the door.

Zoe pushed the bell again. "Doesn't work." Zoe opened the hanging screen door to knock on the inner door, first timidly and then with all her strength.

The sound of a voice calling out came from somewhere in the house.

Trickles of fear made the hair on Jenny's arms stand up.

There was an answering call inside the house.

Then nothing. No one came to the door.

Zoe set the books down quietly on the unpainted porch floor. "I'm out of here," she mumbled and headed back toward the steps.

Jenny flew by her, gone like a shot down the path and out the gate.

They raced to the street and to the car, jumped in, and slammed the doors behind them. Jenny fumbled with the key, then pushed her foot on the gas and took off as fast as she could go.

Zoe, in the seat beside her, waved her hand to go faster, then waved again, all the while looking in the rearview mirror as if something was running after them, coming up the road.

Chapter 5

Back home, they carried the new printer into Zoe's office and set it up without a single word passing between them.

Jenny hurried to her mother's house with the list of the books they'd bought for Emily in her hand. By now she felt a tiny bit of pride—as she did whenever she stood up to fear. Or almost did. A whole life of avoiding that house and now she'd been on the porch. That was something to feel good about. Maybe not the ungraceful exit, but at least she'd gone through that gate. She would never be as brave as her sister, of course. Lisa the Good wasn't afraid of anything. Lisa the Good didn't mind the places where old, bent people answered the door on Halloween and dropped ancient suckers into their pumpkin-shaped baskets with shaky hands. Lisa the Good always had a sweet word for everybody— didn't matter who. *No discrimination*, Jenny thought sourly as she walked to the kitchen.

Dora wanted to know which books they'd bought and looked a little skeptical. "Sounds as if they might be *too* modern."

Jenny waved the idea away. "If Emily's any kind of poet, she'll want to know what poets are writing now."

Dora conceded slowly. "If you say so, Jenny. I only hope she takes the gift in the spirit in which we meant it." She started the dinner, talking from time to time under her breath, but saying no more to Jenny.

That evening, sitting on the porch, there was an underground hint of what lay ahead of them in the small snakes of cooling air that wrapped around Jenny's feet. The maples lining Elderberry Street were already tinged with yellows and reds. Jenny thought about going over to Lake Michigan in the morning and taking a long, hard swim before the water got too cold. She thought about calling Tony to see if he wanted to come along. She'd decided not to tell him she'd seen him on his way to town. She didn't want trouble. What she hoped for was a pleasant, quiet day. And after all, he could have been out for so many different reasons. Maybe a friend had called. Maybe he forgot to pay a bill—nope, not on Sunday. Maybe somebody in Traverse wanted a library house.

"I'll be working at home all day, Jenny. Sorry." A blatant lie.

No hold on him, she grumbled to herself, but the words were boulders dropping around her. There was a certain weight to them that felt too heavy and cold to hold.

She decided to forget it. But she would watch— she wasn't a fool. She would watch and see where things between them went next. *Keep your eyes open*, she warned herself. *Keep your eyes open.*

Later, Zoe and her flashlight coming through the pines was a welcomed distraction. Zoe climbed the front stairs with her usual grunt at every step, came through the screen door, and settled with a huge sigh into a rocking chair. Jenny was happy to have her friend there and shook off her anger at Tony for the moment.

Dora heard Zoe talking and came out of the house with a bottle of wine to celebrate Zoe finishing the edits to her new book.

"Didn't finish, Dora," Zoe said to a slightly embarrassed Dora. "But let's celebrate anyway—like an unbirthday. Everybody should celebrate unbirthdays, don't you think? And almost finishing manuscripts?"

She drank deeply from a glass of the very good Pinot Grigio, then looked toward Jenny out of the corner of her eye.

When Dora went back into the house, she asked, "You call Tony and ask him what he was doing driving into Traverse City when he was supposed to be at home?"

"Nope."

"You call him and tell him you know he was lying?"

"Nope."

"So what'd you do?"

"Nothing."

"Sounds dumb. That guy likes you and you know it."

"Yeah. Sure."

"So you're just going to stew about it."

"I'm not stewing."

"Okay, so, you're hot under the collar. Boiling mad. Stick a carrot in it and you've got a stew."

"You're ridiculous . . ."

Dora was back with napkins and shook her head at the two scrunched up in their big chairs. "You act like sisters."

She poured more wine. "I was always yelling at Jenny and Lisa for bickering. But then those days went so fast." Dora sighed. "Now let's lift our glasses and toast to Zoe's fine literary endeavor. And by the way, we'll also toast to the award you won in New York last month and . . . well . . . anybody think of anything else we should toast to?"

"Your friend, Emily Sutton. For coming out of her literary closet." Zoe lifted her glass and started to drink but was interrupted by Jenny.

"And my sister, Lisa, who finished her documentary. I hope she comes home soon. I miss her."

"And let's not forget you, Jenny." Zoe lifted her glass one more time. "For divorcing that crazy person you were married to and coming home."

"He divorced *me*, Zoe. Makes a difference. I can't drink to that."

"Now, Now. You did see the value of his decision, Jenny."

"His decision was based on his testicles, which I base no value on at all."

"He wanted you back, remember?"

Jenny frowned. "To help him get his office open again. I don't think that qualified as a declaration of undying love."

Zoe clucked. "I'm drinking."

The wine glasses were refilled. The bottle was empty. The three sat rocking faster and faster until they were in a race, which was finally stopped by Dora, who was out of breath and laughing.

Zoe sang: "*A very merry unbirthday to me, to me. A very merry unbirthday to you.*"

Jenny muttered under her breath that little people should watch how much they drank since the wine didn't have as far to go.

Dora, in a deep voice, began to quote random lines of verse about the horrors of drink:

If you drink too much
A drunkard you will be . . .

* * *

Zoe was the first to see the light coming up the street. There was a dance of flashes cutting the dark into circles and squares and triangles. It continued on, passing in front of Zoe's house, the light running over her manicured flower-beds, then over the fairy houses. Diving moths danced shadows through the light.

"Is that her?" Dora sat forward, whispering. Her hands clutched the arm of her chair.

The light stopped in front of the Little Libraries. They heard one of the lids open.

The three of them stiffened. They made no movement for fear of frightening the figure off again.

The light swept the street—up one way, down the other. And then it flashed over them, frozen in place behind the screening, in their row of still rockers.

The dark figure behind the light took a step forward, then another, and was soon coming toward them, up the walk.

Jenny felt like a bug, caught in the bright beam shining directly into her eyes. She threw her hands up to deflect the light.

Fida sat up, barking shrilly until Zoe snapped her on the nose.

"Good evening," Dora called and struggled from her chair to the door, pushing it open. "Come on up. We're just sitting here enjoying this fine evening."

"No. I shouldn't. I . . . can't . . . Oh, dear. I'm not good at things like this."

"Things like what?" Dora bent down toward her, as if to appear smaller and of no threat.

"Oh, you see . . ." The dark figure turned from side to side as if wanting to run, then came up one step. "I'm Emily Sutton, from Thimbleberry Street. You don't know me but . . . I need . . ."

"And I'm Dora Weston. My daughter, Jenny, is here with me. As is our neighbor, Zoe Zola—a fine writer, just like you."

"You do know who I am?"

"Of course. I've always loved your poetry."

"I'm . . . overwhelmed." Her voice cracked on the words.

The flashlight shook as the woman joined them on the porch. After a long time she spoke again.

"I came to thank you for the books, Dora Weston. What marvelous minds you've given me. Is there a special way, do you imagine, to thank someone for the gift of majestic words?"

"Well, I don't know. I was a little worried. They are very modern writers."

"But a poet's mind is timeless, dear Dora."

The small woman, with light from inside the house shining on one side of her plain face, waved a hand then turned to Jenny and Zoe. "I think I might need your help.

I don't know where to go or whom to ask. I tried to get to the door today only to see you pulling off down the road."

Remembering their awkward escape, Jenny slid down in her chair.

Zoe's face drew into an embarrassed frown.

Dora invited Emily Sutton to sit with them.

Emily Sutton perched at the edge of a rocker, looking uneasy and ready to run. At first they spoke of the weather and of the cold to come, waiting until the poet relaxed back in her seat and turned to smile at each woman again and again, as if having stumbled on rare and fantastic creatures.

Jenny finally dared to look directly at Emily Sutton. She was small but somehow looked strong. Her smile came with a dip of her head as if it was only for her—an inward smile. When she initially spoke, her voice had been very low—almost a whisper—and then, with time, she grew loud enough to hear. Now she turned to each of them and smiled as if enjoying herself. Her eyes were enormous globes absorbing the light. She turned from curious face to curious face.

"I don't know . . . I haven't been anywhere in many years. I don't usually see people."

"You're here now. We'd like to help."

"I'm glad of that. I'm truly appreciative. You see, my sister Lorna's disappeared and something's happened to my cousin, Althea."

"That's terrible. You poor thing." Dora planted her feet solidly to the floor. "Whatever is going on?"

"It's a terrible thing."

"Where did your sister go?" Jenny felt timid even talking to the woman. It seemed intrusive to step into a place where Zoe's fairies would be more at home.

In the near dark of the porch, with light streaming from the house behind them, Jenny felt the woman's large eyes turn to her with a probing, even searching, look.

"There was a man." The voice wasn't weak now, only far away. "He came and she packed a bag. Lorna left with him."

"And your cousin?" Zoe spoke up. "Where has she gone?"

Emily lifted her shoulders high then shrugged.

"You should call the police."

"Oh, I couldn't. I just couldn't do a thing like that. Imagine men in uniform in my house. There's been no one there since . . . well . . . when we were a family."

"You're completely alone?" Dora's voice was sympathetic.

"Yes." The woman melted back into her chair. The toes of her dark shoes barely touched the ground. She took three deep breaths. "My mother left us. Went away like Lorna. Althea came from Traverse City with my groceries. Like clockwork every week. I don't know what's happened. I've called and called but she doesn't answer her phone. So you see, I have no one left in my miniscule world. The house is nothing but echoes and shadows, and soon I'll be out of food. I don't shop. I don't go to the bank. I don't look for clothes. I don't do anything a woman should do." She moved self-consciously in her chair. "But I never imagined I'd be left alone. Your kindness touched me—with the books. You needn't have done so much. I only wanted to bring a few of my poems to share with your readers. I

47

thought . . . well, I thought maybe, if I offered my words, you might think me deserving of your concern."

"Why don't we all go inside, Miss Sutton?"

"Emily."

"I'll make us a cup of tea, Emily." Dora got up and led the way into the house, with Emily Sutton following reluctantly. Jenny pretended her head wasn't doing a silly little spin from too much wine. Zoe followed, unhappy that her nose was itching and things buzzed through her brain that she didn't want to pay attention to.

The woman put her hands up to cover her eyes when Dora snapped on the overhead kitchen light. She shook her head and pointed to her face. "The light's so strong. I don't live with such harsh light."

Jenny jumped up to dim the overhead fixture, then sat down, transfixed by this apparition. The woman wore a cult-like gingham bonnet, twisted strings hanging down the front of her plain cotton dress, mother-of-pearl buttons incorrectly buttoned. Her shoes were black oxfords. On one, the dark laces were untied. She wore grayed anklets. She was pale, her very plain face almost blank. Her hair, sticking out everywhere under the bonnet, was a deep, unnatural red.

When she looked up at them, her bulging eyes moved from one face to another—not unkindly—but avidly taking in each woman and assessing her.

She licked at her lips, then pulled her tongue back into her mouth as if it were a secret she didn't want to share. "You are kind." She took the cup Dora offered, but shook her head at anything more.

"I shouldn't," she kept saying as she looked around Dora's large yellow kitchen, white sheers draped across the large window to the backyard, framed photos of spices hanging along the walls.

"What a pretty home you have, Dora Weston."

"Thank you."

"Lorna knew who you were. She's the one told me about the library box and, though she didn't want me wandering out alone, she agreed I might put a few of my poems in it one day. I don't want to be forgotten, you see." Emily set her cup down. "I see you have two boxes now. I hope I've used the right one. I'll stop, if you think I shouldn't leave the poems for fear children might find them."

"I don't think the children will mind," Dora hurried to assure her.

"And how can we help you, Miss Sutton?" Jenny bent toward her, feeling the need for sleep, but too entranced by this fey woman to leave.

"Oh, no, call me Emily. Like bees and butterflies, I prefer being called by my given name: Emily. An Emily. A hive of Emilys. A flock. A murder. A rainbow of butterflies a rainbow of Emilys." She smiled playfully.

"I'm not asking for charity. I have money," she went on. "I get a government check each month. My mother arranged it all. What I need most is someone to go to the market for me. Maybe an errand or two. Althea did all that, except paying the bills. The bank manager takes care of that."

"Jenny and I could go into town to check on your cousin." Zoe finally spoke, her voice too loud, making Emily wince. "Maybe she's been sick."

49

"She would have called to let me know." Emily waved a hand, dismissing Zoe.

"Maybe in the hospital. An accident."

"Althea would be so angry if I set someone on her. I'm sure she's just gone away or has company."

"And didn't call to tell you?"

Emily blinked her large eyes. There was a stupefied look to her, like someone startled awake.

"I don't have a car," she finally said to the others. "That's why I need help. Getting groceries, you see. As I said before, it's come down to food."

"I think we should go looking for your cousin . . ." Zoe pushed herself closer to the table and bent in Emily's direction. Dora stopped her with a hand on her arm.

"I don't drive. Lorna did, but as I said, she's gone now."

"That's all right," Dora said. "I can do your shopping."

"Nope. I'll do it," Zoe spoke up. She was tired, felt slightly drunk, and wanted to go home. When she got out of her chair, Fida, at her feet, looked around bleary eyed and gave a single woof.

"I couldn't ask." Emily raised a hand as if to ward off a threat, though she didn't look at Zoe.

Dora saw and sat back, folding her arms across her chest. Jenny didn't offer.

Emily looked from face to set face then finally turned directly to Zoe. "Well, if you don't mind. I hope it won't prove to be too much for you."

Zoe, puffing up in a way Jenny recognized, said, "Oh, I think I can handle it. As long as you don't throw big parties."

Emily didn't seem to get the joke and hurried on to say she didn't see people and wouldn't be throwing parties.

She turned to Dora with something like relief. "And may I visit you from time to time, Dora Weston?"

One of her hands fluttered up like a wounded bird. The hand lighted in her lap, then flew to cover her mouth, then pulled at a long curl of red hair before dropping to grasp her other hand, holding on as if fearing it might run off on its own.

"I've never known such kindness. Not even when I was out in the world, reading my work to crowds of people. That took so much out of me. I would feel empty after my poems went sailing off, never to sound the same to me again. It was so much better when I came back home and rested."

She turned her needy eyes to the women then stopped to catch her breath, as if so many words at once had worn her out.

"I used to have a dog, you know," she said after a long pause, looking sideways over at Fida, who sat up, her one good eye pinned on Emily. "He was a very large New-foundland. His name was Carlo. Things seemed better when I had Carlo. When he died I couldn't replace him. How could I? You don't replace people you love . . . but now Mother and Lorna and Althea are gone."

Zoe set her cup aside and slid off her chair. "You should really go to the police," she said again.

"Maybe I shouldn't have come . . ."

"Now, Zoe, Emily said the police would be of no use. Her sister went off of her own accord. And her cousin simply stopped coming." Dora frowned.

Zoe shrugged her shoulders. "But 'a person gone missing cries for the discovering voice.'"

"Lovely," Emily said without looking at Zoe. Her hands came together at her chest. Her face was transformed by a large smile that faded fast. She stood. "But I have to get home. I get nervous when I stay out too long."

"How can we get in touch with you?" Jenny asked.

"I don't answer the phone—hardly at all. Lorna used to do that, too. You know, answer the phone for all of us. But you can come to the door." She slid a look toward Zoe. "You know where I live. Knock and call my name. The bell's broken."

She was almost out of the kitchen when she stopped to turn. "Have you heard anything about a woman in town who wants to present a reading of my work? Althea mentioned something about such a thing before she left."

The women frowned at each other. Jenny shrugged.

"Abigail Cane," Dora said. "I think she's got something like that in mind"

"Oh, but I would love to attend." Emily nervously knotted one hand in her skirt. "Imagine being a fly on the wall."

She turned to leave, then stopped again to ask, "So you will come for my list in the morning?"

Zoe sighed. "If that's what you want. Then yes, leave your list stuck in your door and I'll pick it up sometime tomorrow."

"And an envelope with money. Don't forget I want to pay you." Emily turned to smile sweetly at the ceiling.

Zoe watched Emily scurry from the kitchen then bent to pick up Fida, holding her tightly.

After a silent time, Zoe shivered and headed toward the back door. "Anybody but me feel like somebody's stepping on your grave?" she said over her shoulder. "And by the way, that line of poetry I quoted? It was from one of her own poems. Strange she didn't recognize her work."

"She said it was lovely, Zoe. I wouldn't look for trouble," Dora said.

When she was gone, Dora and Jenny exchanged an exasperated look.

"I wish Zoe hadn't offered," Jenny complained, leaning back to yawn. "Could be the slightest bit of jealousy there. After all, Zoe's been the closest thing to a famous writer we've had recently."

Dora pushed herself up from her chair. "Then there will be Abigail Cane to deal with. Wait until she hears Emily's visited here. I wish I could hide for a while." She sighed as she gathered the dirty cups. "Or . . . maybe this is the beginning of a grand event in American literature. We'll be a part of it. I suppose I should be excited. But I'm not."

Jenny yawned, too tired to work up enthusiasm for anything but her bed.

"I feel sorry for her." Dora ran hot water in the sink. She'd used her best cups and wouldn't trust them to the dishwasher.

"Emily? I get the feeling she'll be just fine."

"No. Zoe. She's busy. I wish she wouldn't have offered to do the woman's errands." Dora rubbed her arms.

She turned to lean against the sink. "Remember what Minnie Moon was talking about a few days ago?"

Jenny waited, not sure what Dora was getting at. She shook her head.

"She said something about the fire at the Suttons' house."

"I know. Terrible thing."

Jenny waited for a point to be made.

"Emily's mother didn't just 'go away' as Emily said." Dora bit at her bottom lip. "The woman died in that fire. All they ever found were her bones. Doesn't it strike you as odd she didn't mention it?"

Chapter 6

Minnie Moon, in a peasant blouse and purple stretch pants, hurried into Myrtle's Restaurant just after nine o'clock the next morning. She peered hard around the large, open room with tables at the center and booths around the walls, hunting for Dora and Jenny.

She spotted them in a corner booth and headed straight over, sat across from the women, pinched her lips tight, and squeaked out, "I am truly, truly mad."

Dora put a calming hand on the woman's arm. "What happened, Minnie? Can we help?"

"Doubt it." She shook her head. "Still, I've got to tell somebody or I'll bust wide open. I went to your house. Your neighbor told me you were here."

Jenny, never as patient as Dora, only wondered how long she planned to stay. There was something about Minnie that looked ready to explode, and that kind of mess could take a long time to clean up. She planned to drop Dora off at home and go to Tony's, have a talk with him and find out what the devil was going on. Then she'd promised Zoe she'd drop over to take a look at something new she was writing. "Just another pair of eyes and ears," Zoe'd said when she'd asked if Jenny would mind.

"It's those girls." Minnie picked at a thread sticking from a seam in her purple stretch pants. "It's Deanna, and Candace, too. The both of them. I had to get out of my own house and run to get away from those alley cats this morning."

"Oh dear, what happened?" Dora patted her friend's very worn hand.

"Can you imagine? All over Candace's birthday party. I planned it for tonight. A couple of weeks late already because Candace wanted this boy she likes to be there and he went to the Upper Peninsula with his family, but now he won't be back until next Saturday. I've got everything ordered. Got the cake from Suzy Q. Daisies all over the cake because daisies are Candace's favorite flower. Then ham and cheese sand-wiches. Myrtle here is doing them for tonight. I even got the pants Candace wanted from Sears—too tight for a fourteen year old but still better than some of the things Deanna wore at that age."

She pulled in a long breath.

"So then, wouldn't you know it, Deanna starts kick-ing and screaming that she's eighteen years old and not a baby. She says she's got a date that night and wasn't going to hang around to help with, what she calls, 'some crappy kid's party.' That set Candace off hollering that she didn't want Deanna there anyway because she always went after boys who liked Candace and started trouble because she couldn't keep a boyfriend herself. That she's so nasty to people."

Tears crawled down her cheeks. Jenny thought how awful it must be to be Minnie Moon: a husband in prison up at Marquette and two ungrateful girls at home.

"I'm telling you, Dora. If I don't find something for me to do to get out of that house soon, I'm going to go crazy." She gave Dora a pleading look. "I heard Emily Sutton was over to your place last night."

Jungle drums, Jenny thought and felt her mother's body stiffen next to her.

"I was thinking, what if I go see Abigail Cane and offer to help her with this Emily Sutton business? You know, I could talk to Emily for her, see if we couldn't set up a time for that reading Abigail wants. I've been hearing she wants it either here—in town, when they pull old Joshua Cane down—or maybe at the opera house in Traverse City. Personally I'm thinking that's the right place. Big city and all." The look she gave Dora was sad and pleading. "Then I was wondering if maybe you could talk to Abigail for me. I don't think she likes me much."

"Why, Minnie, I'm sure Abigail Cane likes you as much as she likes any human being. That father of hers kind of ruined her capacity to love. Maybe even to be nice, sometimes."

Minnie nodded. "I know. Funny, don't you think? That in some ways she's just like the old man. Mean, miserable old bastard—excuse my language, but that's what he was. Used to chase me and my brothers off his place on Halloween. Can you imagine? Called us thugs."

Dora's face didn't move. "I wouldn't hold anything her father did against her, Minnie. She's trying so hard to be good to the town now. Really a different woman from what she used to be."

Minnie leaned closer over the table. She checked the booths around them, seeing who could be listening other than Dora and Jenny. "To tell you the truth, I already went over there to that Sutton house. I was just so frustrated with everything at home. Not just the girls, but James, up there at Marquette. If I don't send him money he won't write to me, and I don't have a lot, and he likes to gamble with the other men."

"You went to the Sutton house?" Dora shook her head. "Did you speak to Emily?"

"This morning. Right after Judith Small told me Emily came to your house." Minnie stared at her hands laid flat on the table. "I shouldn't've done it, I suppose. It's just that I need . . . Oh, I don't know for sure." She searched Dora's face. "Being poor's no sin, you know."

"Of course not, Minnie. Whoever said such a thing?"

"I can feel it. People talk to me different than they talk to somebody like you."

Dora found nothing to say. She glanced over at Jenny to see if she could jump in here, but Jenny's blank face only said she had nothing to offer.

Minnie sniffed and looked away. Her plain, round face was sad. "I thought I'd help out by getting things set up and then going to Abigail and showing her how I could handle just about anything."

"And?" Dora prompted when the woman stopped talking, taking a long time to think of what to say next.

"I'll tell you. It was odd."

"What was odd?"

"The whole thing. I went right up on her porch and rang the bell but the bell's broke."

Dora waited, open mouthed. Jenny nodded, trying to hurry her along.

"I knocked. Nobody came, though I could swear I heard somebody talking in the house. I waited on the porch a while and then thought I might as well take a look around since I was out there. I figured she'd come out eventually. You know, now that she's wanting to see people again.

"So what I did was go around the house to the back. You know, where that fire was. Back of the house still not fixed. Nobody there, but I saw a path leading down toward the swamp and figured maybe Emily goes out there from time to time. I don't know . . . I mean . . . how would I know where she likes to hide?"

"What'd you do?"

"Followed that path into the swamp a ways." Her chin went up like a kid caught doing something she shouldn't have done.

"You didn't!" Jenny thought about her own abrupt run from the house. "That was probably a mistake. If she saw you . . ."

Minnie nodded. "Seemed all right to me. The path was pretty worn down. Looked like people used it."

"Did you find her?"

Minnie looked directly at Dora. "I don't know."

"Don't know?" Jenny was back to being impatient.

Minnie shook her head. "I was at this place—like a wide place in the path. Some kind of flower lying around in the weeds, and all of a sudden somebody screamed. I almost jumped out of my skin, I'll tell you. The thing was, I did actually jump off the ground, and when I landed my foot slid back into the water, and I had to grab a tree branch to keep from going straight down. I was scared; I don't need to tell you. Scared the living crap out of me. Since someone was back there, and I didn't think it was an animal screaming, I called Emily to come help me, thinking it had to be her. There I was, half in that awful swamp water and calling her name and nobody came. Not a soul."

"Probably an animal. You shouldn't have gone . . ."

"I'll tell you what I did. I laid down on the ground and crawled, dragging my foot out of the water, then crawled all the way back up that path until I could get off my hands and knees and run to my car. Shoes are still wet. I don't care. All I wanted was to be away from that place."

"Are you certain it was Emily out there?" Dora asked, her face deeply worried. "Maybe she was screaming for help."

Minnie thought hard. "I'm not sure now. Didn't sound like somebody in trouble. That was me. More likely it was an animal, I suppose. You know how they can sound like people. Even some of those herons. Maybe she was nowhere nearby, and I got myself all worked up for nothing."

Dora looked around at Jenny. "You think we should call the police chief and ask him to go take a look? In case it was Emily, and she's hurt or something?"

"I don't think Emily would like it."

Dora nodded. "We'll call Zoe. She's going there for the grocery list."

Minnie shook her head. "All I wanted was to be of help to Abigail, not throw a wrench in the works. I hope I didn't ruin things."

Dora patted Minnie's nervous hand again, reassuring her. "Let me talk to Abigail for you. I won't tell her what happened at Emily's. We'll just see if she can use your help to get this big event going. I'll get back to you."

Minnie stood, smoothing the creases across the front of her pants and beaming down at Dora and Jenny. "I would appreciate it. Can't tell you how much, Dora. I need something to make me feel like a . . . well, somebody that other people like to have around." She turned back to smile. "I've got to go talk to Myrtle, out in the kitchen. Hope she didn't start those sandwiches already. Party will be next week, like Candace wants it. Cancelled the daisies. Cancelled the cake."

Minnie straightened her back and walked off toward the kitchen, leaving Dora and Jenny to exchange open-mouthed stares.

"She went into the swamp?" Jenny leaned toward Dora. "Is she crazy?"

"Into the swamp and out again. Something screaming at her." Dora shook her head. "You have to admit it, Jenny. Minnie Moon's a lot of things. A coward isn't one of them."

* * *

It was midafternoon before Zoe got to the Sutton house for the grocery list and money. It wasn't something she looked forward to, climbing the rickety steps again, but she had agreed to help the woman—at least for a while, until Emily found her bearings and learned to take care of herself. If there was something Zoe took pride in, it was keeping her word. At least most of the time, unless people annoyed her too much.

61

Actually she was ashamed of the way she and Jenny ran that last time, like ten-year-olds. She imagined they'd looked like cowards to Emily. That was another thing she prided herself on—not being a coward. Well, most of the time.

She stepped right up to the porch to retrieve the list.

The screen door hung as it did the last time, the screen in the wooden frame loose and flapping. She pulled the door open and searched around the inner door for a list. Nothing. No envelope.

Thinking maybe the envelope had blown out on to the porch, she looked behind her but there wasn't a piece of paper anywhere. No grocery list and no money.

Crap. Zoe frowned as hard as she could frown. Now she'd have to knock on the door again. She stepped up, lifted her hand, and knocked as high on the glass as she could reach. If that curtain twitched and Emily didn't open the door, Zoe told herself she was out of there and never coming back. And it wasn't out of fear. She'd just be too damned mad to ever speak to this person again.

She knocked. The window rattled. She knocked harder, leaning in and watching the curtain for movement.

The curtain twitched back and a huge eye stared out at her.

Zoe took a step away. And then another. Thirty seconds, she promised herself. *Maybe I'm short and slightly off-kilter, but I can run when I have to.*

There was the sound of the lock turning, and then the door opened just enough for Emily Sutton's face and a length of her body to appear.

"Yes?" she said, as if she'd never seen Zoe before.

Zoe cleared her throat. "I'm here for the grocery list."

"Oh." The door opened wider. Emily's face settled into an embarrassed smile. She bit at her bottom lip while her huge eyes stayed wide open. "Of course. I wrote it out then forget to put it in the door. I've been so busy . . ."

She stood with her head tipped to one side, looking sad or silly. It was something Zoe recognized: the tip of the head to signal she wasn't threatening, couldn't hurt anybody.

Emily wore a printed cotton dress this morning. Wrinkled, as if it never saw an iron. The dress fell almost to the floor, stopping just above a pair of dirty bare feet. Her oddly colored red hair was pulled back into a messy bun and wrapped with a blue ribbon tied into a bow. A sad bow. The kind a neglected kid would tie for herself.

Emily Sutton stuck a finger in the air and stepped back into the house, closing the door behind her. As the door closed, Zoe thought she heard a sound inside. It was the kind of sound you sometimes heard under other sounds. She thought it might be Emily Sutton talking to herself or singing.

She concentrated on being grateful that she hadn't been invited in. She imagined cobwebs hanging from the ceiling, portraits with eyes that followed her, insects scurrying along the molding. She snickered at her overheated imagination and put a finger to her lips.

Emily Sutton was back, this time stepping out to the porch and pulling the door closed behind her. She handed a folded piece of paper to Zoe, along with an envelope.

"The money's in the envelope," Emily said, one hand to her pale cheek. "I hope it's enough. I have very little experience with such things. Lorna used to take care of us. Then our dear cousin Althea. How I wish she were still around." She sighed and patted her own cheek. "It's terribly lonely, you know. Now that they've all gone."

"I thought I heard someone inside with you."

Emily's eyes flew wide, almost terror-stricken. "No. No one." She shook her head again and again. "There is only me. Oh." She put a finger into the air. "I have the radio on in the kitchen. I forgot. The quiet can sometimes be oppressive."

She smiled and drew her fists together at her chest then bent forward as if to bow. "I'll see you this afternoon?"

"Probably first thing in the morning. It's getting late and I'm meeting someone . . ."

"But I'd hoped for today." The pout on Emily's face wasn't pretty.

Zoe dug her heels in, feeling she'd better stop this trick right here. "Can't. Has to be tomorrow."

"Well, if that's the best you can do." Emily stepped back inside the house. "Please leave the things on the porch, right here." She pointed to a particular spot that didn't look any different from any other spot on the porch. "I'm often busy with my work. I don't like to be disturbed."

Zoe started to protest that the weather was too warm for food to be left outside. But Emily was gone. The door closed behind her.

Chapter 7

Jenny called Tony in the afternoon, but he didn't answer. She called a half hour later, figuring by then he'd realized he didn't have his cell on. And then she called again until she decided she was going a little nuts about this whole thing. Just another guy. What she needed, she decided, looking directly at her cell phone, was to get back to Chicago and kick-start her new life.

She spent the next couple of hours calling friends who might know of a law firm looking for a paralegal. The voices were familiar, as happy to hear from her as she was to talk to them. Women from Ronald's old firm said they would call as soon as they heard of an opening. A couple of them knew Ronald was trying to get back into business. One almost whispered that the word going around Chicago law circles was that nobody who knew Ronald Korman would work for him.

"He's having a tough go of it, Jenny," Carol, who'd been his secretary and Jenny's friend, said. "Old clients he dropped when he went to Guatemala say they wished now that they'd sued him. Most are saying he should go back to Guatemala—or maybe North Korea, where he'd fit right in. If you talk to him, you might tell him to try some other state."

There'd been a catch of laughter in her voice as they said good-bye and Jenny whispered, "*Or some other planet.*"

In the afternoon, Jenny pushed her dark hair back behind her ears as she checked the sweet potatoes in the oven. Her big surprise for dinner: a cold sweet potato soup she'd found on the Internet. She'd been home since June and had barely helped out beyond a little garden work and house cleaning. Guilt drove her to promise Mom that she'd fix dinner at least three nights a week, though her cooking skills were limited and her interest in cooking almost nil.

The growing heat in the room made her think it was dumb to warm up the kitchen to make a cold soup. Too late now. Cold sweet potato soup it would have to be. She closed the oven as Dora walked in the back door followed by Her Grand Eminence of Bear Falls: Abigail Cane.

Abigail was in full swing about something. None of the usual "How are you" or "Warm day" or "Looks like rain." Abigail barely nodded to Jenny as she took a seat, her back as straight as a tree trunk, and thumped both fists on the table.

"I'm telling you, Dora, I was shocked. You could have knocked me over with a feather."

"Really?" Dora peeled dirt-covered garden gloves from her hands and headed to the sink to wash. "Minnie Moon called you?"

Jenny noted the irritation in Dora's voice. So much for running interference for Minnie.

"I barely know the woman, and here she is, calling me with news of Emily Sutton."

"What news is that, Abigail?"

"She says Emily's coming out of her house and even writing new poetry. She says Emily left some of her poems in that Little Library box of yours. Is all of this true? Minnie seems to have intimate knowledge of everything."

Dora hesitated. "Well, yes. It was Minnie who found the poems. And the woman has . . ."

Abigail prompted, "Has what?"

"Well, Emily did come down to see me."

"You have got to be kidding! You mean like paying a neighborly call?"

"Not quite."

"Then what in heaven's name are you talking about?"

"Emily came over."

"Tell me all about it. You know I've been planning an event to honor her. I was thinking of the day my father's statue comes down. You know, lose one town figure, gain another. I thought we'd read her poems—one after the other until we've read them all. Maybe a picnic in the park to follow. Do you think she'd like that? Wouldn't it be amazing?"

Dora went to the fridge, took out a pitcher of iced tea, and filled glasses for all three of them. As she sat down, she turned to frown at Jenny.

"You have the oven on, dear?"

"Making a cold soup for dinner."

"Roasting tomatoes?"

Jenny shook her head. "Sweet potatoes."

"Oh." Dora turned back to Abigail. "Why don't we go out to the front porch? Be cooler there."

Jenny followed along behind, still listening for the phone to ring, and then telling herself she wouldn't answer if Tony called. He'd made her wait too long.

Settled in a porch rocker, sweating glass in her hands, Abigail quickly went back to why she'd come to visit.

"The thing is, Dora, I would like you to speak to her and tell her my plans. I'll be very happy to meet her, if she says that's all right. Or I was thinking of getting an even bigger event going. Maybe form a committee to look into an evening at the opera house in Traverse City. Actually, Minnie mentioned it. I might have misjudged the woman. Anyway, if Emily has new work, she can read and answer questions. Or read her old work." She frowned, planning hard. "I'll bet we can make it a fundraiser for the National Poetry Society in Traverse. Just imagine, that woman hasn't been out in public for twenty-five years. Think of the splash news of her reemergence will make across the country?"

"The only reason she's out is because her sister, Lorna, up and left home," Dora said quickly. "Then she had a cousin doing the shopping, and now that woman's stopped coming. She's asking for help, Abigail, not notoriety."

Abigail set her empty glass on the wicker table beside her and waved a hand. "If she's come out like this, I'll bet anything she's ready to make her poetry known to the world again." Abigail nodded to herself a few times. "Are you helping her with the shopping and such? If not, I can hire someone to do it."

"Our neighbor, Zoe Zola. She'll see to things for Emily."

Abigail's face lit up. "Now there's a one. I'll bet anything she'll get after Emily to publish her poetry. Your Zoe is getting famous in her own right, I understand. You know how we Bear Fallsians like to celebrate our own. We'll have to talk about doing something with Zoe soon, but as for now . . . I'm absolutely stunned at the news. You should have called me immediately."

Dora looked to Jenny for help. Jenny rolled her eyes and bit her lip. She had her own problems, and whether Emily Sutton read her poems anywhere—or didn't—wasn't high on her list of things to worry about. Though, she had to admit, Emily certainly was big news in town.

Jenny took a swipe at the sweat on her forehead. She scratched at a place low on her back where a mosquito bit her. She got up when she thought the phone was ringing, stood in the doorway to listen, but heard nothing other than lawn sprinklers whirling and kids ringing their bicycle bells.

"I didn't want to betray her," Dora, seeing she was going to get no help from Jenny, was saying. "She's a fragile person. It might not be a good thing for her . . ."

"Don't be silly. I'll bet she'll be happy to know we want to laud her, alert everyone to the kind of people we have living here in town. The more I think about it, you really must introduce me. I would be so honored. And it must be soon. I mean today or tomorrow. Oh, and Dora, I hate to ask you this, but I must. Would you see to it that any more poems Emily puts into your library box be taken out and given to me? We don't want her thunder diminished by familiarity now, do we?"

"They aren't mine to . . ."

"Did you by any chance mention that I was planning a reading of her work?"

Dora nodded. "She seemed to know something of it. Maybe her cousin heard."

"And what did she say?" Abigail's voice trembled.

"As well as I can remember, she said she would love to be a fly on the wall at the occasion."

"'A fly on the wall'! That's amazing. We must begin. And how I shall love working with the real Emily Sutton. Oh dear, her words: 'A reef, a rocky shoal, a whirlpool. / A ship within the eye. / No greater tragedy than a friend gone missing.' How I look forward to our meeting. I'll plan a luncheon."

"Please, Abigail. I don't know if I can arrange what you want. I'll ask Zoe to talk to her but I can't promise . . ."

"Of course you can, Dora. I'll be waiting to hear. And don't forget about those new poems. Get them to me as soon as you can. New work! The literary world will be aghast. People will come from everywhere for this astounding event. The world press . . ."

"Now, Abigail."

But Abigail was on to something else. Nose up, she sniffed again and again. "I smell something burning," she said, looking directly at Jenny, who hopped out of her chair and ran back to the kitchen to grab her blackened and withered sweet potatoes from the smoking oven.

* * *

With no cold soup for dinner, Jenny and Dora, along with Zoe, climbed into Jenny's car and headed for Myrtle's. It was too hot, even at eight o'clock, to think about food, but Zoe was too angry with Emily Sutton to stay home and do nothing. Dora was upset about Abigail Cane's uproar. And Jenny, while living down the ruined soup, got a call from Tony that she'd been happy about at first, then mad as hell about when he'd acted distracted, said he was calling about a missing blueprint and wondered if she had it.

That was it.

"No, I don't have it."

"Oh, sorry, thought you did."

When he hesitated to hang up, she dared to ask why he hadn't called lately and got the old, "Sorry. Busy."

* * *

The restaurant was almost empty. The early diners had already been in to deplete the meatloaf with hamburger gravy and mashed potatoes—Myrtle's year-round signature dish.

Jenny ordered an iced tea, thinking how she wished it was a shot of bourbon, which she'd missed since coming home. Wine and beer that's all the people of Bear Falls seemed to drink. But bourbon was what people drank while blowing off steam in cities. She'd blown off a lot of steam over Ronald.

"Who was on the phone earlier?" Dora asked, smiling across at Jenny as they waited for Delaware Hopkins to come take their orders.

"Nobody," she mumbled.

"I thought maybe it was Tony," Dora said. "He hasn't been around in a while. I don't know what's happened. Probably busy."

Jenny shrugged.

Dora looked closer at her daughter. "Was it Tony?" she asked, this time in a quieter voice.

Dora gave up waiting for an answer and said she was ordering the potpie. They all agreed that was probably best since the meatloaf was gone. Delaware Hopkins, seeing them put down their menus, hurried over, squeaking across the tile floor.

Delaware leaned close to Dora's ear. "Minnie was in a while ago." Her voice went down to a secret, gossip level. "Said that famous poet of ours paid you a call. That true? Think she'll be coming out of her house for good soon? We're all just dying to meet her."

"Minnie talks too much." Dora frowned as hard as her companions were frowning.

"Do you blame her? Biggest news she's had to spread in years." Delaware flounced around, looking hard from face to face.

She turned to Zoe. "You in a better mood than your buddy here?" She pointed her pencil at Jenny.

"What do you mean?" Jenny sat up straight, ready for battle. "I'm fine."

"Yup. Don't say hello when you come in. Sit down like you're here for a hanging. I'd say you're all in moods tonight so I'll just get your orders in and mind my own business."

Jenny almost laughed. The two of them, Delaware and the other waitress, Delaware's mom, Demeter, were the town criers. The pair knew everything, heard everything, told everything, though they were known for spreading censored news so as not to hurt people too badly. Jenny figured it wasn't a good thing to do, making Delaware Hopkins worry about them. If they weren't careful, Delaware would be seeing to casseroles coming to the house, then anonymous people would be sending them happy cards meant to cheer up poor, miserable souls. They'd be writing thank you notes until their fingers fell off. Too much stress to take, making Delaware and Demeter worry about you.

They ordered their potpies and small salads, which didn't fit into Delaware's idea of what people should be eating that time of night. She mumbled that they were going to have bad dreams, with chickens chasing them, unless they switched to maybe just a bowl of soup and half a cheese sandwich. With nobody changing their order, she was off to deliver the news to Myrtle, out in the kitchen, that there were potpies to ready, which would heat up the kitchen all over again. "Guess I don't get out of here early," Delaware yelled from the kitchen door, turning to smile at the women's table.

When she was gone, Zoe reached across the table and tapped Jenny's arm. "Why did you let me offer to get that woman food?"

"Huh?"

"You should have seen the size of the list Emily gave me." Zoe didn't look happy. "First of all she forgot to leave it stuck in the door the way she was supposed to. Then she was angry because I dared knock on her door. Then she had the nerve to get upset when I said it was too late to shop today and that I would get the groceries back to her in the morning. Honestly, Jen. That woman is a diva. She made me feel like a lackey, there to wait on her."

Jenny made a face. "A poet. What did you expect?"

"I expect manners. A little gratitude."

"Look at this." Zoe pulled Emily's list from the pocket of her flowered top. "Two pounds of butter. Hmmm, one chicken—dead I suppose. Chickpeas. Coffee. Ipana toothpaste." She looked up at Jenny. "Do they make that anymore?"

Jenny shrugged.

"I'll just get her any old toothpaste." She made a note and finished reading the list. "Toilet paper. Well, I would hope so. Oatmeal. A half-pound of sugar. Plain cookies . . . hmmm . . . some other stuff. A light pink lipstick. Oh ho! Red hair dye. Well, I guess we know how she keeps that hair of hers so red."

"Did she give you money?" Dora leaned forward to ask.

Zoe shook the envelope at her.

"How much?"

Zoe opened the envelope, then counted the money. "Fifteen dollars."

"For all those groceries?" Jenny laughed.

Zoe moaned. "It'll be a lot more than that. What do I tell her?"

"Tell her she owes you."

"I won't see her. She said to leave the groceries on the porch."

"Days are too warm for that," Dora joined in. "Just keep knocking until she answers the door. If you have to leave things out there, why, I'd leave her a note saying you won't set the groceries out like that next time because you don't want to poison her. Make sure you tell her in the note how much she owes you."

"You think I'm going to be doing this forever?" Zoe's eyes shot wide open.

"If you're going to be such a complainer, you shouldn't have offered in the first place," Jenny said, too filled with her own misery to worry about Zoe.

"I thought I'd like her. Is it my fault that I don't?"

"You haven't given her a chance," Dora said.

Jenny was tired of the whole subject. "I'll help," she said. "As long as I have the time."

"You've got nothing but time."

"Thanks." Jenny stared straight at her.

"Sorry." Zoe looked away. "It's just that the woman's weird. Runs like a cat one night then comes back wanting help. Gets me to do the grocery shopping for her but forgets to leave a list and gives me about a half the money it takes, then doesn't even ask if it's enough."

"Abigail Cane heard about Emily and her new poems." Dora slipped the news in while she could. "She said she could hire somebody to do the shopping for Emily if you didn't want to."

"It's not that I don't want to help her out. I just don't like the way this is starting. Nothing smells right to me. And you know how good my nose is for trouble. I've been thinking. We better go into Traverse and see what happened to Althea. If she feels the way I do already, she's probably just hiding out."

"Abigail Cane wants to meet Emily. She wondered if you could set it up."

"Me!" Zoe gave Dora a startled look. "I'm not Emily's social secretary. Tell her to go over there herself."

"Don't be so angry, dear." Dora gave Zoe one of her bad-little-girl frowns. "All Abigail wants is an introduction. I don't think that's too much to ask."

Zoe put a finger to her nose and slid down in her seat. "Too much. Too little. Maybe just enough. Emily was snotty to me. I don't like being treated that way. She looks down on me like I'm the hired help."

"She has to look down on you," Jenny popped in. "You're short."

"And you're crabby," Zoe shot back as the chicken pot-pies arrived.

* * *

"Myrtle's on her way out." Delaware leaned over the table, removing plates and whisking crumbs to the floor. The restaurant was empty except for Dora, Zoe, and Jenny.

The women sat up straight. Myrtle coming out of her kitchen was big news. The thing about Myrtle Lambert was that though she'd won the family restaurant from her brothers in a court case, she didn't have the personality of a business owner. She didn't much like people. Didn't much like talking to people. And she was rarely seen except on her way to and from work, her floppy green hat the only thing that marked her.

The hat was plopped on top of Myrtle's head when she came through the swinging kitchen doors. Apron wrapped around her middle, she stopped to check the front door, making sure nobody was coming in, then scuttled to the table and slid in beside Zoe.

"I don't think we've met," Zoe said. She put out a small, limp hand but Myrtle ignored her.

Myrtle thumped a fist on the tabletop and turned to get in Dora's face.

"I heard Minnie Moon talking in here today."

Jenny thought this visit was too unusual not to savor. Myrtle was known as one of the odd people in town. But she did her business. Shopped for supplies. Cooked her food. Nobody questioned her right to stay in her kitchen if she wanted to. There were a lot of people in Bear Falls who weren't exactly sociable and kept to themselves. Odd people everywhere.

Jenny looked at the wrinkled woman in her green hat and tried not to smile. "What was she saying?" Jenny played dumb, while the other two only stared.

"That Emily Sutton's come out of her house. Put some of her poems in your library box." She nodded to Dora. "You people all see her?" She glared from one to the other.

"Sure did," Zoe answered for them all.

"Talk to her?"

They all agreed.

"She say anything about her sister, Lorna?"

Jenny looked at Zoe, who watched Myrtle carefully. "She said her sister was gone. Packed a suitcase and left."

Myrtle nodded fast at all of them. "That explains it, I guess. Emily could be hard to get along with."

Jenny and Zoe waited.

"Okay," Myrtle said, putting her hands flat on the table and beginning to rise.

"Explains what?" Jenny asked.

"Nothing." Myrtle shook her head. "Just . . . always figured she'd end up alone."

"Alone?" Jenny asked. "Why?"

Myrtle put her head down, got up, and scurried back to the kitchen as the bell rang and a customer came through the door.

"What the heck was that all about?" Jenny watched the woman disappear, kitchen doors swinging behind her.

"The two of them, coming out within just a couple of days of each other," Zoe said. "I told you I smelled something strange in the air."

Chapter 8

It rained during the night; the unpaved parking lot of Draper's Superette was pocked with water-filled holes. It was never easy, even at the best of times, for Zoe to push a cart all the way across the lot to the store door. She had hit potholes before, sometimes sending her ass over teacups, with people running to help the little person flat on her face in the gravel and brush at her as if she wasn't a full-grown woman.

All that over a grocery-cart failure.

She maneuvered around the holes that morning. Maybe they'd be dried out by the time she finished with Emily's list. Or maybe she'd slip a stock boy a five to push the cart back out.

Most days she didn't think about her height, or lack of it, nor her strength or lack of it because she'd been that way for thirty-three years, and what was, was. Once in a while she thought about being tall and willowy and gorgeous and looked at for the right reasons as she walked down the street. But not often. There were usually more important things on her mind.

She pushed her cart past the coffee shop and tried to get by the checkout stands, but there was Cassandra Hatch, one of the cashiers, calling and waving.

"How ya doin', Miss Zola?" Cassandra pushed items over the scanner as fast as she could push. "Heard you've had some excitement at the Westons'."

Zoe smiled and shrugged as if she had no idea what Cassandra was talking about.

"Heard about that poet, Emily Sutton. She was over to Dora Weston's house. If you ever see her there, say 'Hi' for me. We're all so thrilled to have her out again. Can't wait to hear her read some of those new poems I'm hearing about. Minnie Moon says Abigail Cane's planning a big affair for Emily. A reading. A meet and greet. Something like that. I'm hoping to volunteer, as long as it doesn't interfere with my job here."

Zoe pushed her cart out of the reach of Cassandra's eyes and tongue. She stopped behind a cooler to read over Emily's list again and make a map in her head: produce, meat, household goods, dairy, checkout. With luck, Cassandra's line would be too long, and she could go to the quiet girl who kept her head down.

Zoe crossed off every item as she put it in the basket, noting the price of each and adding it up in her head. With her cart full, she went to the checkout, happy that Cassandra had six people waiting in her line.

Zoe watched the total on the register mount, then counted the bills in the envelope again. Fifteen ones. The bill was thirty-seven dollars and seventy-one cents. She groaned.

Should she tell Emily Sutton she owed her or keep quiet? Would everybody else say, "Poor woman. Doesn't have a clue what things cost"?

She counted out the ones and then dug the rest from her purse.

On the way to her car the cart got snagged in every single pothole. Too much on her mind to remember to ask one of the stock boys for help, so she pushed and grunted and finally reached her car.

By the time she got the bags in the back, she was worn out and talking to herself about how Emily Sutton wasn't going to take her for a fool again.

Driving around toward the Sutton house, she was thinking about being poor and what poverty did to a person, especially a creative person like Emily. She thought about chalking the extra money up to charity, then thought of how she didn't like to be taken for a fool and didn't have that much herself. But what would she say to a poor soul who'd been virtually locked away for so many years? *Cough it up?*

Zoe quashed that silly side of her brain and told herself she would present the woman with the bill. Then she decided to wait and see how she felt about the whole business when she got there. *Let fate decide*, she told herself.

"*Fiddle-Dee-Dee, Fiddle-Dee-Dee. We'll see. We'll just see,*" she sang one of her happy songs as she drove. "*We'll just see.*"

* * *

Mist from the swamp lay around the Sutton house as Zoe parked at the curb in front. The mist moved slightly with every breath of air. First shifting in one direction, then swirling back in the other. She got out of her car reluctantly, thinking how lucky she was not to have to live in such a place, happy all over again for the little house her grandmother left her.

She pulled the two bags from the back and made straight through the gate and up the steps. She set the bags down in the exact spot Emily had pointed to then thought of that plastic wrapped chicken. The sun was high, middle of the afternoon. It was warm. The porch felt like a desert, the slanted, old boards with peeling paint giving off heat.

Be stupid to leave a fresh chicken out in the sun.

Dumb, really.

She set the bags down and knocked at the door. Only common sense, despite what Emily ordered.

She waited, then knocked again, making this one into a *rat-a-tat-tat* that shook the door and rattled the window.

No answer.

Now what was she supposed to do? She looked around to see if Emily might be out in the yard. The chicken would be garbage if it sat outside too long.

She was torn one way and then the other. Maybe Emily knew she owed her money and wouldn't answer until she left. If so, the chicken wasn't her problem.

She got as far as the top step and stopped, going back to knock at the door again.

She decided she would stand there forever, if that's what it took. Nobody pulled tricks on her. She might be small, but her brain wasn't. She could outfox the best of them. And that included Emily Sutton, who was really annoying her at this point.

She knocked again, shaking the glass in the door.

When nothing happened, she turned the knob and pushed the unlocked door open far enough to stick her head in and call out. "Emily!"

She listened. A radio voice came from somewhere at the back of the house. Maybe Emily was in the kitchen.

She stepped into a crowded entryway with a coat rack on one side. An ancient, dusty coat hung on each hook. On the other side of the small area, an ornate, tarnished, gold-framed mirror hung—cracked and blackened. Beneath it was a bench filled with old boots. What she could see of the room beyond was just as overstuffed with things of all sorts: boxes, bags, antique furniture, shadeless lamps. There were piles of books and magazines. The walls of the room hadn't been painted in years. The color was a faded shade of blue with steaks of white, as if someone had begun to paint at some point in the past and lost interest.

The smell of the house made Zoe want to cover her nose. Dust. Garbage. Years of both of those. She called to Emily again.

Maybe the hall, directly across from where she was standing, led back to the kitchen. At least she could put the chicken in the fridge, then get the heck out of there.

There was a noise from overhead. A footstep or maybe just a creaking board. She went slowly over to the staircase on the far wall of the living room and called out Emily's name, looking up the stairs for the woman to come down.

"You have a great deal of nerve, haven't you?" A voice came from behind her, making her jump and grab at her chest.

When she turned, she bounced into Emily Sutton, standing with a bunch of goldenrod in her hands, her small face bunched into a heavy scowl.

"I thought you'd leave everything outside, the way I asked," Emily said without a "Hello" or a "Thank you" or a "What the devil are you doing in my house?"

"I was afraid to. Not with the chicken," Zoe found herself apologizing.

"I'm never far away." Emily's oval-shaped face was flushed. Her eyes looked as if they might fly out of her head. "I wish you wouldn't impose this way . . ."

"Impose!" Zoe straightened her shoulders. She'd done nothing more than any normal person would do.

"Well, well, well . . . I see you're upset. Then I'm sorry. I should be grateful, shouldn't I? It's just that, I don't have company—ever. You frightened me."

"*I frightened you!*" Zoe rolled her eyes and pointed at the street. "My car's right out front. You might have guessed who was here."

"Yes." Emily thought a while. "I might have guessed. I sensed you were the inquisitive sort."

"Inquisitive!" Zoe felt herself blowing up like a rooster.

"I mean," Emily went on, a sad smile on her face, "a writer, after all. Aren't we an inquisitive bunch though?"

"I did your shopping and brought your groceries . . ."

"I said I was grateful." Emily smiled, which did nothing to soften her face or her distress. "Was the money correct?"

Zoe couldn't open her mouth for fearing of exploding. She shook her head, meaning "no."

"Then thank you." Emily motioned toward the front door as she headed to the kitchen, grocery bags in her arms.

She turned in the archway. "If you hear anything about that reading people in town want me to have, tell them I will be honored. I'm getting a book of new poems together. In fact, I heard you are a writer. I was wondering if you'd speak to your editor about me. I'll bet anything he'd be thrilled to hear another Emily Sutton book of poetry was in the works."

The plain face split in half, taking pleasure in her own words. Her head tipped to the side as she waited for Zoe to express her elation at the news.

Zoe didn't dare open her mouth. She took one step and then another, heading toward the door.

"Oh, and maybe in a few days, I'll need a few more things. I have your phone number. I'll call and let you know when to drop by for the list."

Zoe held herself tight as she crossed the living room, then the vestibule—stepping on an ancient boot—then out the doorway to the porch.

As she drove off, she made a mental note of how much Emily Sutton owed her. Next time, she promised herself, she would get the money and then tell the imperious queen to go get her own groceries.

Or better yet, she'd find Althea.

Chapter 9

"I called her again," Zoe said from a chair in her living room. "Still no answer."

"You mean her cousin?" Jenny brought herself into Zoe's Lilliputian living room, where the furniture legs had been cut down as far as they could be cut and where one chair was reserved for Fida, who growled at anyone daring to walk too close, her little white face knotting into a terrifying smile.

"Hmmm . . ." was all Jenny could come up with. "If you're still so upset, why don't we take turns shopping for her? As you said, I don't have much to do. Time on my hands."

Zoe turned her head. "Whew! You're a Pitiful Pete. 'I'm nobody! Who are you? / Are you nobody, too? / Then there's a pair of us—don't tell! / They'd banish us, you know.'"

"Royal pain," Jenny snapped back to her.

"You're a royal pain. That was Emily Dickinson. I'm doing research. She might be the subject of my next book."

"I knew it was Dickinson. I'm not completely illiterate, you know."

"And not without talents of your own, which you no doubt had before the worm divorced you. And probably still have."

"Many talents. I can look up legal precedents. I can track case law. I'm a woman of extraordinary gifts."

"Then start using them, Jenny Weston, before you bore the hell out of everybody."

"Well, if that's all the skill you have for friendship . . ." Jenny started to get out of the chair to go back home but had trouble pushing herself up. She fell ungracefully backward then laughed until she was crying.

"You Jabberwock!" She slit her wet eyes at Zoe, who'd rushed over to help. "'The jaws that bite, / the claws that catch.'"

"Ah ha! You know some important things after all."

"Like a Jabberwock?" Jenny was surprised at how much lighter she began to feel.

"Of course. The Jabberwock. The Mock Turtle. So many instructive characters in the Wonderland stories."

"So now, how long will I have to hear about death and eternity in Emily Dickinson? Talk about boring."

Zoe narrowed her eyes. "Infidel! You wait and see. I'll teach you how to think yet."

They agreed to split a beer and speak of other things.

"Like this Althea Sutton. Do you want to go with me to see her tomorrow?" Zoe asked.

Thinking she didn't have much else to do but not daring to admit it, Jenny took a while to nod that yes, she'd go into Traverse City with Zoe, and then to say that she hoped they would find a cousin who might lay claim to Emily Sutton and all her troubles.

* * *

It was lunchtime when they got to Traverse. Jenny was driving because Zoe made her nervous with all her controls and handbrakes, especially since she did a lot of talking with her hands.

"You want to get some lunch before we go to Althea's house?" Jenny asked as they drove by the big bear welcoming them to town, then down Munson to Front Street, where the downtown area began.

"Brew okay?" Jenny asked as she stopped for crowded crosswalks.

"Downstairs at Horizon," Zoe suggested.

"Or the Green House Café. Love their soup."

"Wherever there's a parking place." Zoe checked out the crowded sidewalks where tourists walked five across and the stores did the kind of business they never did in the winter months.

Jenny spotted a woman getting in her car just down the block. She put her signal on and waited until the woman got back out of her car and toddled off to do more shopping.

"I'm hoping Althea Sutton still lives here." Zoe sat forward, on the edge of her seat, taking the search for a parking place seriously. "First thing I'll do after we talk to her is tell Emily. The second thing I'll do is tell Emily I can't fetch her vittles anymore and that she'd better apologize to her cousin for whatever she did to her if she wants to go on eating."

"If she drove, it would be different," Jenny said as she saw a car leaving just ahead. She sped up to grab the spot but a car next to her cut over and pulled in.

She gave the rude driver the finger as she drove slowly past, liking the power of that finger and finding she felt more at home now. Kind of like being back in Chicago: rude drivers, crowds, circles of talking people blocking sidewalks. Who would have thought she'd miss Chicago? She'd already started planning a trip back there in her head. Maybe Zoe would go with her. They'd shop and see a show and go to a restaurant where meatloaf wasn't the height of cuisine. She was smiling broadly when a car ahead pulled from the curb directly across from the Brew. With their lunch place decided for them, she couldn't help but think this had to be her lucky day.

It wasn't.

Zoe saw him first. Tony Ralenti was sitting in the window of the Brew. His dark curly head leaned toward the woman next to him as if to catch what she was saying. The woman smiled and reached up to put a hand on his cheek as she spoke.

Zoe swore under her breath and hurried around the car to stop Jenny, who was coming back from putting money into the meter.

"I was thinking," Zoe said hurriedly. "Maybe we should get over to Althea's house before she leaves . . . or . . ."

Jenny looked down at her watch: twelve thirty. Zoe could be right. The restaurant might be packed. She squinted toward the front windows. Usually if all those seats were taken, there was no hope of finding a table inside.

She squinted again and saw Tony. She put her hand up to wave, then stopped herself, feeling Zoe's hand on her arm.

"Let's go somewhere else," Zoe said, her small, pretty face deadly serious. "Plenty of other places."

The woman beside Tony turned to him, talking. Her head was low. Her face was close to his. Jenny didn't recognize her. Certainly not from Bear Falls, not with that angular haircut and made-up face. More New York than Traverse City.

Zoe pulled at her arm. "Probably an old friend."

Jenny swallowed hard and said nothing.

"Maybe she's a relative. I wouldn't worry about it."

Tony got up to leave. The woman reached out, stopped him, and pulled him close. Jenny wasn't sure if he kissed her or just said something near her ear.

She wasn't able to turn away. Didn't believe what she was seeing.

He came out through the door to stand in the middle of the sidewalk. He glanced over at her and then looked up and down street. He squinted, looking across the street again, this time narrowing his eyes to see better. She thought he was going to wave but didn't stop to find out. Getting back in the car, she slammed the door then waited for Zoe to hop in the other side. She couldn't help but look in her rearview mirror as she pulled from the curb, driving off as fast as traffic would allow.

Tony was still standing near the curb, one hand up over his eyes, watching her go.

While Jenny drove, Zoe scratched her nose repeatedly. They were on the way to Slabtown, where Althea Sutton lived. Zoe kept her head turned, obviously not wanting

Jenny to notice and know the nose was at it again. Only too late this time. The damage was done. Terrible, about Tony—they were thinking the same thing—oldest crummy trick a man could play on a woman. Zoe's estimation of him fell to zero. "Creep," she muttered to herself, though Jenny heard.

Jenny looked once at Zoe, daring her to say another word out loud. She wanted no pity and no Wonderland philosophy. She wanted to drive and nothing else. Just keep driving the few blocks over to Slabtown to speak to the woman, get whatever assurances Zoe wanted from her, and then head home where, just maybe, she was ready to pack a bag and head off to a new life.

Places she might go streamed through her mind.

Chicago. Maybe.

Montana. A sister had to take a sister in when the sister was mad as hell and not going to take it anymore.

Or maybe turn the car around, find him, then drive along beside him shouting insults. She liked impossible scenarios like that. There was always a little satisfaction in pretense.

As she drove, she let red lights and stop signs and even *Do Not Park* signs take all her attention. Better than the picture in her head: Tony leaning close to kiss that woman good-bye. The thought that he'd rather be there with that flamboyant, skinny, phony . . .

What man wouldn't? She gave herself credit for all the wonderful, authentic qualities she was sure she possessed, then blew the thought right out of her head. What man wanted authentic when he could have sexy and showy?

Crummy bastard was the best she came up with, but it suited her mood.

"We don't have to go there if you don't feel like it," Zoe said, hunkered down in her seat, getting nothing back from Jenny.

They drove in silence, except for Zoe's rumbling stomach, which hadn't been fed as it expected.

* * *

Althea Sutton's house, a small white bungalow, was set back between older, two-story houses, each with a large, imposing porch. The house had an attached garage on the left side, two small squares of neatly cut grass in front, and untended flowerbeds running along a small concrete porch with a white-and-green aluminum awning above it.

Zoe rang the bell. There was an echo deep inside the house but nothing else. She pushed the bell again.

No one answered.

"She must be out." Zoe turned away from the door, her small face drawn up in a puzzled look.

"Or maybe she's on vacation." Jenny toed the doormat. "People still take them, you know."

Zoe looked around at the other houses. Next door, in front of a large square-brick house with green trim, an elderly woman stood watering her lawn, hose in hand.

"Why don't you go ask that lady if Althea still lives here?" Zoe nodded toward the woman in a straw sun hat.

"This is your baby. You go."

Zoe shook her head. "People sometimes don't keep their mind on what I'm saying. They're too busy looking me over."

Jenny had been with her enough now to know that Zoe always got attention, just not always the right kind.

Jenny headed toward the lady next door.

The elderly woman looked up from under her wide gardening hat and greeted Jenny with an inquisitive smile. She turned off the hose and dropped it to the ground, then stripped off her pristine gardening gloves. "Yes?" she asked pleasantly.

"We were wondering about your neighbor, Althea Sutton."

The woman's eyes wrinkled with curiosity. "Yes? What about her?"

"Do you know where she is?"

"I'm sorry." The woman's lined face showed confusion and then irritation. "I don't understand what you mean. Or what business it is of yours?"

"It's about her cousin. She lives in Bear Falls."

The woman nodded. "The cousin Althea takes care of? Or at least helps out?"

"That's the problem. She's stopped coming and her cousin is wondering what happened to her." The lie was a little one.

The woman looked up and down the street and thought a while. "I thought she must have gone away, but she usually tells me where she's going: a church outing or even bird watching from time to time. Just so I can keep an eye on things, but . . . well . . . this time she didn't say a word. I was beginning to wonder if there could be something wrong. The woman's in her late sixties and lives alone. Always good to look out for each other."

"Why did you think there might be something wrong?" Jenny asked.

"Well, you see, Althea has a man who does her grass, but look at those flowerbeds. Filled with weeds. Nobody's done anything there for at least a couple of weeks." She leaned around Jenny and pointed toward where Zoe stood.

Zoe waved.

"For goodness sakes, who's that?" The woman turned quickly back to Jenny.

"A friend."

She waved back to Zoe.

"Has anyone else been around looking for Althea?" Jenny asked.

"Young lady, I don't spy on my neighbors." The woman was getting suspicious and a little testy at being pressed.

"I didn't mean . . . we're just concerned about her."

"This cousin you're talking about. That wouldn't be the famous poet Althea's always bragging about, would it?"

Jenny nodded.

"In that case. Yes. I've seen a car in the driveway from time to time. Mostly in the evening. I've never seen anyone going in nor out, though I have watched. Purely for Althea's sake, you understand. Maybe that was the cousin in the car."

"You saw the driver? It was a woman?"

The woman thought again, then shook her head. "I didn't see the actual person."

"What about the car?"

"Do you really think I take down the license numbers of everyone who visits a neighbor?"

"But maybe the kind of car."

"I don't know one from the other."

"The year?"

"Please! Do you know the year every car on the road was built?"

Jenny thanked the woman and headed back to Zoe.

"What'd she say?" Zoe was impatient. "Where's Althea Sutton?"

Jenny shook her head. "Doesn't know. She's seen a car in the drive from time to time, but that's all."

"So where'd Althea go? And why would she drop Emily flat?" Zoe frowned. "Unless Emily got to be more than she could take. I can understand that well enough."

"Maybe it's like tough love. Get your own food or starve to death. You've got a pair of legs—use 'em." Jenny wasn't feeling particularly charitable at the moment, unable to shake the face of the woman in the Brew. Then unable to shake Tony, standing on the sidewalk.

People could be such . . . crap.

She stepped back to look again at the front, curtain-covered windows of Althea's house. Nothing moved behind them. Nobody was peeking out and deciding not to answer the door. The woman was obviously not at home.

They gave each other a "What now?" shrug.

"I'll check the garage," Zoe said. "If she moved away, she would at least take her car."

"And put the house up for sale."

"True."

The windows on the overhead garage door where way above Zoe's head. Jenny leaned across her and cupped her hands against the glass. At first her eyes had to adjust to the darkness inside. When they did, the car inside was obvious, taking up most of the small space surrounded with what looked like rakes and shovels and a potting table.

"There's a car in there." She turned to look down at Zoe, face and voice puzzled.

"Shouldn't be." Zoe started around the side where she found an unlocked door and opened it as, behind her, Jenny whispered, "I hope that neighbor's not watching. She'll call the police for sure."

She put her hands on Zoe's shoulders as they stepped inside the garage, then fell back. Coughing. The air inside was thick and hot and smelled overwhelmingly of decay.

"Wha . . . ?" Jenny gagged, tasting the thick odor in her mouth and throat.

"Let's get out of here," she said, pulling her cell from her pocket as she stumbled back through the door.

Zoe waved off Jenny's hand and shook her head. "We don't know anything for sure. You know animals get inside garages and die." She went in and walked around the elderly Chevy, her hand over her mouth and nose.

"Don't, Zoe." Jenny took another step back out the door.

Zoe moved up the far side of the car, swatting flies away from her face. Jenny watched as Zoe stood on her tiptoes, hands resting on the car door. She could see Zoe's face through the car window, which was buzzing with more flies. Zoe's eyes got huge. She put her hand to her mouth, then looked over at Jenny.

"Call the police," she yelled. "It's got to be Althea Sutton. She's dead, Jenny."

Chapter 10

Zoe Zola bent over in a weedy flowerbed, sick to her stomach among the straggly daisies. She wiped at her mouth with the Kleenex Jenny handed her, then bent again.

The dead woman in the car was flashing in and out of Zoe's head. The smell came back—a terrible sensory memory—mixed in with the sound of a thousand black flies buzzing at once.

The thought bent her back over the flowerbed but there wasn't much left to bring up. She was thankful there'd been no time for lunch.

Jenny stood beside Zoe in the front of Althea Sutton's garage. She looked this way and that, avoiding the next-door neighbor who'd stopped all pretense of watering and watched them closely.

She hoped the police would get there fast and wished she were anywhere else but here, with a dead woman in the garage, Zoe heaving in the bushes, and the now quiet neighborhood around them soon to be torn apart by death.

Jenny had no intention of taking a closer look at the body. Zoe's condition was enough to tell her whatever she'd seen was as bad as a thing could get.

"Terrible," Zoe finally choked out, getting a hold of herself. "She's sitting behind the wheel of the car. But dead." She made a face up at Jenny. "Oh, so dead. And . . . things . . ."

"I get the picture," Jenny said, grateful for the sound of a siren and then for the police car skidding to a stop at the curb behind her car.

Jenny waved the cops toward the garage. She tried to warn them, only to be told, gruffly, to wait outside—as if she had planned to do anything else. When the men came out, their faces weren't any better than Zoe's had been. One of the cops made his own bend-over in the bushes. The cops had only a few questions before directing them to wait in Jenny's car. Other squad cars and plain sedans arrived, and a large bald man ambled over, leaning in the open window to introduce himself as Detective Minty, then to say, kindly enough, that he'd be back to talk to them as soon as he could.

"Why do I feel like I've got a noose around my neck?" Zoe grumbled as she settled back against the hot leather seat.

"Same reason I hear bars clanking shut around me."

Jenny scowled at the wheel. All she could think was how this had become the worst day of her life—well, second worst. Her dad's death trumped everything.

"Can't get my head around this," Zoe said after a while. "Emily didn't know what happened to her, and here she is dead. Looks like for quite a long time, too."

"Maybe she committed suicide."

Zoe shook her head. "That's no suicide, Jenny. You'd have to see her to get what I mean."

Jenny put up a hand. "Don't tell me. Let's just sit quietly and see what the detective wants from us. I need to go home so bad." Her voice broke. Then a thought hit: What if Mom heard about this on the radio?

Couldn't happen. Too soon. They had time. She prayed there wouldn't be any reporters rushing over to get interviews from them while they were still white faced—maybe a little vomit running down the front of Zoe's blouse.

Zoe looked over, her small, pretty face sad. "What a rotten day this turned out to be."

"You think?" Jenny said and closed her eyes.

Neighbors gathered as men scurried in and out of the house and garage. Men in hazmat suits went in the garage and stayed. It was almost an hour before Detective Minty came back, ambling over as if he had all the time in the world, then leaning in the window, apologizing, shaking his shiny head, and asking if they'd been inside the house at all. He went on to say that the house had been ransacked. "Thinking a burglary," he said.

"What about the woman? That is Althea, isn't it?" Zoe asked, meeting with his quizzical look.

"Dead more than a couple of weeks, the coroner said."

"Not suicide, was it?" Jenny leaned up to ask.

Zoe scoffed. "If you mean the lady didn't beat herself over the head while sitting in her car. Yes, I'd say that's a safe assumption." She turned to the detective. "Murder, right?"

"We're not giving out any information yet, but it's safe to say you're right. Miss Sutton was murdered."

Zoe narrowed her eyes at him. "We'll be happy to tell you why we were here. It wasn't to do her harm."

"In a little while. Back at the station. I'll take your statements then and send you on your way home. Awful thing to find." He stepped away, and then back. "Why were you here again? I forgot what you said."

"Because she hadn't shown up to take care of her cousin for a while," Zoe spoke up loudly.

"That's right." He nodded. "You're from Bear Falls, right? Something about a woman who lives alone and needs help. Is that it? You two must've been mad at this lady, eh?" He motioned toward the house.

Jenny eyed him. "Officer. She's been dead for a while you said. We just got here today. I'd say that pretty much lets us out as your suspects."

"You know, ma'am," he smiled coolly in the window, arm resting on the car, "you'd be amazed what murderers do and how they think. For instance, with this incident now. If I killed a lady and never saw anything more about it in the papers or on the TV, maybe I'd start to wonder what was going on. Maybe I'd even go back to look at the body, make sure it was still there."

"And would you call the police?"

He looked away then leaned farther in the window. He chuckled. "Got me there. Pretty dumb killer, to do a thing like that. And you ladies don't look dumb to me at all."

He gave them a probing look then pulled back and straightened, tugging at the belt around his waist.

"You don't have to stay here. I've got your names. Why don't you go on over to the police station. I'll be there as soon as I can to take your statements."

* * *

"Hungry?" Jenny asked as she drove up Eighth Street. "We missed lunch."

"Yuck." Zoe gave her a sick look.

They pulled in front of the station on Woodmere and went in. The woman at the front desk was waiting for them and showed them to Detective Minty's office, pointing to chairs, even offering coffee, setting their stomachs bouncing again.

They'd been there for an hour and a half before Detective Minty bustled in, his tanned face deadly serious, his large body dropping into the desk chair as he first apologized for keeping them waiting then took a pad of paper from a drawer, slapped it on the desk, and settled back in his chair. He wrote on his pad of paper before looking up again, first at Jenny and then at Zoe.

His small eyes narrowed to slits. "Althea Sutton's a friend of yours?"

Both women shook their heads fast, as if innocence would be measured in headshakes.

"Then what were you doing in her garage?" He folded his hands on top of the pad of paper as if he was only asking a casual question. Had nothing better to do with his time. He played his pen across the back of his fingers.

"Look, Detective," Jenny wanted this miserable day to end. "We're tired. You've got our names and contact information. I'm upset. Zoe's upset. We don't usually find bodies . . ."

Detective Minty put a hand up in a "stop" motion.

Zoe elbowed Jenny in the ribs, making Jenny turn to her.

"What? You want to stay here forever? I'm tired and hot and also hungry, despite watching you heave up your guts."

"Let's hold on a minute here." The detective eyed Jenny as if assessing guilt and scoring her pretty high. "Let's start with why you were there again, and how you found the body."

Zoe repeated the story of Emily Sutton and why they came to town to find the cousin who used to buy groceries for her but had left her alone with no help.

He wrote as Zoe spoke and Jenny filled in.

"And you went in the woman's garage—why?"

"Because it was there." There was a slight hiss to Zoe's words. She was beyond tired and hungry now. Any minute, she expected to fall right out of her chair.

"Try again, Miss . . . eh . . . Zola."

Zoe sighed. "I wanted to see if her car was there. She didn't answer her phone when I called. Didn't answer the door. I figured if she'd moved, the car would be gone. It wasn't. I went in to take a look and found her like that."

"Got any ideas what happened to Miss Sutton?" He laid his pen down and stared from Zoe to Jenny and back.

"She's dead, I know that much." Zoe almost groaned.

He nodded. "Hope neither one of you had anything to do with it."

Zoe said nothing. Jenny fought to keep her anger in check.

"Did that look like fresh blood to you?" Zoe spoke fast.

"How long ago did this Emily Sutton say her cousin stopped coming out there?"

Zoe looked at Jenny then back to the detective. "She didn't really say. Maybe three weeks. Emily probably had enough groceries for that long and then panicked."

He seemed to have run out of questions other than rechecking their addresses and phone numbers so he could reach them.

He asked for Emily Sutton's address. "Have to go break the news." He shook his head. "Always a tough thing to do. I'll get out there soon as we've got things wrapped up here. Have to talk to your police chief first. He'll be brought in on this. You won't be going over there, to the cousin's house, will you? I'd like it if you left that to me. I'm not a tough guy. I don't want to hurt the woman, it's just that sometimes it's better if we're there when the family gets the news of a murder. Actions and reactions, it's called. Watching to see if the response is what we think it should be. I don't mean to be cruel. It's just the way things are in a murder investigation."

"Emily Sutton won't answer the door," Zoe warned. "Not the phone either, unless she knows ahead of time that you're going to call."

He looked puzzled. "She an invalid or something?"

"Kind of eccentric. She was a well-known poet—once. She doesn't like strangers. Rarely sees anybody, or talks to anybody at all."

"You two see her."

Jenny nodded. "And my mother's seen her."

"Think you could go with us, then, to see this Emily Sutton? Make it better all around if I don't have to burst in on her. I wouldn't want you saying anything though. You'd be there in case she needs you."

He smiled, a kind of peace offering, as he took them to the front waiting area. At the door he offered his hand, then told them, with a chuckle, that he didn't think either of them had anything to do with Miss Sutton's murder. "If that will make you feel any better," he smiled. "Looks like she was hit on the head inside the house then stabbed when she was trying to get away." He watched their faces, seeing how they took the details.

"You know anybody who was mad at Miss Sutton?"

They shook their heads. "Didn't know her, Detective."

"So there's only this cousin—that's all the family?"

"There's Emily's sister. But she's gone."

"Got a name or address?"

Zoe shook her head. Jenny said, "Her name is Lorna Sutton. That's about all we know."

He thought awhile. "Looks personal, the way that house was torn apart. Sure would like to talk to that other cousin."

"Ask Emily, but I can tell you now, she doesn't know where Lorna went."

They assured him they knew nothing more but would go with him to break the news to Emily.

"Have a good day." He waved from the doorway as if they'd just shared a pleasant social call.

"Oh, we certainly will," Zoe shot over her shoulder.

Jenny pulled her arm, hissing at her to be quiet. The last thing they wanted was to piss off a cop after they'd found a dead body.

The ride back to Bear Falls was long. Every mile could have been a hundred. It wasn't only the horror of finding Althea Sutton dead, but there was still Tony's treachery stuck in the back of Emily's mind. Or not treachery at all. Maybe they'd never been anything but friends. The rest was in her head.

Nope, Emily assured herself. She wasn't an idiot. She'd seen the looks, the smiles. Damned if he hadn't been flirting and she'd flirted back. Flirting wasn't a prelude to being cut out of his life completely. Or maybe it was. Her experience in these things wasn't that extensive.

Damn, she told herself. There should be a book—with diagrams—that listed the ways men got out of relationships. And another book that warned women about men who couldn't commit in the first place. Women needed to know these things. It wasn't that dating was a waste of time. It was just that if a woman invested the slightest bit of feeling, a light should go off. Red—run like hell. Green— looking good.

Maybe there was a look a man gave another man—like "HELP!" Or maybe a secret code he used, thinking the woman would pick up on it and cut the cord before things got beyond critical mass.

She made herself angry all over again, but at least the problem with Tony was real and human, maybe even explainable. There was nothing explainable about Althea Sutton sitting in that car. The awful smell in that garage. The flies.

Jenny's cell rang as they drove through Acme, still miles from home.

"Jenny? Is that you?" It was Dora, in a state. "Minnie Moon called. She said Randy Solomon got a call from a friend in Traverse. Is Althea Sutton really dead? That's what he told her. He lives right down the street from Althea. I knew you two were going to town to see her so I wanted to warn you not to go over there."

"Zoe found her, Mom."

"What? Dear! Dear! Dear! Is she all right? I mean, poor Zoe. You know how excited she can get."

"She didn't kill her, Mom."

"Kill! You mean somebody killed Althea? Why, this is just awful. Terrible."

"We're on our way home."

"Were you there, too?" Dora demanded.

"I was."

"For heaven's sakes. Poor Emily! What now! I can't think . . ."

"We'll be there in half an hour."

"But what about Emily? Who's going to tell her?"

"A detective's coming out to Bear Falls. He said he'd pick up the police chief and meet us later. He wants me and Zoe there when he breaks the news."

"Well, yes. You both should go. Poor Emily. Imagine, and after all the heartbreak she's suffered in her life."

Dora was quiet.

Jenny thought the call was over and was about to hang up.

"Oh, and dear. I hate to bring up anything else at a time like this, but there was a young woman here this afternoon. Police Chief Warner sent her to our house because she'd been to Emily's and there was no one home. Well, that's what she said, but we know Emily won't answer the door to a stranger."

"What did she want with Emily?" Jenny glanced over to see that Zoe was, understandably, sound asleep in the seat beside her.

"Well, it's the strangest thing . . ." Dora hesitated. "I'm . . . anyway, this young woman claims she's Walter Shipley's niece. He's quite a famous poet. Probably a lot better known than Emily. It seems he's disappeared. Quite a while ago, according to this Alex Shipley. I might have heard something, but I don't remember much about it. She's here because Walter Shipley and Emily were friends. Or they knew each other. Something like that. Her parents live in Europe but she goes to school here in Michigan and thought she'd try to track down Emily. To see if she knows where he went. The police in Maine—that's where he lives . . . or lived—have come up with nothing."

Dora sighed. "I'm sorry now I invited her back, what with the day you've had. I think I'd better call Abigail, too. You know how she's being about Emily. This will be a blow and you know how upset she was with me last time." She stopped talking, then said, "Did you say Althea was killed?"

"Not really, Mom. More than that. She was murdered."

That Jenny lost the signal right then felt almost like divine providence. If Mom was any indication, the town was already buzzing. All she could hope was that no one took it on herself to tell Emily.

In the seat beside her, Zoe's head tipped, blonde hair hung over her eyes. Her small hands were crossed in her lap. Jenny already knew this woman to be tough and hard-nosed . . . and vulnerable. If only she could spare her some of what was ahead of them.

Back home, Zoe popped awake, jumped from the car, and ran through the trees to her house, hurrying to Fida to hold her and hug her, while Jenny went to her mom—each to her own point of comfort.

Chapter 11

"She's here, dear." Dora hurried out to the porch to hug her daughter and then to break the news. "Walter Shipley's niece. She's in the backyard."

Jenny groaned. "Detective Minty and Ed Warner are coming later. They want me and Zoe to go to Emily's with them. Break the news about Althea. All I want to do now is lie down awhile. Can't you explain to her?"

"I know. But the poor girl is deeply worried."

Jenny hurried into the house and dropped into the first chair she came to. "I wish I didn't have to deal with something else right now. I didn't see the body up close, but poor Zoe was in that garage. I don't think she needs another worry, if you plan on bringing Zoe into this, too."

She leaned her head back and closed one eye. "Didn't you say this man's been gone quite a while? Could she hold off at least until Emily's been told her cousin's dead?"

Dora shook her head. "Come out and meet her. Please. She is such a sweet girl. I think you'll like her."

"Mom!" Jenny complained, but Dora was headed back toward the kitchen, leaving Jenny with nothing to do but follow.

The girl sat in the backyard, on the ground under the huge walnut tree. Her head was bent, examining a leaf, long fingers running over the rough surface of the fanning veins.

Alex Shipley was in her early twenties, wearing the uniform of her age group: long narrow-legged jeans, a striped T-shirt that hugged her curved shoulders, and strappy sandals. Her face was thin and lovely. She saw Jenny and Dora and jumped to her feet, swiping her hands along her jeans, then sticking a hand out to take Jenny's.

Classic bone structure. That was what Jenny noticed first. And billows and billows of messy blonde hair caught on top of her head with combs. Long strands of hair hung around her face. A crammed backpack lay on the ground at her feet. A nervous little smile ran across her full mouth as she brought one shoulder up to her right ear as if, turtle-like, she was trying to disappear.

Dora shepherded them to a table on the back porch where they could sit.

"Your mother told me what happened today. Awful." The girl set her backpack down and flicked strands of glossy blonde hair from her eyes.

Jenny could only nod. She was wrung out.

"I'm sorry. I wouldn't have come if I'd known. I went to Emily Sutton's because the last I knew of my uncle, he was going there. I have letters. He and Emily Sutton exchanged quite a few. I only have hers. It seemed as if there was something between them." She rubbed one hand hard over the other. "I knocked and knocked but Emily didn't answer.

Your police chief—I didn't know where else to go—said to come talk to you. That you might be able to get Emily to see me."

"You're in school in Michigan, dear?" Dora leaned in to ask, giving Jenny a minute to absorb everything.

"Yes, ma'am. U of M. Grad school."

"And what are you studying?"

"English literature."

"What do you know?" Dora glanced at the figure coming across the lawn, through her garden, Fida snapping at her heels as if getting even for the hours Zoe'd been away. "Here comes someone you should meet right now."

Zoe came up the steps without her usual thump and waddle. One step at a time. Holding on to the bannister. She took Alex's outstretched hand, sat down with a huge sigh, and listened to why this Alex Shipley was there, on the Westons' back porch.

"She studies English literature," Dora said, smiling wide at Zoe. "Imagine that."

"I've heard of you, Miss Zola. One of my professors gave me a book of yours to read. Wonderfully thought-out. I hope to write the same sort of thing someday. I love research and tying thought and the writer's life and work together."

Soon Zoe was smiling, perking up at having someone of like mind sitting at the table with her. For just a minute, she seemed to be herself again.

"I've read your book on characters in Grimm's Fairy Tales. Scary, all that death and horror. Comparing them to Freud and Adler was genius." Alex leaned forward, as close as she could get to Zoe.

Color slowly came back to Zoe's face. Her eyes glowed again. Back to places inside her head, populated with all sorts of weird creatures and the weird thoughts that followed when ogres and monsters were allowed to run loose.

And then they were back to Alex's reason for being in Bear Falls, and everyone grew deadly serious.

"Three years?" Zoe shook her head after she heard.

Alex took a deep breath. "My parents haven't heard anything from him since August of 2013. I was living in Maine then, so I went to Kennebunkport to check on him. His landlord had already put his things in storage. My father's been paying the fees ever since, thinking Uncle Walter will return from wherever he went to and need his belongings. He's done this before. For maybe a month or so at a time, gone off to write where he can be alone. But never this long."

"And"—Zoe moved her chair closer—"what brought you to Bear Falls?"

"I found letters from Emily Sutton to Uncle Walter. She invited him to visit here. They'd been writing back and forth for a few years. The summer he was supposed to come here is the summer he disappeared. I was hoping . . . well."

"I can imagine what you were hoping." Jenny knew the girl wasn't going to find her uncle at the house on the swamp. No man in that house. "But I don't think Emily can help you."

Zoe nodded. "She's alone. There's nobody else with her. Her mother's dead. Her sister's gone. And well . . . her cousin . . . just died."

"Mrs. Weston told me what happened. That's awful. She was murdered?"

Zoe nodded.

"Then this isn't the time for me to be bothering her."

Her disappointment was palpable. She looked down at her hands, opening them wide as if considering why those hands couldn't reach out and find her uncle.

"Have you thought maybe your uncle found he needed to be away from everyone? Emily's like that. She left the life she had and disappeared into that house and stayed there. Writers are an endangered species, Alex," Zoe said, meaning to be kind. "The world is such a constantly demanding place. Poets need to replenish. Some go away for years."

"But I can't get it out of my head that he wouldn't do that to us. Our family's always been close. And I have these letters . . ."

She patted her backpack then pulled it around to her lap. She took two faded envelopes from one of the pockets. Looking at the women, she carefully opened one of the envelopes and scanned it before reading a couple of lines: "*I don't often see people, as you know, Walter. But I will certainly see you. I look forward to it like nothing I've looked forward to in years. Please come so I can show you my swamp. Like you, I need silent places. And places where I can hear the breath of small, slippery streams. You will laugh, as I do, at the turtles, and the frogs. We can shiver in the cool shadows and be frightened by wet earth that grabs at our feet and threatens disappearance.*"

"Goodness, that sounds exactly like Emily." Dora sat back and clapped her hands together.

Zoe made a noise. "I'm amazed." She snapped her mouth shut. Not a word of what she truly thought about Emily Sutton leaked out.

"She was expecting your uncle's visit?" Dora asked.

"It seems so. I don't know if he came here or not. But I'd like to find out. She included a poem in this one." Alex opened the second letter.

The girl handed two sheets of paper to Dora, who took the pages reverently and read the poem to herself, lips moving slightly. She looked up at the others. Her face glowed.

"Oh, it's Emily at her best. One from her book."

She read,

Silliness in the cosmic swamp.
High dudgeon greets the spring.
A million seek immortality
Beneath the spackled pollen screen.

Black water and I hold my breath.
An over populated log spins, set in place.
A dread superfluity of turtles,
Now each a flying carapace.

Drawn to dark phantasms
Entailing trespass in the brave.
In boots and stick, sent flying
By the slither of a snake.

Alex turned the envelope over in her hands. "August fifth, 2013. There are ten letters all together. I think there was an attraction. But maybe it was only that they respected each other's work." She put her head down. "I even hoped he might be here with her. That's why I came. To make sure he's all right."

There were tears in her eyes when she looked up. "I've been hoping they were in love and he's here, and happy. Then I thought maybe, if not that, at least I could find his car. Something. I need proof he's still . . ."

"His car?" Jenny interrupted.

"A red Saturn. He loved that car. If he came here, he would have driven it. I'm trying to find anything connected with him. He never renewed his license. The car wasn't sold, as far as I could find. Not in Maine, anyway. What would he have done with it?"

They talked on until Detective Minty called to say he and their police chief, Ed Warner, were on their way over. Alex got hurriedly to her feet, grabbing up her backpack and thanking them for their time. Dora reached out to stop her, taking her hand.

"Where will you be staying? I'm sure we could set up a time for you to talk to Emily. There's got to be a way."

Alex dipped her head and gave a half grin. "You can call me. I'll leave my number."

"But will you be close by? There aren't many places to stay in Bear Falls. Maybe Traverse. That's a big town."

Alex grinned again. "No problem. I'll hang around."

"But . . . how old are you, dear?"

"I'm twenty-three, Mrs. Weston." Alex laughed and put her arm around Dora's shoulders. "You don't need to worry about me."

"But I will. Please let me know where you'll be. I don't like to think of you some place that's not, well, safe for a girl your age."

Alex shrugged. "I'll sleep in my car. I've done it before."

Before Detective Minty arrived to pick up Zoe and Jenny, Alex was settled into Lisa's old room, still protesting, saying she'd be fine, but she was no match for Dora Weston.

* * *

Long shadows lay over the Sutton house when Ed Warner's police car pulled in front and parked. Silhouettes of tree branches moved across the darkened rock walls, setting the house in motion, making Jenny think of cartoons where houses moved and chased people.

The two policemen, in the front seat of the Bear Falls police chief's squad car, gathered folders together and got out, following Zoe and then Jenny through the gate up to the porch.

Zoe went through her usual routine—knocking then calling Emily's name.

They got the usual response—nothing.

"Here, let me." Detective Minty leaned in and knocked, then called out, "Emily Sutton? I'm a detective with the Traverse City Police Department. Could you come to the door please?"

Nothing.

Ed Warner, Bear Falls police chief, a long, tall man with a head that sat loosely on his shoulders, adjusted the gun on his hip and walked to the end of the porch. He looked first at the already dark swamp and then stretched his body over the rail to get a look at the back of the house.

"She go out into that swamp?" Minty asked, frowning at Jenny and Zoe as if they were hiding Emily Sutton.

Zoe shrugged and spread her arms wide. "Who knows? All I've done so far is deliver groceries. I don't know her daily routine. Except that she doesn't answer the phone or the door."

"How do you get ahold of her? To pick up this grocery list you talked about?"

"She calls me."

"Then she's got to be in there." He tried again, knocking and calling out her name.

Nothing. The two cops ambled close together and mumbled to each other. Ed Warner's loose head wobbled a few times. They headed for the steps, motioning for the women to follow.

Zoe could have told them, just from looking at the ground, that they'd chosen the mushy side of the house to take toward the backyard. Zoe and Jenny stepped on the highest hillocks of grass they could find, picking their way behind the men, who swore as they sank down into mucky dirt, then shook their heavy shoes and swore again.

There was nobody around the back.

"What happened here?" Detective Minty stood with his jacket open, hands at his hips, looking up at the burned stone wall that was the whole back of the house.

"There used to be an ell tacked on." Jenny told them what she'd heard from Dora. She'd only been ten when they moved to town so didn't know a whole lot of history. "Emily's mother died in the fire."

Minty nodded. "Terrible thing. Seems to be an unlucky family."

"Thought Jenny would've filled you in on the Suttons." Ed Warner looked vaguely guilty of something, then frowned over at Jenny.

"Anything else?" Minty asked when Jenny seemed about to answer, then didn't, thinking he could learn about Emily when he met her.

The four of them stood in the weedy yard looking around at the outbuildings: a chicken coop, two sheds close to falling down, and one unpainted garage, the windows covered with cardboard.

They looked out toward the street, Minty asking if this had ever been a farm and Jenny about to tell him what she knew.

"What are you people doing on my property?"

Startled, they turned to a woman standing behind them as if she'd popped out of the ground.

Emily Sutton's face was flushed with anger. She was dressed in nondescript old pants that must once have belonged to a man, and an outsized sweater. She wore boots that were covered with muck.

In her hands she held a strange bouquet of white stems, blackened pipe bowls at the end of each stem. Jenny had never seen anything like them.

"Well?" Emily sniffed and reared back to demand an answer. "And you, Zoe Zola, have you taken it on yourself to bring people to my home?"

Zoe puffed up and would have pushed right up to Emily if Detective Minty didn't put his arm out to stop her.

"I'm with the Traverse City police, ma'am. Detective Minty." He stuck his hand out, then let it drop to his side when she ignored it.

"What do you want with me, Detective?" Emily kept her large eyes focused on Zoe.

"I've come with some bad news. Could we go inside?"

Emily shook her head. "Why should I invite you into my home if you're all only here to upset me?"

Emily's defiance slipped away as she looked from face to face. She grew concerned.

"Miss Sutton." Ed Warner had his thumbs stuck in his gun belt. He took a step toward her. "How are you doing? Remember me? I was out here a time or two when you thought you saw prowlers."

She looked him up and down, then shook her head. "I don't *think* I see prowlers. Like now, people will intrude from time to time. And I don't believe I've ever seen you before, Officer," she said to Ed Warner.

"But, ma'am . . ."

Emily turned from Jenny to Zoe. She shook her head. "I hope I won't be sorry for confiding in the two of you. Here you are, knowing how I value my privacy."

Tears sprang to her eyes. Her head tipped to one side. The change was instant.

"Ma'am," Minty stepped in, exasperated and sounding ready to have this over with, "there's been a death."

"A death?" Her eyes popped wider. "Who's dead?"

"I believe you're related to an Althea Sutton."

"Althea? My cousin?"

He had her full attention. Her hands came down, the odd flowers she held fell to the ground and scattered in a small heap at her feet.

"What's happened to Althea?"

"She was found today. In her garage."

A hand flew to her mouth. "Not suicide! Oh no. I warned her. Always depressed. Every time I saw her. I told her she had to see somebody."

Minty shook his head. "Sorry, ma'am. Worse than that. Somebody murdered your cousin."

Both hands flew to her mouth. Tears flooded her eyes. She took a step toward them, crushing her dead-looking flowers underfoot. And then another step before she turned and ran toward the house, feet flying over the muck. She was out of sight before any of them reacted.

Minty watched her go, then followed, saying that he had to talk to her.

The three of them watched the man go after her and waited until they decided it would be best to go back to their cars.

"Know what she was holding?" Zoe spoke into the uncomfortable quiet of the car.

Jenny looked over and shook her head.

"Indian Pipes. Emily Dickinson's favorite flower."

Jenny nodded. Ed Warner turned to look over the back of the seat but said nothing.

"They don't last if you pick them. Emily Sutton should have known that."

"Is that so?" Jenny pretended interest, then bent to check the front porch of the house where Emily stood, talking to Detective Minty. She looked at her watch. Six thirty. She was hungry. She was mad. She was disgusted with just about everything and, unable to stop herself, leaned toward Ed Warner.

"Can I walk home? No reason for me to stay, and I'm tired."

Surprised, Ed turned and shook his head. "Not until the detective comes back. I have no authority to let you go."

"Oh, Ed." She'd known him from their school days together. "You know where I live."

She reached out to open the door, with Zoe pushing up behind her.

"Hey." Ed grabbed Jenny's arm. "I'm not kidding. You're not going anywhere until Minty's through with her. You ever think maybe she might need your help? Just hearing her cousin's been murdered and all? Usually ladies like to offer."

Zoe muttered something that sounded like "ladies" and didn't wither at the chief's look.

Minty came down the steps. Emily went into the house and shut the door behind her. Jenny and Zoe were driven home.

Nothing more was said beyond Minty's warning that he might still be calling on them for information. No clue as to what Emily told him. Just a big, unexpressive back turned, then a wave out the window as Ed Warner drove away and Jenny turned to find a familiar truck parked in front of the house.

Zoe's eyes filled with pity when she saw the truck. She shook her head at Jenny and went as fast as she could go back to her own house.

Chapter 12

Jenny felt as if she'd been trapped by some crummy trick of fate. *Why now?* Her eyes kept closing on her—she was that tired. The last thing she needed was a reunion or some big confrontation when she couldn't think, or even feel.

Maybe she *had* done something to him. She tried to think hard enough to come up with a terrible sin she'd committed. Nothing there. He was the one who was curt to her. He was the one who didn't call. He was the one with that woman in town.

Whatever happened between them wasn't her fault. And now—between a dead body, hours in a police station, and Emily Sutton's nuttiness—she'd had as much as a woman could take in a single day.

She walked quietly through the house toward the kitchen, where she heard voices. Mom was there. And Alex Shipley. Then Tony's voice. How could she talk to him in front of everyone?

Jenny whispered a firm "shit" under her breath and stood in the doorway, looking around—from one face to the next—ending with Tony.

They stopped talking when she walked in.

"How'd it go?" Dora got up and hurried over to hug Jenny.

"Bad." Jenny wanted to stay there, with Mom's arms around her, but Dora pulled back to point to Tony.

"Look who's here. We were showing Alex Tony's new designs for Little Libraries. You'll be interested."

"Not tonight," Jenny said and skipped his face.

"They're wonderful." Alex, thoroughly at home in a pair of Lisa's pajamas, smiled. Her long hair was down and lying across her shoulders. No makeup. Beautiful.

Perfect homecoming, Emily thought sourly.

"You should take a look," Alex said.

"Not tonight," Jenny said again. "I'm going to bed, if all of you don't mind. Long day. My brain's fogged. I couldn't tell you good from bad right now."

She started toward the hall leading to her room.

"Heard about what happened. Sorry for what you've been through." Tony's voice had a deeper rasp than usual.

She stopped halfway across the kitchen. She looked directly at him. Was he talking about what he'd done to her or just the rotten day?

"You go on to bed, dear," Dora said, looking from Jenny to Tony.

"I was wondering . . ." Tony was out of his chair.

Dora put out a hand to stop him. "Maybe now's not a good time, Tony," Jenny said as he started toward her.

He took Jenny's wrist and held on.

She looked at his hand on her and almost smiled. It felt good to have him that close. Reassuring. Or something else. She was too tired to figure it out.

"Not now," she whispered, looking into his eyes for something that probably wasn't there.

His shaggy, dark head was too close. The drawn lines on his face sent a message she had no name for. "When? I have to talk to you," he whispered, close enough for her to feel his breath on her forehead.

Jenny shook off his hand and hurried back toward her bedroom. There, with the door closed, she fell on her bed and was asleep in seconds.

By the time she got up the next morning, there was no one around. A note from Dora lay on the table. It said she was having lunch with Abigail and would be home later. The note also said that Zoe had called and wanted her to call when she got up. Next was the news that Alex was going into Traverse to check with the DMV about her uncle's car and to take care of other business. The note ended with the news that Zoe was coming to dinner later so they could all talk about what was going on and what they could do about it.

Jenny read the note again and again, having the strangest feeling the paper had nothing to do with her. There was no one she wanted to talk to. She didn't want to see anybody—least of all Zoe, around whom terrible things seemed to swirl. And there was no way she was going to sit through dinner while they talked as though they could change anything.

"Tony." She said his name aloud and supposed he would have to be faced, but not today. She had nothing left inside to deal with him right then. Disappearing sounded like a great idea. Gone. Out of there. Like jumping in a hole and pulling the earth down after her.

* * *

She found a lonely beach on Lake Michigan and walked barefoot, bending to examine every stone in case one was a Petoskey stone, state stone of Michigan. She walked at the very edge of the waterline, playing an old game with the lake, daring the water to get her. It always did, and made her jump as spray wet her jeans.

Up in the grasses, she searched for fish skulls or empty clamshells—treasures she would stuff into her pocket.

Then she went wading into the lake to rescue a solid piece of driftwood, holding the wet wood in her hands and imagining the sinking ship it came from or, more likely, the old dock broken by last winter's waves.

She thought about murder, holding the driftwood. A middle-aged woman slaughtered in her own house. As if nothing she'd done until that moment mattered or could have changed the ending.

She thought about reasons to kill: hatred, jealousy, money, fear . . .

And reasons to be cruel. The way Tony had been to her.

The air got colder. She'd brought a sweater, tied around her neck. She untied it and pushed her arms inside. When she stood to look out at the horizon, she hugged herself, searching the place where the sky and water merged. Nothing but an infinite gray. No sun. A thin dark line began to form above the lake's outer limit. A storm coming from where most Michigan storms began, over Minnesota, or farther north, in Canada.

From time to time she shivered, but refused to leave. There was no place to go. No better place to think.

At first she thought of nothing. And then she thought about Zoe and her belief in reading the signs to understand your life and in a sensitive nose that smelled trouble. Zoe rolling her eyes as a piece fell into place for her and she knew—as she always emphasized with a blunt finger in the air—"You see? If I hadn't seen that old man sitting in the park I'd never thought of Thoreau and embraced my country life here in Bear Falls."

Always a "See! You have to stay alert. Nothing's either all bad or all good. Everything is a part of something else. You just have to wait to find out what that something else is."

She'd tried Zoe's way all morning and come up with nothing except that she didn't understand herself and didn't get Tony at all. Maybe he was hiding a killer in his house and couldn't tell her. Maybe he had a terrible disease. Maybe that woman at the Brew was a long lost sister.

And maybe she was the Queen of England, and he knew he wasn't good enough for her.

She wasn't even sure she felt anything for him. There'd been a few kisses. Nothing beyond that, though she'd been coming to think just maybe there would be a time soon when he'd lean over to kiss her and she'd look into those eyes that laughed at her so often and "that" would be "that."

"That" was always "that" when sex came into the picture. At least for her. Some old-fashioned ancestral belief stuck in her head like a magic kernel: sleep with the guy, marry the guy. So three men in her life. All starting here on this beach with Johnny Arlen, where she'd lost her virginity and never missed it.

She dug her toes into the sand and wondered how old each separate grain could be. Old enough to have been through an awful lot. Old enough to watch the earth change again and again. Old enough to know that nothing much in the short life of a human being was worth suffering for.

The storm came up fast, the gray disappearing into rolling clouds. Wind blew the lake into waves falling over each other. Jenny stood watching the storm coming at her until it began to rain.

By the time she got back to her car, she was soaked. Her hair hung in pasted bunches. Back in the car, with the heater on, she smelled like wet wool.

She drove toward Tony's house. How she looked had nothing to do with what she had to ask him.

* * *

She pushed the heavy wooden door to his carpentry shop open and went in with the wind rushing behind her.

Tony was bent over a long table, drawing a pattern onto a piece of wood. When he looked up, at first he was bothered, then surprised to see her.

"Come on in." He took small pieces of plywood from a chair and brushed off the sawdust. "Sit down. You're soaked," he said and filled a kettle with water to set on the two-burner stove at the back of the shop.

He made her a cup of tea while she shivered, hunched in the chair.

"I couldn't talk to you last night," she finally said, the cup of tea warming her hands. "Yesterday was awful."

"I can only imagine." He pulled a chair up in front of her and sat down. "Do they know anything? Was it a burglary? They're saying today that the house was ransacked. The police are asking anybody with any information, something they noticed or saw while driving by her house, to come forward. Doesn't look like they've got a suspect. Usually, in a place as small as Traverse, somebody always knows something."

The questions wound down as she looked at him but didn't answer.

He rubbed at his grizzled face, then ran a finger over a scar on his hand. When he looked at her, he shook his head and then looked down. "We've got to talk about this."

"I don't even know what 'this' is, Tony."

"I know." He shook his head. "How the hell could you? I haven't been able to face you."

"Something big," she said and tried to smile but failed.

He tried to take her hand between his, but she slowly pulled away from him.

"I should have told you from the first." He looked down and shook his head.

Jenny wanted to touch him so badly. She wanted to put her fingers in his hair.

"I haven't been honest. Not with you or anybody else. Not since I first came here." He looked up, his eyes going over her face. "Honest to God, Jenny. I didn't think it mattered. This was a new life. I didn't have any plans beyond setting up this shop. See if I could make a living here. That's all I was thinking about. As far as who I was or about my personal life . . ." He shrugged. "I didn't think it was any-body's business."

"What's changed?" she asked. "Me?"

He nodded. "And me."

"You better get it over with." Her body was tight. She felt the same way she did every time things blew up on her.

"I'm married."

She took in what he said and sat there looking at him. She finally nodded.

"I see." There didn't seem to be anything else to say, or at least she couldn't find the right words. "Maybe you should have mentioned it before."

He nodded his head again and again. "I didn't know what to do. I'm so sorry."

"You're right. You never mentioned you were married. Guess I should've asked."

He took her hand and held it. She didn't pull away.

"Where's your wife?" she asked.

"We're separated. Jan went to live in New York, with her mother. We were going to give it a year."

"You've lived here longer than that. Why isn't she with you?"

He shrugged. "Wasn't right. She didn't want live in Bear Falls, and I didn't want to move to New York. We just let it go. Jan's in no hurry to get married again. I didn't think I would ever find somebody."

Jenny looked away from him. "You could have told me before . . ."

"I know. I'm a coward. I didn't want to mess up any-thing. When I met you I thought you were a great person, but not for me. Just coming out of a divorce like you were. Next thing I knew, all I wanted to do was talk to you and see you."

"What's changed? We could have talked about this."

"Jan wants us to get back together."

Blindsided again. The woman with him at the Brew.

"So you just kept on lying. Pretending she'd go away and I'd never know."

"No." He shook his head hard. "Nothing like that. I had it all planned, and then Jan showed up and I didn't know what to do. So damned mad at myself."

"Is she moving here?"

He shook his head. "I told her about you."

"But you're still married to her."

"I'll file for divorce."

"Why haven't you?"

"I will. I promise I will. It's just that she needs a little time."

"And what do I need?"

He didn't yet understand and didn't answer.

"All you had to do was tell me. Instead you chose a lie. And maybe it's still a lie." She got up from her chair, avoiding the hand reaching out to her.

"I'm not lying to you, Jenny. I wouldn't. She needs a little time. For a year she's been trying to figure out what to do, and then she made a decision and called me."

Jenny went to the door and opened it, letting rain blow in. She turned back to him.

"You know what, Tony? I've been lied to before. I just don't want to be lied to again."

She hurried out into the wind and lashing rain. Out to her car, and home.

She felt as if there was a tiny hammer pounding just above her eyes as she drove through town. Rotten weather. A rotten headache. A rotten man she'd been falling in love with. She pounded the wheel with her open hand.

So there. He was married. And sorry for lying to her. As if Ronald hadn't been so very sorry, so very often.

There was no going home. Dora's note said Zoe was coming for dinner. Alex would be there. They were going to figure out how to get Emily to talk to Alex about her uncle. They were going to talk about Althea's death. They were going to talk about all kinds of things she didn't care about right then.

When she got to the center of town, she turned on Oak and headed out toward Highway 31 and Traverse City. Maybe this was the perfect day to go back to Chicago. How much more of a kick in the ass did she need?

If the rain hadn't gotten worse, if her head had stopped hurting, if she had so much as a toothbrush with her—she might have kept going to Chicago. Instead she checked into the Comfort Inn on Munson and planned to hole up there for as long as it took her to crawl out of this old cocoon and into the next one.

Once in the room, she turned on the television and watched the worst shows she could find. When her phone rang and Dora left a message that she wondered where she was, Jenny ignored the call.

When Dora called again, Jenny didn't answer.

When Tony called she let it go to voicemail then listened to him say only, "I'm sorry."

The next time Dora called, she answered and told her she needed to be alone and she would be home in the morning.

"I understand, dear," was all Dora said. "Take your time. I've known something like this was coming. I only hope you'll be all right."

Jenny didn't promise anything, only that she'd be back.

Chapter 13

There was a light scrim of early frost on the grass when Jenny left the hotel and headed back home. An inkling of winter. *Perfect*, she thought, pulling into light traffic. She considered breakfast at Bob Evans until she remembered she was still in the slightly damp clothes she'd worn the day before and that they were wrinkled, her hair was barely combed, and her teeth were unbrushed.

Breakfast was out. Tony was out. She wasn't going to cry one more tear. They weren't engaged. Nothing was promised between them. It was over. No more drama. She had plenty to think about. Things going on back in Bear Falls. That was what she'd decided overnight. She was going to start all over with building this new Jenny Weston. She was going to help Alex Shipley. She was going to apologize to Zoe—as fast as she could—for being snotty, for standing her up last night, for making fun of things she believed to be true when all the while she had a better handle on life than Jenny did. Lots of reasons to go home. To stay there or not stay there. To go back to Chicago or not go back to

Chicago. She was a free woman. She still had alimony coming in. Maybe she'd open a business. Maybe she'd go work in a vineyard in California.

She was already feeling better when she parked in the drive at home and Fida ran over, almost hitting a tree trunk because of her blind eye, and jumped on Jenny's leg as soon as she got out of the car.

"Hey," she called out to the small person wrapped in a sweater way too big for her. Zoe was kneeling in her garden, beside one of her fairy beds.

Zoe turned, squinted up, and made a face at her. "Where have you been? We were supposed to have a high-powered planning meeting last night, and you never showed up."

Jenny only said that she was sorry and bent down to throw her arms across Zoe's back, hugging her and almost forcing her facedown in the dirt.

"What the heck's that all about?"

"Just a friendly hug. Between friends. Because we're friends. I mean actual friends."

Zoe sat back on her heels and shook her head. "Quite a night, huh? You and Tony make up?"

Jenny winced and shook her head. Zoe shut her mouth.

"Why don't you come on over. I'll fix us both breakfast." Jenny pointed toward her house.

"I ate. Usually do before eleven o'clock."

"Have a cup of tea with me."

"Got to write most of the day. Christopher Morley called this morning. Wants me in New York in a week or so. We're meeting with PBS. They want to make my books into a TV series. They're thinking of combining the stories with the writers' lives. Something like that. He's already told them about my upcoming *Two Emilys*. Pretty exciting stuff."

"Dinner then?"

"Again? How do I know you'll be there?" Zoe frowned up at her.

"Of course I'll be there. I'll even cook."

"Now there's a reason to stay home."

Jenny made a noise and turned away. "Do what you want. You will anyway."

"Okay, I'll come. But only because all I've got for dinner is one wrinkled ham hock in my fridge."

"Good," Jenny waved. "Bring it. I'll cook it."

"By the way," Zoe called after her, "you don't know who's at your house this morning, do you? Abigail Cane and Minnie Moon. It'll be like having breakfast with a set of electric hens. You sure you want to go home?"

Jenny headed up the steps. She heard the voices from outside the house. Taking a deep breath and remembering she was an all-new Jenny Weston, she put a smile on her face, flicked her messy hair back over her shoulder, and entered the kitchen.

Dora smiled and nodded, relief written on her face. "Glad you're back, dear."

Jenny bent close to hug her mother, feeling the need for warmth from someone. Dora held on to her and whispered, "Tony called. He wants you to call him. Poor man. He sounded terrible. Is he sick?" She looked hard at Jenny, then turned back to their guests.

"See who's here?" Dora gestured toward the two at the table.

As if she could miss them. Abigail Cane, proper and prim in her two-piece blue sweater set and black slacks, gold chains wrapped around her neck, sat up expectantly, waiting for homage to be paid. Minnie Moon, in an orange muumuu covered by a camo jacket, sat across the table from Abigail, feet stuck out to the side. She was wearing flip-flops over white socks, the fabric bunched between her toes.

"They're worried about Emily," Dora said and nodded to the toast and jam on the table, then put a kettle on to boil for tea.

"Everybody is. Poor thing. Losing her cousin like that." Jenny joined them at the table, reaching hungrily for the last piece of toast.

"Well," Abigail pushed herself up straighter in her chair. "That goes without saying. But what I'm talking about is her reading at the opera house. I'm very worried things are going to be derailed by all that's happened."

"I must have missed something." Jenny smiled from Abigail to Minnie, who made a face and shook her head from side to side.

"What's going on? I didn't know there was an event planned at the opera house. Does Emily know about it? Will she show up?"

"I only verified the date yesterday," Abigail said. "It was all they had open. Monday, October third, seven in the evening. The opera house is handling ticket sales, but Minnie—who's been such a great help to me—is seeing to incidentals like ushers and flowers for the stage." She reached across the table to pat Minnie's hand, bringing a proud smile to Minnie's face. "If word of Emily Sutton's return to literature spreads, as I expect it will, the opera house will be filled. The proceeds from the night are going to the National Poetry Society, right there in Traverse City. Emily can hand out scholarships to the Interlochen School. I don't need to tell you how important the event will be."

"But I'm guessing you haven't talked to Emily about it yet."

Abigail looked pained. "How could I, with her cousin dying the way she did? I'm willing to go over there, but will she let me in? And what about the funeral? Will there be one? When? Heavens, I feel like a ghoul, and yet what can I do? I know Emily wanted this. She told you she'd be pleased, didn't she, Dora?"

Dora, reluctant to be stuck directly in the middle, nodded. "She mentioned she would like to be a fly on the wall if there was a reading of her work. But I don't know if that meant a huge event like you're planning."

"Please, Dora." Abigail shook her head. "Even Zoe Zola mentioned something about Emily writing new poetry."

"And I gave you what she left here," Dora said. "What did you think?"

"Wonderful. If she doesn't have more, then those, along with her published work, will do fine. And about the funeral? Have you heard anything?"

Jenny leaned back to see if the teakettle was boiling, craving a cup of tea—maybe one of her very special teas she'd found in Traverse. Today was a Berry Chai day. "I know the funeral can't be held until the medical examiner releases the body. I don't know how long that takes in a murder case. Zoe might know. She knows a lot of things most people don't."

"Yes, well, we do need Zoe's help, too. She's the only one, it seems, who sees Emily regularly. Isn't that right, Minnie?"

Minnie, who appeared to be Abigail's immediate source of information for just about everything, gave a gracious nod of her head as she kept an eye on a plate of fresh toast Dora was bringing to the table.

"I heard the police were over to Emily's night before last." Minnie leaned forward for a slice of toast, then reached for the homemade strawberry jam. "Weren't you there, too?"

"I was. Zoe, too. A detective from the Traverse City police came out to break the news about Althea. He thought Zoe and I could help, in case Emily took it badly."

"And did she?" Abigail asked. "Take it badly?"

"Bad enough, I guess. But she didn't need our help. She's not the kind of person who leans on others."

Abigail didn't say anything at first, only thought hard. "Well, I'll have to admit something to you. I just came from Emily's. Minnie and I were there to leave sympathy cards. Along with the cards, I left a note about the opera house event. And that we've got a planning meeting scheduled for next Tuesday. I asked Emily to come. I put my number in my note. I'm sure she'll call, but I was hoping I could count on you and Zoe, too? Could you talk to her? Explain, please, what this will mean for her career. And for young poets in the area. Three o'clock. The meeting is at three. In my home."

Abigail pushed her chair back slowly, then stood. Minnie hurried out of her chair, taking a half slice of toast and jam with her.

"And Dora, I'm only saying this to you and Jenny. If you think about what happened to Althea, it is certainly a tragedy, but she's only a cousin to Emily. It's not as though she has to go into months of mourning. You might mention that to her."

"Abigail." Dora was shocked. "I'm surprised at you. You of all people. You shouldn't tell other people what to feel."

Abigail flushed. "You're right, Dora. I just don't want anything to go wrong with the event now that everything is set in motion. I want it to be grand, for Emily Sutton and for Bear Falls. We'll be known as her home forever afterward. That old swamp house will probably be a shrine one day. I see this as making up for my father. A gift with deep meaning."

"Are you still trying to get his statue removed from the park?" Dora asked.

Abigail smiled as she nodded. "The council has agreed. We have only to set the date."

"Congratulations. I know that's what you wanted."

With tears in her eyes, the woman thanked Dora and put a hand out to Minnie.

Abigail and Minnie left together.

* * *

For the next few hours, Jenny holed up in her bedroom as Dora entertained neighbors who dropped by to get details of Althea's murder firsthand. From time to time, Jenny heard the phone ring in the living room, but Dora never came to get her. If he called she didn't know what she would do. Talk to him? About what? He'd destroyed the possibility of anything between them with his lie. Maybe they could talk about it someday. She'd deal with that when his face in her head didn't hurt so much and when her ego had come back up to at least half of what it had been.

She lay on top of her teddy bear quilt and read poetry for hours. The perfect day for it. Curious about the two Emilys of Zoe's new title, she'd found a volume of Dickinson's poetry on one of Dora's shelves of favorite books and then a Dickinson biography. Zoe's books followed the course of a writer's life as it was bound to the work they created. Jenny had read a few by now and was fascinated at how the authors' lives worked out in their stories or poetry. For good measure, since her day was going to be spent in other worlds—where she didn't have decisions to make about anything—she pulled down Emily Sutton's book even though she wasn't one of the two Emilys Zoe was writing about. Inside the book were folded sheets of paper.

Jenny went back to her room to sit on the window seat with a pillow at her back and read Emily Sutton's poems, finding that, despite herself, she was comparing her to Dickinson. It seemed to her—though she wouldn't say a word to Abigail Cane—that Dickinson dug deeper. Especially about death, where her brevity cut like a knife.

In Dickinson, Jenny read, "Death is a supple Suitor / That wins at last."

In one of Emily Sutton's new poems, she read again,

Echoes in the house
Predict the universe.
Simple sounds that
Only death can know.

A gong, as time hangs waiting.
The rasp of winter's cough.
A crack marks temperature descending,
From silence to divinity.

Jenny thought hard about the woman she knew. It wasn't easy to put the brittle woman together with the words in front of her. Certainly, Emily Sutton was alone. Echoes in the house made sense, but the rasp—whose "winter's cough"? Was she talking about herself? That she'd been sick? But "silence to divinity" sounded as if the person in the poem had died and was looking back from the grave.

Jenny felt goose bumps run up her arms. Did poets ever write about their own deaths, imagining the moment? Probably. What else did Emily have to think about, in that stone house all alone?

She put the new work down and thumbed through the book of Emily Sutton's published poems, searching for the poem Zoe quoted that first day; the line Emily didn't recognize or seem to know. As Jenny remembered, it was "A person gone missing cries for the discovering voice."

She found it in a poem called "Illusion":

A space. An emptiness of breath.
A lightness in the air where she once stood.
The phantom waits beyond the edge of being
As the one gone missing cries for my discovering voice.

My instead of *the*, but the right poem. Odd that Emily didn't recognize her own work. Or maybe she'd been too excited that night, her first interaction with people since her cousin had stopped coming. So nervous. So ethereal. One of those people out of time who could make you believe in an afterlife. Emily had come asking a favor, not knowing what her reception might be. Jenny put herself in the woman's place and forgave Emily her lapse, even her odd ways of being. What would *she* be like—being raised in that terrible, cold house? What would *she* be like—after a mother's awful death? What would *she* be like if she came home and never left again?

But the big "WHY?" just sat there. What drove Emily Sutton home to begin with? What was there at home that never let her leave? Then she was all alone and still she stayed. But writing poetry again. Coming back to herself?

Jenny leaned her head against the wall and closed her eyes. She thought how relative things were. In her own life, love, or the misery of love, was huge. Then there was Emily, her young life cut short, as if disappearance was a goal.

Mental illness? Agoraphobia—the sickness Emily Dickinson probably suffered from? Maybe, as with Jenny, there had been a cruel love. Maybe there was a man, still out there somewhere, who'd failed her.

Jenny had to smile. She'd found a place of kinship with Emily Sutton, something she didn't think was even possible. Couldn't stand the woman. Didn't want to be anywhere near her. But now she'd dug deep enough—as Zoe always said to do—and there it was. They were probably sisters after all.

Jenny thought of the weird eyes and the weird clothes and the changing face, either mean or pathetic, and felt tepid warmth toward her. Enough to make Jenny vow she would never get like that. No damned cats in fancy dresses. If she ever considered a tea ball, she'd have herself committed. A good solid mug with a crack in the handle, not a fluted cup with a golden rim atop a fluted saucer, a small round cookie sitting at the edge.

She'd come to Dickinson and Sutton to understand how they had lived and why. She thought she had a handle on her own life now. What the hell was she thinking? So much invested in being loved when life really wasn't about that kind of love at all. It wasn't about being loved. It was about giving love. Love had to go where it was welcomed. No more of this victim shit, she told herself. No more silly Hollywood movies. She was Jenny Weston. Thirty-six years old. Plenty of life ahead of her to find her place out in the working world, where she belonged with other people—like her new friend, Zoe Zola—and where she was as a daughter, a sister, a human being standing on her own, no matter if it was in Bear Falls, Michigan, or in Timbuktu, which she decided she might visit one day soon.

God! But she felt good. The poets had done it, handed her a life back. Jenny got up and sat down at her dressing table. She pulled a strand of long black hair out and looked at it. Did she want it long or was it long because she thought men liked long hair?

She liked it.

She looked at the makeup littering the table's top and wondered if she wanted to wear that phony stuff anymore. She put on a little pale lipstick and decided she liked that better than the bright shade she usually wore. She looked at what she had on—a faded yellow T-shirt, with a sagging bra underneath.

In the closet there were a few halfway decent outfits she'd brought home with her. She took one out—slim white pants with a blue silk top.

Who cared if it was a weeknight? Who cared if she had nowhere to go? Who cared, even, if no one but Dora would see her? Nothing was going to be about other people anymore.

She put on her pretty clothes, brushed out her hair, applied more of the pale lipstick, and went out to shock the crap out of Dora, who widened her eyes and whistled when she saw her daughter looking beautiful. She took note of the confidence in Jenny she'd been praying would come back.

* * *

Sitting on the porch later, Dora set her newspaper down. She sighed. "First Abigail and Minnie, then people calling about you and Zoe. Others calling to get as much dirt as possible: *'Who was it that got killed again? Is that a relation to our poet?' 'What's Jenny got to do with all this mess?'* I tried to be nice but I can't tell you how many times I wanted to hang up."

Dora searched Jenny's face.

"Was it about you and Tony? The thing that happened yesterday? And who you became today?"

Jenny made a face and sat down to rock, looking over through the pines to Zoe's house, where she heard Fida barking at someone or something or perhaps at nothing, just to hear herself bark.

"I'd like to help," Dora said.

"It's all right, Mom. I'm handling things."

"If he's done anything to hurt you, I won't ask him here again." Dora's face was set.

"It'll be fine, Mom." Jenny got up and leaned down to kiss her mother's curly hair. "I'm starving. I'm cooking dinner. I've asked Zoe over to make up for last night."

"What are you cooking? I was going to make a vegetable soup."

"Great! You make soup. I'll make a salad."

"You call that cooking dinner?"

"Close enough." Jenny shrugged. "Will Alex be here? I guess we've still got to talk."

"She didn't say. Let's wait and see."

Dora made her vegetable soup, though the soup heated the kitchen and the house reeked of cabbage, not one of her favorite smells. Jenny tossed her salad, adding in walnuts and cheese—anything to make it special. She felt a little guilty about claiming she would cook.

Dora set the table for four, not knowing if the Shipley girl would be back for dinner or not. The yellow dishes with green and red apples were bright on her yellow cloth. She felt deeply that there were times that called for special touches and soothing meals, like a hot vegetable soup.

Jenny ran out for an hour to find something to wear to Abigail's meeting since they'd all been invited. She couldn't wait to see what she would buy now that she only had herself to please.

"Don't want to get the fish eye from the movers and shakers," she'd said before leaving, only to be back in an hour with a short, flowered dress that made her look like a flower box and would certainly set the women to talking.

"Good enough, don't you think?" she'd asked, parading in her dress of muted flowers.

Dora's praise was as colorful as the dress. She understood the need. She knew how small-town life could tie you into cords of similarity. How she'd always wanted to fit in, until she fit the life of Bear Falls perfectly but wasn't sure where the old feisty Dora Findley had gone.

Dora laughed at her daughter. "When your father and I first moved here, people looked at me as if I were a rare thing, never seen before. A big city girl. A librarian to boot. And then they got to know me, and I got to know them, and that rare thing melted away." She sighed. "And still, I try to fit in. I'm wearing my blue dress. They've all seen it before."

Jenny laid the napkins around at each of the places, linen instead of paper, then pulled the linen napkins off the table and set out paper because she wasn't a linen kind of person.

Jenny sat down to wait for Zoe and Alex while Dora headed outside to pick flowers for the table. Asters had survived the early frost, she said. And there were a few roses left.

"I'll fill in with fall leaves, if I have to." She slipped into a light jacket and was out the door with scissors in her hand.

The evening ahead was wearing Jenny out already. Back to Emily, at the center of everything, when all she could think about was Althea Sutton. She'd called Detective Minty earlier, but he didn't call back. She'd call Ed Warner, but he didn't call back either. Probably her use to both of them was finished. She'd have to watch the newspaper and the nightly TV news for updates on the murder.

* * *

"She pooped all over the house" was the first thing Zoe reported, though not unhappily, when she walked in, setting Fida on the floor and bending down to shake a finger in her face.

"Yes, I'm telling on you," she said, though the dog, completely unembarrassed, rolled her good eye toward Jenny and settled under a chair to sleep.

They all sat down to wait for Alex, who had called saying she would be there in a while. Zoe was quieter than usual because she'd been to Emily's house that afternoon. Another grocery order and another delivery.

They talked about Alex and her uncle's red car and were soon interrupted by a call from Detective Minty saying he would like to come over to speak to Zoe and Jenny in the morning.

"Did you get the money Emily owes you?" Dora asked Zoe, worrying about the liberties that woman was taking

"I didn't see her. I left the groceries on the porch."

"I went shopping for a dress to wear to Abigail's tea." Jenny tossed her salad.

"What tea?"

"She hasn't asked you? She said she wants everyone there."

"Am I 'everyone'?"

"They're planning a huge event at the opera house. Emily will read her new poetry."

"Did she tell Emily? Good luck with that one."

147

"I think she left her a note."

Zoe shrugged and spread her paper napkin on her lap. "If I know Emily, she'll eat that right up. I'm telling you, she's nothing at all like her poetry. I expected a good mind. I even thought we would sit and talk about wonderful things. I thought I'd have my own version of Emily Dickinson to talk to as I wrote this new book. But it's nothing of the sort. This Emily runs and hollers and then gets sweet for thirty seconds and is off again, complaining about the soup I brought last time or the hair dye I had to exchange."

Zoe shook her head and looked over at the soup pot as if wondering when they were going to eat.

Dora was mentioning that they were waiting for Alex when the phone rang.

As Dora hung up after a very brief conversation, she turned to look from Zoe to Jenny, her hand at her mouth.

"That was Ed Warner," Dora said. "We have to get over to the police station. Alex is there and might be arrested."

Chapter 14

Alex Shipley was bent forward, hands between her knees, long hair hiding her face, sitting next to a desk in the Bear Falls police station. She looked up when the women walked in, then back at the floor.

"What's going on?" Jenny was the first to greet Ed Warner, who was seated behind his desk.

"Jenny." Ed pushed back his chair and unfolded his hunched back to stand and greet her.

She looked into her old classmate's dark eyes. "I can vouch for Miss Shipley, if that's necessary."

"I already know her pretty well myself." Ed nodded, setting his head bobbing to one side. "I heard the whole story when she got to town. That's why I sent her over to you and your mother. Thought you could help her, what with that neighbor of yours buying groceries for Emily and all. Least, that's what Delaware over at Myrtle's tells me. Only thing is, the girl can't trespass, no matter how much she needs to talk to Miss Sutton."

He glanced at Alex, who looked away, embarrassed. "That's a puzzling story about her uncle. I agree about that. Maybe I should have gone over to talk to Emily for her. As it is now—with the trespassing charge—it'll be very hard to get to Miss Sutton. She might even get a lawyer and press charges against Miss Shipley."

"Trespassing?" All three women turned to look at Alex, who shook her head and stared down at her fingernails. When she got up and walked over to them, she looked younger than twenty-three, and far past miserable.

"I looked in a garage at the back of the house." Alex brushed her hair away from her face. "That was the only place I went on the property. I swear. I just got a glimpse when she started yelling. I was going to go up to the house and explain to her what I was doing but the chief here arrived before I got a chance."

"Shouldn't have been there at all, Miss Shipley."

She turned to Jenny. "I saw something in the garage. I swear I did. Something big. Covered with a tarp. That's got to be a car."

"Lots of sheds have old cars in 'em," the chief said. "Or old tractors. Their place was a farm once. Years and years ago now. Fields were across the road, and the swamp wasn't so big then, from things I heard."

Alex shook her head. "What if it's my uncle's? He loved that red Saturn. He wouldn't have gone anywhere and left it behind."

"If you ask me," the chief was going on, "I think you should get Miss Zoe here, or Miss Weston, to take you over there so you can ask the woman what you want to know. She's a little strange but no worse than a lot of people we've got around here. When I told her I was bringing you back to the station, she asked who you were and what you were doing on her property. I told her you'd come to town to see her. That kind of grabbed her interest. She wanted to know what you wanted to see her about."

"Did you tell her?" Alex leaned toward the man. "What did she say? Can I go talk to her?"

He let his head loose, shaking it again and again. "I didn't saying a thing. Figured that was your business. You and these ladies will have to figure that one out for yourselves. I just got off the phone with Miss Sutton."

"Is she pressing charges?" Jenny asked.

He shook his head. "She called back to get Miss Shipley's name and where she's staying."

He turned to Dora. "Hope you don't mind. I told her it was you she was staying with. Thought that was what I heard."

Dora said no, she didn't mind. That was fine. "And we'll have to see if we can get Alex back over there—legally."

She turned to Zoe. "When are you shopping for her again?"

Zoe didn't look pleased. "Soon. She told me she needs a dozen sky-blue scarves. Lord knows for what, or where I'm supposed to get them."

Dora grinned at Jenny. "No doubt she's making a dress for Abigail's tea party. Emily Sutton's got a lot more to be nervous about than the rest of us."

"She must've got ahold of Abigail, if she knows about the committee meeting." Jenny turned to Zoe. "I guess the opera house event is on."

151

They took a chastened Alex home to soup and a half-wilted salad. Their talk, at first, was about Alex's uncle, then about Alex's plans. "I can't stay here forever." She put her head into one hand and looked up at them like a little girl. "I'm got to get back to school."

"The evening's still pleasant, why don't we take our ice cream out to the porch and I'll make us some tea." Dora ushered the three women from her kitchen and fixed ice cream glasses and a plate of cookies. What she was thinking, as she worked, was how much Alex Shipley was like one of her own daughters. Headstrong. Willful. And plunging ahead until she ended up in trouble. Not so much Lisa, who had grown out of that stage, but certainly Jenny, still butting her head against stone walls, then getting mad because her head hurt.

With nothing left to talk about, the porch was quiet. Zoe talked about going home. She had edits to do in the morning and then a few phone calls.

"Christopher called," she said, leaning toward Alex to whisper that Christopher Morley was her editor. "Can you imagine that he's buying my plane ticket to New York? But not until the week after next now. He had to change the meeting with PBS. To listen to him, he's got almost a book a day coming out and every one of them has a nervous writer behind it."

She bent down to nudge Fida with her toe, getting a grunt and a sleepy woof. A couple of spoons clinked against glasses. A cookie was snapped in two. Dora opened windows along the sides of the porch so they got a cross breeze. A little chilly but nothing beyond what a sweater could fix.

Dora brought up whether or not they could bring Alex to Abigail's meeting on Tuesday.

"I'd rather ask first," Jenny said. "And you, Zoe. She explicitly said she wanted you there. I'll jog her memory. She probably thinks she already invited you."

"'No room. No room.'" Zoe put her little hands, with bright-red nails, to her cheeks, becoming Alice in Wonderland.

Alex, the English major, laughed and leaned in as close as she could get, becoming the March Hare. "'Have some wine.'"

"'I don't see any wine.'" Zoe crinkled her nose.

"'There isn't any.'" Alex lowered her voice to a very serious level.

"'Then it wasn't very civil of you to offer it.'" Zoe's irate face was believable. She was into character.

"'You should learn not to make personal remarks,'" Alex said in a loud voice.

Dora leaned forward and tapped her knee, a finger at her lips, shushing them. "Look," she said and pointed down the street.

A bouncing light wove a path along the sidewalk, coming toward them.

"Emily Sutton," Dora whispered toward Alex. "I think you're about . . . to meet her after all."

They watched the light and the dark figure behind it zigzag up the front walk, then up the steps.

"I hope she's not mad because of me," Alex muttered under her breath beside them and pulled back in her chair.

There was a light knock, and the door opened.

"Hello," Emily Sutton said as she stepped inside. "I hope I haven't come at a bad time."

"Emily!" Dora popped up, quickly pulling a chair around for her. "We've been worried about you."

The woman hesitated and peered through the near-dark at each of them, only to stop squarely at Alex. She took a tentative step onto the porch and stood with her hands crossed in front of her.

"How are you?" Dora, Zoe, and Jenny asked at once, distracting the withering stare.

"I'm happy you're here, Zoe." Her serious face lightened a little as she turned away from Alex. "I want to add to my shopping list. I have no thread. Could you get me thread, do you suppose, to go with the sky-blue scarves? I would say sky-blue thread, wouldn't you?"

"I'm not sure where to go for sky-blue scarves and thread," Zoe said, sounding more puzzled than angry. "I might have to go all the way into Traverse City."

"Oh, would you?" Emily clasped her hands at her breast. "It's so important. I want to make myself something very special to wear for Abigail's tea party. I understand it is to honor me. I've written a few new poems for the occasion."

"I think it's more for planning your event at the opera . . ." Jenny started to say but was cut off by Dora.

"Please, sit with us. Would you like a glass of tea?"

"Oh, no. But a glass of wine would do. To celebrate the moment. That would be wonderful."

Surprised, Dora got up and headed quickly out to the kitchen.

When Dora was gone, silence fell until Emily turned her probing eyes on Alex, who was still hiding in her chair. "We haven't met, have we?"

Alex sat up and agreed they hadn't. "I'm Alex Shipley. Very happy to meet you, Miss Sutton."

"Emily, please. May I ask why you were trespassing on my property this afternoon? Miss . . . Shipley, is it? I called the police. But you know that. I watched them haul you away."

"Not exactly 'haul,' Miss Sutton." Alex sat up and flicked her hair away from her face.

"I can't begin to express the fright you caused me. You do know I've been recently bereaved."

Alex nodded. "I'm so sorry about your loss."

Emily waved one hand in the air, as if brushing away a fly. "Oh, we weren't close. It's too bad, but I'd warned her again and again about the company she was keeping."

Zoe moved in her chair. Jenny sat up straight, catching her breath. They looked over at each other, startled, then back to Emily.

"I knocked at your door. You didn't answer," Alex said.

"I don't." Emily's voice hardened. "For good reason." She stared at the girl. "And did you find what you were looking for in my yard?"

Alex began to say something when Dora came back and busily poured wine for everyone, handing the glasses around.

Emily tasted the wine and made a face, but drank it down in audible gulps.

"Thirsty." She looked at the faces watching her, and smiled, not prettily.

"Shipley?" Emily was suddenly surprised. "Shipley? Did you say your name was Shipley? I used to know a man named Shipley."

155

"That's why I'm here," Alex said, finally taking a deep breath. "Walter Shipley's my uncle. He's been missing for three years."

"Missing? Really? But that's how poets are, Miss Shipley. Time away from a world that reaches out with hooks and grapples to tear us to shreds. You're looking at a poet now, one who is finally brave enough to reenter the world after many years away." Emily cocked her head to one side and squinted at the girl, taking in every bit of her. "One day he will return, as I have."

"The last I'm able to trace him, he was supposed to come to Bear Falls. You invited him."

Emily shook her head almost violently. "That isn't true. I barely know the man. Through his poetry, of course. He has an amazing mind. But to invite him . . ."

"I have the letters you exchanged."

Emily slowly sat up. She set the glass on the floor beside her, finally saying, "Letters? For heaven's sakes. You have my letters? May I see them?"

Zoe, watching everything going on, put a hand out to stop Alex from getting out of her chair. The girl sat back, taking in Zoe's message.

"I don't have them with me," she lied. "I just wanted to talk to you about him. See if he came here that fall."

"If you have letters written between your uncle and me, I'd like them back. Wouldn't you say they are my property?"

"Of course. When I get back home I'll send them. I should have thought to bring them with me."

Jenny understood immediately that Alex had caught on—how to talk to Emily Sutton. She watched Alex's lovely face shift from startled and angry, to confused, and then to sweet, even entranced. She tipped her head toward Emily and smiled a bright smile.

"In one of the letters you invited him to come visit. I even got the impression that maybe he was to stay with you."

Emily drew in a long breath and held it as if she'd stopped breathing completely.

Dora jumped in. "You see, Emily, Alex is very worried about her uncle."

Emily slowly rose from her chair and tiptoed toward the door. She pulled her flashlight from her skirt pocket and flipped it on. Before anyone could stop her, she was down the steps and out the walk.

The flickering light disappeared as she flew back up Elderberry Street.

* * *

After they were all in bed there was a knock at the front door. Jenny heard Dora's bed squeak as she got up, then heard her hurrying down the hall, then talking to someone in the front room. In a few minutes the door was closed and Dora was in the hall again. There was a tap at Jenny's door. Dora stuck her head in. "Tony was here. I told him you were sleeping. Awfully late for him to call."

Chapter 15

The morning of the committee meeting/tea party at Abigail's, Zoe flitted back and forth between their houses, wanting their opinion on one outfit after another. This was her first big social event since moving to Bear Falls.

Zoe bought most of her clothes in children's departments or off the racks in resale shops, so she couldn't find a thing to wear. At least, nothing of sufficient seriousness.

First it was a white flared skirt with a jeweled top. She whirled in front of Jenny and Dora but didn't wait for them to comment before hurrying back out the door. "I look like a pint-sized gypsy," she called behind her. "Who knows what to wear in fall?"

Jenny made a pot of tea and took it outside to sit in a chair under the walnut tree. The air was September perfect. Cool. Only the smallest of breezes. She wished the day were over. There were bigger things to think about than Emily. Like Tony at the door and what she was feeling about that.

She was dressed, ready for the afternoon in her very short and very flowered dress, with sandals that almost matched but didn't quite, and she didn't care at all, thinking of how women used to dress—the corsets and long skirts and heavy tops. All before deodorant. She wondered what those women smelled like on a hot day and if rooms had to be aired after afternoon teas were over.

In a few minutes, Zoe was back, striding head down through the garden. This time it was a red dress with a little red jacket. Her shoes were red. Jenny didn't want to say she looked like a traffic light so she nodded and smiled.

Zoe narrowed her eyes. She bent close to Jenny's face. "I can see you're lying."

She turned to go back home but stopped. "What the devil was Emily talking about last night? That business about her cousin and the company she was keeping?"

"I was going to ask you the same thing. Althea was in her sixties," Jenny said. "Probably not running with a gang."

"From what I heard, her only activities were church related or bird watching. Now how did church people get to be bad company? Is there some mescaline cult in Traverse City?"

"Maybe the birds." Jenny shook her head. "I've heard crows get pretty rough."

"Acting as if Althea's death was nothing." Zoe made a face. "How in the name of all that's worth talking about does that woman write the thoughtful, deep poetry that she writes? The most I'd expect out of her is some moony-spoony stuff. Maybe a bloody mystery."

"Or a long lecture on how important she thinks she is."

"I've been wondering about that sister of hers, too. Lorna." Zoe toed the ground near Jenny's chair. "When Minty gets out here, I'm going to mention her. See if he can find where she went. It's not just that Emily seems to need a keeper, but every time I go over there I get the feeling people are watching me from those upstairs windows." Zoe shivered. "And that swamp. She spends a lot of time out there, it seems. Those places have to screw with a person's mind after a while."

Goose bumps ran up Jenny's back. "And those awful flowers she was holding. Gave me the creeps."

"Hold on! Don't knock those flowers. Those were Indian Pipes. I hope you get to see them in the woods someday. Strange little white pipes sticking out of the ground. Not a flower at all, I imagine. More like a fungus. Something like a mushroom. But unearthly."

"Black, was what I saw." Jenny winced.

"Maybe they're like moonstones. Change colors, depending on who's holding therm."

"You sure don't like her, do you?" Jenny laughed at her friend.

Zoe shrugged. "I'm still trying. Maybe I'll see a better part of her today. She's reading new poetry."

Zoe turned away. "I'll be back. I've got my barber pole dress to show you."

"Jenny." Dora stood at the back door. "Phone call."

Jenny got out of her chair and went slowly toward the house. It had to be Tony. She steeled herself for his voice. She would listen, but that was all. He'd lied to her from the very beginning. Married. Leading her on without thinking about what he was doing. All the while he'd known her history with men. She would have thought he'd be a little bit careful. Her stomach was churning by the time she picked up the phone.

"It's Emily Sutton," Dora mouthed at her as Jenny said "Hello" into the phone.

"It's my dress, Jenny," Emily rushed to say. "I made it myself but now I'm not sure I should wear it."

Jenny, disappointed, assured Emily it would be fine.

"I am probably badly out of style. What will those women think of me?"

"People don't expect style from poets, Emily. They want to see you and hear your work. Whatever you wear will be fine."

"Oh, I don't know, Jenny. I'm not certain I should let this go on. Such a large event. Maybe my work is outdated and my new poems not up to the old. I could be making a fool of myself."

Jenny assured her that everyone would welcome new work from her.

"But Abigail's gone overboard. I don't really think I'm up to it. After all, I just lost my cousin."

"I heard most of the tickets for the big event have been sold, Emily. Snapped up right away."

"Really?" She couldn't hide her excitement. "I suppose it would be a shame to disappoint so many people. Hmm . . ." Emily stopped to think. "Still, what are you wearing?"

"A flowered dress."

Emily was silent for a moment. "Maybe I should wear black," she said. "The color of the deepest, darkest universe—what with the death of my cousin and all. Will people expect me to be in mourning, do you think?"

Jenny didn't dare answer.

"But then, my costume is blue. Waves of blue. Do you think that will be too much?"

"Fine. Sounds fine to me." Jenny turned and rolled her eyes at Dora, who stood listening behind her.

"I suppose with you in flowers, I will be the dramatic one." There had to be a self-satisfied smile in the woman's voice. Jenny fought the urge to hang up. She politely said she would see her at Abigail's house.

When Dora asked what Emily wanted, Jenny only said, "Whether to wear black or blue."

"And what did you tell her?"

"Blue, of course. Black would make her look too normal."

* * *

As Zoe walked back out of Dora's door in a dress of red and white and blue that did truly look like a barber pole, Chief Ed Warner walked in.

He wished Zoe a good morning and smiled broader than Ed Warner ever smiled.

"Your friend looks upset." He nodded to Jenny and then to Dora. "Might be that dress she's wearing. Somebody's going to follow her down the street yelling that they want a haircut."

Thinking he was being very funny, Ed Warner chuckled and shook his head.

Dora looked at the clock. Only an hour before they had to leave for Abigail's. Still, she offered to make the chief lunch, which he turned down, saying, "I'm here to talk to the two of you. Miss Zola, too. If she comes back."

"Zoe's getting dressed for a meeting at Abigail Cane's in about an hour. We're kind of pressed for time," Jenny said.

He put his hand in the air. "Only take a minute. There's just some things I've been thinking about. A long time ago, my dad told me about the Suttons." Chief thought a while as he checked his fingernails. "You see the back of that house?"

Dora nodded.

"There was a fire out there in the ell," he went on. "My dad said it was a sad thing, but I never paid much attention. Kids don't, you know. When I took over from Chief Arnow, he showed me a box of evidence and said not to ever throw it out. That's when I heard that the mother was out there sleeping when the fire started. She went up in flames. Chief had reports in the box. Yellowed now, most of them. I never took it for much until all this started happening. Read over the whole thing this morning."

He nodded and thought awhile.

"The chief wrote that he smelled gas on the burned boards when he was out there. It rained the next day. When he got time to go back out there, couldn't smell it anymore." He looked hard into their faces as they listened. "You know what that could mean?"

Dora shook her head. Jenny crossed her arms and listened hard.

"Well, I called Chief Arnow this morning. Lives in Florida now. Fort Lauderdale. Says he likes it a lot down there."

He cleared his throat and looked out the window at the sound of Zoe calling Fida to come in the house.

"Chief told me something. Made me swear not to say anything, but after thinking it over, I had to come here. I need help working this out. All this stuff around Emily Sutton. Whoever killed that cousin of hers, it sure looked personal to Detective Minty. Nothing taken from the house. A lot of blood, Minty tells me. Guess Althea was hit in the head with an axe, then stabbed out in her car. That's the kind of killing that points to someone she knew. Chief Arnow went on to say that Emily came back to town just a year or so before the fire. Next thing he knew, the other sister, Lorna, was gone. The chief said he didn't know for sure what happened to her. Had an idea, but didn't want to say what it was." He cleared his throat. "You know what to make of any of that?"

Dora shook her head. "What did Chief Arnow think?" she asked. "Did he say? Was he hinting at arson?"

"Didn't say anything else. Just he was happy he was retired now. I kind of got the feeling he meant he was glad I was the one handling this new problem with the Suttons."

Ed left. Zoe trotted in, this time dressed in yellow chiffon that fell to her ankles. Over the yellow dress she wore a pale beige shawl. Her shoes were beige slip-ons, and her purse was yellow. She also had a yellow ribbon wound through her bright curls.

"Now what have you got to say?" She smirked at Jenny, who smirked back.

"Hope you don't get mistaken for a daffodil."

Dora shushed Jenny and told Zoe she looked perfect.

* * *

They walked over to Oak Street because the day was sunny and still warm. There was only the three of them. Alex had begged off going, which Zoe had said was a very smart move on Alex's part.

On the way, under a row of colorful maples, Jenny told Zoe what Ed Warner had come to tell them.

"Gas?" was all Zoe asked.

"Gas," Jenny said.

"Like, did Ed say the chief suspected arson?"

"I think that's what he was implying."

Dora looked around from Jenny to Zoe. "But who would have done a thing like that? Emily's a lot of things, but I doubt an arsonist is one of them."

"What about Lorna?" Jenny suggested.

"I doubt the fire was arson at all." Dora snapped her lips together. "People in Bear Falls don't do things like that."

Jenny gave Zoe a warning look as they met with a few other women headed up Oak Street to the meeting.

It was precisely three o'clock when all the women walked up the steps of the imposing mansion. The grounds were perfectly kept, as always. Flowers bloomed precisely as they were supposed to bloom—no hanging heads on the chrysanthemums. The trees were neatly trimmed so that no branch hung below the other. The grass grew to the edge of the brick walks and not an inch beyond.

Dora took in the perfection and sighed, knowing she would never reach such elegance.

Zoe looked around and said that this was no place for fairies.

The tall front door was answered by Abigail herself, in full afternoon-tea regalia. She welcomed them in, bending close to Jenny's ear to say that Emily hadn't arrived yet.

"I'm a little worried," she confided. "Elizabeth, my secretary, went to get her over an hour ago. I can't imagine what's holding them up. Almost everyone is here now.

Early, I might add," she said, leaving Dora to wonder what "precisely three" had really meant.

Abigail led all of them into a huge dining room where a lace-covered table glittered with polished silver. The rest of the guests were gathered at the far end of the room, around a table where teacups and a huge silver tea urn stood. It was, after all, tea time, time to be social and gossip and greet each newcomer with exclamations on her clothes, on her hair, on things recently heard about their children's prowess on the football field or in the gym or in the new robotics class at the high school.

They knew each other well. Neighbors and close friends. Even Miss Gladys, principal of the elementary school, was there, greeting Dora and her troop from a circle that included Minnie Moon.

Minnie Moon, in brown pants and a fuchsia, flowered blouse, was a surprise. A bigger surprise was that her daughter, Deanna, was with her. Deanna of the sour disposition, of the impressive pout—in a dress long enough to cover every vital intersection of her body. The girl nodded then stood looking around the room, taking in everything from the paintings on the walls to the collection of silver cups locked behind the doors of a huge cabinet. Jenny watched as Deanna looked dreamily at it all and actually smiled, seeming almost pleased to be there.

Or planning a heist, Jenny was mean enough to think.

The women began to ask each other when Emily Sutton was expected. They were all smiles and excitement.

"My mother used to talk about her. We're very lucky to have her," Priscilla Manus of the historical society told her circle.

"Historic occasion," Abigail agreed with Priscilla.

"And when will our star arrive?" Priscilla asked again a little later.

"Soon. She'll be here soon. Elizabeth's gone to get her."

Minutes ticked by, noted in sonorous tones by the large grandfather clock standing by itself on one of the end walls of the room.

Abigail went out to make a phone call and came back to say that Emily and Elizabeth Wheatley were about to leave the house. Abigail bent to tell Jenny that truthfully, Elizabeth was still waiting in her car for the woman to come out.

Abigail looked worried, but there were many details and committee reports to hear before Emily got there, so she put up her hands and asked the ladies to please be seated at the table so the first meeting of the Emily Sutton Reading Committee could begin.

Dora learned that her assignment was to hand out cookies at the sweet table outside the auditorium of the opera house on the evening of the event.

Jenny was to usher and would receive a tiny flashlight for her finger to show latecomers to their seats.

Zoe was scheduled to take tickets at the bottom of the curved staircase leading up to the main hall, though Minnie, who had probably coveted that position, asked if Zoe might not get lost in the crowd. There was an uncomfortable moment until Zoe said she was taller with her arms stuck up in the air, and one by one the women around the table nodded and agreed that Zoe would just be fine taking tickets.

"I really wanted to interview her before the reading," Abigail leaned toward Zoe to say. "But Emily wouldn't hear of it. She said she's used to handling crowds of readers by herself. I hope that's a wise decision. I'd imagined I could praise her in a way she can't possibly praise herself."

Zoe looked as if she was going to say something rude. Jenny stepped on one of her yellow shoes, distracting her.

"Ticket-taker." Jenny leaned down to tease her friend. "So much for being a well-known writer yourself."

Zoe smiled up at Jenny. "And you, with your little light. What a fine usher you will make."

When another report was read, Dora found she was in charge of not only giving out the cookies but baking them as well. She was asked to make the buttery little stars she was known for throughout the town.

Other women raised their hands, offering their specialties. Minnie Moon said she'd make her dump cake but was dissuaded by Priscilla Manus, who said they should stick to cookies, for the sake of tidiness.

The Committee on Ticket Sales reported that the members of the National Poetry Series had taken over ticket sales, and the house was sold out.

"People are coming from everywhere. Even New York, I've been told," Millie Sheraton, a neighbor of Dora's, said.

There were reports on coordination with the opera house, with local press, and with businesses wanting to advertise in the program. Then the design of the program was shown, with a very old photo of Emily Sutton at the center.

Abigail went out of the room to use the phone again, coming back looking much happier. "Elizabeth says they are almost here. I don't suppose I need to remind everyone to keep themselves under control. Don't rush the poor thing. She's been through a terrible time in her life. And let's not forget her recent loss."

Almost as she finished talking, there was a knock on the dining room door. Abigail clacked across the oak floor to answer. Beyond the door, there was a flurry of voices, and then Abigail turned to face the women, her face serious. "Ladies, it is my honor to present to you one of the best poets writing in the world today: Bear Falls's own, Emily Sutton."

She stepped back and Emily Sutton filled the doorway. There wasn't a sound in the dining room.

Emily stood with her hands clasped in front of her. Her head was down. She was dressed in nothing but blue scarves. They hung in points from her shoulders. They hung down both of her arms. They hung from her waist to the floor, over bare feet.

One of the scarves encircled her oddly red hair. Another was tied across her breasts to keep the waving scarves in place, though something with that plan had gone wrong. One small nipple peaked out from the sea of blue.

There were subdued gasps as Emily lifted her head and moved daintily into the room, smiling, looking from face to face with curiosity.

Abigail led her to the head of the table, asked her to be seated, then, under her breath, asked Elizabeth Wheatley to run upstairs and get a wrap for Emily, who seemed chilly. Her usually calm secretary hurried off, her usually perfect hair flying in all directions.

The women kept their eyes turned away from Emily in her diaphanous scarves. Some looked at their hands. Others studied the notes Abigail handed around the table. Nobody said much while they waited for Elizabeth's return.

Dora leaned close to Jenny. "You should have said black," she whispered.

"She only asked me colors," Jenny whispered back. "Not stripper routines."

Abigail saw fit to deliver a long introduction while Emily hid most of her face in a teacup, large eyes shifting back and forth as she slowly sipped the tea and sighed.

The knitted shawl was delivered as fast as Elizabeth could make it upstairs and down. All eyes were again on Emily as she pulled folded papers from a tiny purse hanging from her shoulder. She laid the papers on the table, unfolded them and smoothed them again and again, then looked up at the faces turned toward her.

She began to read in a tiny voice:

A reef, a rocky shoal, a whirlpool.
A ship within the eye.
No greater tragedy than a friend gone missing . . .

When she finished reading the familiar poem, she lifted her head and smiled at the appreciative applause of her audience.

She read another of her older and well-known poems.

"And now," she said when she'd finished and sat forward in the high-backed chair, pushing the knitted shawl back over her shoulders, "I have a new poem."

She waited for the sounds of awe to die down, cleared her throat, and began to read,

I don't walk out where people walk.
I don't enjoy that day.
I walk my rooms, back and forth,
And that is where I stay.

Jenny didn't hear the rest. Her eyes were on Abigail's face, and then on the faces of the women around the table. Some stared at Emily, transfixed with wonder at the words they heard. Some screwed up their faces as if smelling something bad.

When Emily finished reading, she took her time folding the papers together, again and again, then looked up to smile at the women who politely clapped for her.

She pushed her chair back, having trouble when it caught on the rug under the table, and motioned to Elizabeth Wheatley to come extricate her. Elizabeth moved the chair then tried to straighten the shawl over Emily's shoulders but failed. She escorted her hurriedly from the room. The other women got up and followed as fast as they could go.

When Jenny and her group tried to escape with the others, Abigail stopped them, one of her hands in the air.

"We have things to talk about," she said.

She directed them back toward the dining room as she followed the others to the front door.

It was another fifteen minutes before Abigail was back. She swept into the room and, with the women's eyes on her, opened a chest to pull out four glasses and a bottle of Jack Daniels. At the table, she poured a solid shot for each of them.

Abigail downed her drink, poured another, then urged her guests to drink up with her.

When she'd settled herself, she looked around at each startled face and asked seriously, "Wasn't that the damnedest thing you've ever seen? What'd she think she was coming to? A carnival show?"

Zoe laughed, then put her hand over her mouth when Abigail frowned at her.

Dora bit her lip.

Jenny tried to think of other things and clamped her teeth together.

"Well? What was that?" Abigail demanded again, shrugging herself out of the silk jacket she wore and stretching out in her chair.

"I think she needs wardrobe advice," Dora offered, sneaking a look at Jenny.

"That's pretty obvious." Abigail poured herself another shot, offered the bottle around, downed her drink, and stared hard from face to face. "Elizabeth's an idiot for letting her leave the house the way she was."

She turned to face Jenny. "You've got to be in charge of getting her to the opera house dressed decently."

Jenny shook her head. "I don't think I'm the one . . ."

"Somebody's got to do it, and she seems to like you better than the rest of us."

Jenny shrugged, uncomfortable. "I don't think that smile she gave me meant 'like.'"

"Close enough." Abigail slapped her hands on the table and turned to Zoe.

"You're the writer. What did you think of that new poem she read?"

Zoe thought a minute. "Kind of slight. Maybe she's out of practice."

"She can't read that kind of crap at the opera house. We'll be laughed right out of town. Could you take a look at what she picks out to read? I mean that you should direct her to the good stuff and away from the kind of garbage she just read. If nothing else, get her to stick to old work. We'll handle questions about it later."

"Emily doesn't like me much either." Zoe slid down a little in her chair.

"What about you, Jenny? Could you handle the outfit and the poems?"

Jenny wanted to go home. She nodded at Abigail, not knowing how she would handle Emily's wardrobe, nor caring what she read that night.

"Maybe you should cancel the whole thing," Dora said, looking quickly from face to face.

Abigail knocked her glass sideways as she leaned toward Dora. "Don't say that. It's too late. Tickets have been sold. We'd look like a pack of fools. What's going to happen is that the three of you will dress Emily and get her to the opera house. Okay? You will take her sheets of paper, whatever it is she chooses to read, and go over every one of them. She's going to be vetted within an inch of her life. She will read. She will take her applause. She will go home. And I will never bother her again."

"Oh, Abigail." Dora pushed her chair back, ready to get up. "Let's not be cruel. It's as if we're using the poor soul for our own aggrandizement rather than for the glory of American literature."

Abigail eyed Dora. She seemed about to say something but changed her mind and sat back. She put a hand over her eyes and moaned.

They left her like that, quietly filing from the room. They walked home, feeling as though they should tiptoe, as if they were leaving the scene of an accident. They didn't have a word to say to each other.

On the way Jenny checked her cell and found two calls from Tony. He'd left no messages.

Chapter 16

The house was silent when Jenny woke up a few hours after going to bed. Rain lashed at her half-opened windows in ferocious waves. She could hear the wind in the pines, a sloughing of sighs.

Jenny got out of bed to close the windows, then sat down to watch lightning cut straight across the sky to the west, out over Lake Michigan. After only a few seconds, the house shook with thunder.

The thing about electrical storms was that they cleared the air, she told herself. In the morning, everything would shine. One huge bath. One huge cleansing. She thought about that instead of the damage the storm could do.

Another lightning strike, turning trees into monsters with waving arms.

She checked her bedside clock. One o'clock. If she went out to the living room to watch television, she would wake Dora and Alex. Anyway, the cable always failed during thunderstorms. She checked through the books on her nightstand—nothing she wanted to read. Nothing she wanted to do.

She paced the room—five good paces each way.

The storm passed overhead. Lightning weakened. The last of the thunder faded off to the east.

There was nothing for her to do. She had nothing she wanted to think about.

She dug out a pair of jeans and a red sweater. She found her sandals where she had kicked them.

She grabbed a jacket, her purse, and keys and then closed her bedroom door quietly behind her.

* * *

Strong winds pushed at her car again and again. Tony's small ranch house on Maple Street sat under waving trees. The only light on was at the back of the house. Jenny could just see its glow through the picture window at the front the front.

His truck was parked in the drive so he was home, but probably sleeping. Maybe not alone.

She pulled in at the curb across the street from his house and settled down to watch.

She could always drive off before anyone saw her. She thought about those phone calls she'd ignored and wondered if he'd been calling to try again to explain what he'd done. Or maybe he'd been calling to tell her he was back with his wife and to say he was sorry but good-bye.

She watched the house for a sign, any sign, that she was where she should be. Nothing happened.

When the rain stopped, the wind died and the night cooled. She turned the motor on from time to time for heat. The darkness was complete. She wrapped her arms around herself and nestled farther down into the seat. She practiced what she was going to say—how angry she was going to get, just how she would put him in his place and tell him never to bother her again—as soon as she saw him.

An hour went by.

The thought hit her that his wife was probably in there with him.

What would she do if they both came to the door?

She thought those thoughts for a while, watched the trees become still silhouettes, and told herself that this whole thing was a new low for her.

A thin sliver of a moon came out, casting random shadows into the darkest places. She looked at her watch: two thirty. The last thing she would do was cry. Damned if she would give any man that much of her again.

Another fifteen minutes, she promised herself. That was all. If nothing happened, she would go home and move on. No turning back this time. No forgiving. Love wasn't supposed to work that way. If there was no sign from wherever signs came from, she'd drive off and forget him.

A light came on in Tony's living room.

She leaned hard back into the seat, afraid he might look out and see her.

His porch light came on. He didn't have a dog that needed to go out. Maybe he heard a noise. Or maybe a neighbor had called about the car parked across the street from his house.

At least there was no one with him. Maybe that was all she was going to learn.

She started the motor, praying she'd get away before he realized it was her car. He stayed standing on his porch, hands on the railing, looking over toward where she was parked. In just a minute, he was down the steps. He hesitated only once, at the bottom of the steps, then walked across his grass to the curb.

Jenny turned the motor off and was out of her car before he walked into the street. Her hair, already wet, hung in her eyes. She ran though deep puddles. She tripped on the curb and almost fell. Tony caught her.

She looked into his face and couldn't read anything there except that he was wary.

"I'm returning your calls—for the last time." She looked up, her body stiff. Rain ran down her face and into her mouth. "I came to tell you that I won't put up with another liar. I can't. Who are you, anyway? Are you my friend or some jerk out to use me? Are you this person I was beginning to trust or a cheater? Are you married or not married? Do you still love her . . . damn." She balled her hands together at her sides. If she let go, she would hit him. The unstopppered rage inside her was running red hot.

"Come on in, you're shaking," he begged, his arm going around her. "I'm so damned sorry and mad at myself and sick to my stomach that I let it go that far."

She pulled her arm away. "You mean, letting me trust you . . ."

Water ran from his face to hers as he bent close. "I never meant . . . I didn't think . . . I mean, I didn't know this was going to happen. All of a sudden you were there and something was going on and I . . ."

She tried to pull away from him; too many words wanted to spill out and they weren't the words she'd come to say. She wanted to stay mad. She wanted to be irrational and scream and kick and do anything else it took to wake him up.

"The past is over, Jenny." He put his face close to hers. "I meant what I said before. I filed for divorce. Won't be contested. It'll be quick. I promise you, Jenny."

She wanted to believe him. Wanted it so bad.

She stood in the middle of the road with Tony's arms around her, with her hands on his chest, with new rain soaking them, and wondered how two people who loved each other could be so stupid.

"Come in the house," he whispered next to her ear. "Please," he begged when she hesitated. "We need to talk. I promise I will never hurt you like this again. Not ever, Jenny. Words aren't easy for me but . . . I love you. I want us to be together forever. Me and you. Us."

When she kissed him, it was like melting straight into another human being. Not a make-up kiss. Not a sex kiss. More than any kiss she'd shared before—his lips hard on hers, her fingers twisted in his dark hair.

"I love you," she whispered back to Tony, as if it were the first time she'd ever said it.

* * *

He made coffee in the morning. She got two cups from one of the tall double cupboards he'd built when he redid his kitchen. Double cupboards. Pullout cupboards. Shelves for tall boxes and shelves for can goods. There was a pullout drop drawer for the long kitchen utensils that there was never a place for in ordinary kitchen drawers.

"This is a cook's heaven." She opened drawer after door and drawer after door, marveling at the utility of the space. Not a large kitchen, but one designed for the cook. Cupboards for large pots. Slots for the lids. Dora would swoon, Jenny thought as she toured the room while he cooked.

"I didn't know you could cook." Jenny put a hand on his arm and looked into his face.

He looked up from the restaurant-style stove where he carefully basted eggs for both of them. "I know," he said. "One of my hidden talents."

She smiled. "I think I know another one."

He reddened, then motioned for her to watch the basted eggs as he went to find his cell, which was ringing faintly off in another room.

The ringing phone made Jenny come back to the world beyond the walls of Tony's house. *Mom! I never called her.* Dora didn't know where Jenny was. There would be only the empty bed this morning when she went in Jenny's room. With so much going on all around them, maybe Mom had already called Ed Warner and reported her missing, or figured she was hiding in a Traverse City hotel room again.

Thinking hard about what she was going to say, she found her purse on a chair, where she'd left it last night, but her iPhone was dead. She'd have to borrow Tony's when he got off.

Maybe she would even tell Mom the truth about where she'd been all night. Or not worry about telling her because it would be Tony's phone number she'd be calling from, and Mom would know immediately.

Tony walked into the kitchen, still talking into his phone until he held it out to her.

"For you," he said. "Zoe."

She made a face at him, mouthing, "How she'd know . . . ?"

He shrugged.

"Hello." She ran excuses through her head. She was at Tony's because he'd called this morning. There was a carpentry emergency. Or he'd called early because he'd lost a set of plans for a Little Library and needed her to come look for them. Or—

"Emily called me," Zoe said, asking nothing. She sounded perturbed. "I'm shopping for her, and she asked if you and Alex would come over there with me this afternoon."

"Why?" Jenny resented being dragged back to that world so fast. She wanted to sit and have breakfast with Tony while she watched him eat. She wanted to smile at him from across the table, watch him smile back.

"Don't ask me. You know Emily. It will be about any idea that struck her during the night."

"Zoe. Will you call my mom and tell her where I am?"

"Huh! Oh, yeah, that's right. You're at Tony's house. Have fun. I'll tell her."

She hung up without the remarks and snickering Jenny had expected.

"What'll your mom say when she finds out you're over here?" Tony asked.

Jenny smiled up at him and thought only a minute. "I hope she'll be happy for us."

"Was Zoe? Happy about us?"

"You know Zoe. Distracted. She's got another Emily Sutton emergency. Emily wants me and Alex over there this afternoon."

"What for?" He leaned down and kissed her.

"Probably to see what we thought of her performance yesterday."

"Are you going to tell her the truth?"

"I'm going to lie through my teeth."

"What time?"

"Not until three o'clock."

"That gives us lots of time." He took her hand and led her to the table where she sat next to him, not thinking about what she was eating, only about the next smile she wanted to give him.

They never got to the fruit salad. They didn't clear the table.

The next couple of hours were just theirs. Jenny didn't think of Dora, nor Zoe, nor Alex, nor anybody but her and this odd man who seemed to love her.

Chapter 17

When Jenny walked in the house at noon, Dora looked up from her newspaper and frowned.

"Next time have the courtesy to call me directly if you're going to stay at Tony's all night" was all she said before asking if she wanted lunch. "Alex is out with a friend who came up from U of M to see her. She'll be back in time to go to Emily's." She paused. "Oh, and that detective from Traverse City called. He was supposed to be here yesterday, I think. He asked that you call him back."

Jenny did, immediately.

"I've been looking into Emily Sutton's background. Seems there are a lot of empty years where I can't find anything out about her. Can you, or anybody else there in town, fill in those blank years?" he asked.

"There's not much to fill in, Detective. She was back at home before we even moved here. There was a sister. Her name was Lorna. She was here until a couple of years ago when she left. Emily claims she doesn't know where Lorna went."

Another long silence. "Okay. That's a place to start. I'll see what I can find out about her. Lorna, you say? Lorna Sutton?"

"I guess so. Unless she got married."

"Anything else."

"There was a fire. I think it was around the time Emily came home."

"I know about that. The mother died in the fire. I talked to your chief about it. He says it was suspicious, but they didn't have arson investigators to look into it then."

"That's all I know."

"Personally," he went on, "what do you think of Emily Sutton?"

"You want gossip?"

"Half of our investigations rely on gossip, Jenny."

"Okay. I think she's very, very odd. She's one kind of person one minute, another the next."

"How do you mean?"

Jenny thought, wanting to be fair. "Emily can be shy and artistic—you know, otherworldly—one minute. The next minute she's ordering people around and acting as if somebody made her queen of the British Empire."

"I'm coming back out there to talk to her. I called, but she didn't answer, so I'll just show up again. If you've got a couple of minutes, I'd like to talk to you and Zoe Zola."

"Actually, I'm going to Emily's this afternoon."

"Why?"

"She asked for me and Alex Shipley to come over."

She told him she'd let Zoe know he was coming.

"And who knows?" the detective said. "Maybe I'll see you at Miss Sutton's house later."

* * *

They set the bags of groceries on Emily's porch at exactly three o'clock, as instructed. The door opened before Zoe could knock. Emily didn't invite them into the house, but took the bags of groceries in—one by one—and shut the door, saying she would be back in a minute.

There were no chairs on the sagging porch to sit on, so Zoe, Jenny, and an excited Alex sat on the steps, taking turns looking at each other, then away. As one, they stood when Emily came out and closed the door behind her. She waved them back to their places on the steps then stood above them, looking down. She had on navy pants that ballooned to the tops of old sneakers with knotted laces, and her white, lacy blouse was long-sleeved, elastic at the wrists. Her hair had been swept up into a fire-engine pouf at the very top of her head. A blue ribbon was wrapped many times around the pouf, then tied into a bow at the back. Her smile was pleasant, almost smug. Her shoulders were drawn up to her ears. She clasped her hands tightly in front of her.

"Well?" She looked from face to face. "Do you think the world is ready for my new poetry?"

Zoe and Jenny looked at each other. Alex, who wasn't at the meeting, looked out toward the swamp that was quickly changing to a coat of many colors.

"Oh, dear." Emily searched their faces, her bulging eyes bulging even more. "I hope I haven't misjudged the intellect of the audience."

Zoe was the first to shake her head. "You fascinated them."

Jenny knew Zoe was pleased with her own answer. "Fascinated," Jenny echoed.

"Tell me what they said after I'd left." Emily settled her shoulders back and waited. "I want to hear every word."

Alex, who'd heard about the meeting, watched as Zoe and Jenny squirmed.

"Most didn't have words to describe what they felt," Zoe said then looked to Jenny for support.

"You heard the applause," Jenny put in.

"Yes." Emily's eyes wandered to the sky, as if the scene of her triumph was permanently written somewhere up there for her to visit again and again. "It was a magical event. Then we will move on to the night at the opera house. All the tickets are sold!" She clapped her hands. "Since that is the case, I can't possibly disappoint my public, can I?"

Everyone agreed, loudly, in ardent, dishonest voices.

Satisfied, she nodded, and Zoe got up from her cramped space on the steps.

"Well, I suppose we'll get going . . ."

"Oh, no. That wasn't all I asked you here for. Please." She motioned Zoe back to her seat, then sat down on the very top step where she could look down at the women while making them keep their necks turned. She quickly got to the real reason for inviting them to her house.

"I have things I must tell you. And only you three." She looked from one to the other.

Alex bent toward Emily. Her face was avid, as if hoping she'd learn where Walter Shipley had gone.

"First," Emily smiled down at her, "I'm sorry for calling the police when you were here."

Alex shrugged off the apology.

"I'm so much alone. You understand. There is a certain fear that lingers when a house reverberates with echoes, you see."

Alex gave an almost imperceptible nod.

"This is what happens when the world has turned its back. I'm trying so hard, Alex." She put a trembling hand out to the girl, who took it and held on. "Do you understand? Can you understand what it is for a poet, a woman who's lived inside her head for so many years? Do you have any idea what that kind of confinement entails?"

Jenny and Zoe watched as Alex, as if hypnotized, nodded again and again, agreeing that she understood.

Emily bent down closer, her voice hardening. "Then you know why I can't have people breaking the frail circumference of my life. I'm often locked in different houses as I try to work." She abruptly dropped Alex's hand. "Your intrusion was a jolt. No telling what I would have written that day, if not for you flitting across my backyard."

Jenny was incensed for Alex. "She knocked," she spoke up. "You didn't answer." If this is why she wanted them there, Jenny figured it was time to go.

"Oh, don't misunderstand. I don't mean to be cruel. I just want the girl to know the mechanics of my life."

"I do," Alex said, her normally self-assured voice made small.

Emily bent toward Alex again, a drop of white spit in the corner of her mouth. "You do see then, I hope, why I can't be disturbed the way you disturbed me."

"Was he here?" Alex found her voice, speaking up as if shaking off a trance. "That's all I wanted to know. Is that his car out in your shed?"

Emily's eyes flew as open as they could get. "A car? In my shed?"

She turned toward the swamp and said nothing. After long minutes, she turned back to Alex.

"How I wish it were, dear, but that car is an old one that belonged to my mother. Lorna used it from time to time. She drove. I didn't. Walter's car is gone."

Zoe, cramped from the hard steps, started to get up but Alex put a hand up, stopping her.

"Before he came," Emily continued, "I warned him about Lorna."

She drew a long breath.

"His first letter was nothing more than praise for my poetry. He asked why I'd gone silent for so many years. I wrote back to tell him how his poetry blessed my life— his wonderfully microcosmic poems: *An ant on cosmic shores . . .*' How do I answer his question: *'Where are your poems, Emily Sutton?'* How do I say that I had no choice?"

She put a hand out for Alex to take again. "You have the letters. You saw for yourself what grew between us, didn't you?"

She waited for Alex's nod.

"I thought he felt the same. Our minds fit so perfectly together." The emotion on her long face slowly drained away. "One day Lorna came to me and said she was in love with Walter. Lorna often fell in love. I didn't think much of it. I didn't warn him about her. I should have." She glanced at Alex, tears in her eyes.

"How could I tell a man like your uncle that my sister couldn't be trusted? How could I say I'd come home to stay because of her? How do you tell a man that you can't go away with him? That you are tied to your sister and this house forever?"

Her listeners could have been statues.

Alex whispered, "What happened?"

"On the morning that I was going to tell him he had to leave, I got out of bed and heard the silence. Silence everywhere, as if the universe had gone deaf. I looked out my window. Walter's red car wasn't at the curb. Red became a blankness, even a blackness out my window. There was no need to go downstairs. No need to move from my room. No use, my waiting for them to come back. They were gone. Together."

Jenny asked, "But why would he stop calling his family, Emily? The man liked to be alone but he wasn't a hermit."

Alex nodded and watched Emily's face move from emotion to emotion.

"I know," she whispered, leaning toward Alex. "But who knows what power Lorna had over him? There's more." Emily bent in half, as close as she could get to Alex.

"Lorna started the fire that killed my mother. My mother asked me to come home to protect her." Emily nodded, looking from face to watching face. "I found the hidden gas cans later. When I asked her, all she said was that our mother wasn't necessary anymore. Can you imagine? Our mother 'wasn't necessary anymore.'" She stiffened her shoulders. "When the police chief asked too many questions, I had Lorna committed to an institution. She came home when the hospital closed."

Her lids dropped halfway over her eyes. When she opened them completely, it was to look from face to horrified face.

"These are my phantoms," she said. "No one must know or I will die. I promise. These things cannot be told to anyone else or I will die."

Chapter 18

Given the late hour, since most diners came for the five o'clock specials and were gone, Myrtle's was almost empty when Zoe walked in. She was alone. The last thing she wanted right then was any more talk about Emily Sutton. All the way home they'd talked about nothing else. Then they swore Dora to silence the way they'd been sworn to keep Emily's secrets, and that started the talk all over again.

Alex was relived, she said, to finally know what happened, even if it didn't bring her any closer to knowing where her uncle had gone.

She told them she planned on going back to school in the morning since she'd found what she'd come to find—that Uncle Walter'd gone off with a woman he loved.

Zoe had been happy to leave the Westons' house and go off by herself. She felt as if her head would burst wide open if she heard Emily's name mentioned even one more time that night.

Delaware, over at the register checking the last couple out, raised a hand and called a loud "Hi," which Zoe returned with a grudging wave as she slid into a booth in the farthest corner of the big room.

When Delaware came to take her order—which was easy since Zoe asked for the daily special: meatloaf and mashed potatoes with green beans and applesauce—Delaware hesitated next to the table, looking down, with half-closed eyes, at Zoe.

"Heard you were over to Abigail's house for that meeting."

Zoe squinted as if staring into a bright sun. She nodded.

"Heard there was quite a show."

Zoe frowned. "What do you mean?"

"Come on, Zoe. Heard that poet came to Abigail's half naked."

"Really?" Zoe looked puzzled. "Where'd you hear that?"

"Never mind." Delaware made a face. "Is it true?"

Zoe shrugged and shook her head. "I don't know what you're talking about, Delaware. Emily Sutton was there. She read a new poem but she had clothes on. At least as far as I could see."

"That's not what Minnie Moon told me." Delaware bit her lip at letting the name of her source slip.

Zoe made a noise and shook her head. "I thought Emily's dress was pretty. Sky blue. Perfect for a poet."

"Minnie said one of her boobs was hanging out."

"You mean bulbs. Breasts are more like flower bulbs—filled with life. Someday I may be calling on them to give life to some wee little baby. I'd never call them my boobs." She looked up at Delaware, one eyed. "Boobs are screwballs. They're kooks. They're dolts and fools. I would never call a treasured part of my body a thing like that."

"Guys would."

"Then maybe we should come up with silly names for their parts, too."

Delaware waved a hand at her. "You're nuts."

"Yes, well." Zoe shrugged her shoulders and stared down at her hands to hide the laughter in her eyes.

"Anyway, that's what Minnie Moon said. Half hanging out of whatever she was wearing, with a hand over it as if pledging allegiance to a flag."

"Minnie's a prude."

"You think Minnie's a prude? Never thought of her like that."

"Well, look what she wears, nothing but muumuus that hide everything. Must have—what do they call it? Body issues."

"Minnie?" Delaware brought her thin, plucked brows together. "I know she's religious but I never thought of her as having . . . what'd you call it? Body issues?" She thought awhile. "Her kids don't have issues like that."

"That's true. Minnie probably went out of her way to set her daughters free—considering what they wear in public."

"You can say that again. I've seen more of those girls' behinds then I've seen of my own."

Delaware stood on one foot, then the other. She looked out the window as the neon lights along Oak Street went off. She turned back to Zoe, liking the company and the chance to talk a little bit now that she wasn't rushed with customers.

"Everybody's going to the opera house to hear Emily. Hope nothing goes wrong there. I got tickets for my mom and me. Biggest thing that's happened to Bear Falls, Mom says, since the winter of 1978 when it snowed so hard that Chief Arnow declared Bear Falls officially closed. No electricity. Big excitement over that. Even more talk now, about the poet. Woman's been spotted, kind of flitting around in her yard and sneaking off places."

Delaware smiled a tight smile and went off to turn Zoe's order in to Myrtle, who was out in the kitchen, unseen as usual.

Zoe got her iced tea and, along with it, more of Delaware.

"How are Jenny and Tony getting along?" Delaware asked. "Haven't seen them in here together in a couple of days."

Zoe gave Delaware a narrow-eyed look.

"What?" Delaware said. "I'm just asking. Hope there's no trouble. I like the two of them together."

"Trust me," Zoe said. "They're fine."

"Glad to hear it. That makes me happy. My Larry and me have been together for ten years now. I think that's a pretty good record, though Mom wants us to get married."

She walked off, looking to retrieve the dish of meatloaf pushed through the opening to the kitchen.

Just behind the dish of meatloaf came Myrtle herself, scurrying from the kitchen, wiping her hands on her spotted apron. She pushed into the booth across from Zoe.

"Everything okay?" Myrtle looked hard at Zoe. "Heard you been having trouble."

Zoe swallowed a chunk of meatloaf. "What do you mean by 'trouble'?"

Myrtle's eyes disappeared into a cluster of wrinkles.

"Didn't you find that body?"

Zoe nodded.

"What's the body got to do with Emily Sutton? I heard about that."

"Emily and Lorna's cousin, Althea."

Myrtle threw her head back and stared at the ceiling, watching a big fan circling. Then she looked hard at Zoe. "If I was you, I'd keep my eye on Emily Sutton. She's not what she pretends to be."

Zoe felt her patience slip. She'd had enough of slightly cracked people for one day. Enough of hearing about Emily Sutton. Enough of just about everybody in Bear Falls. She cut her meatloaf into tiny pieces and stuck the pieces, one after another, into her mouth, chewing very slow so the process absorbed her.

Myrtle ducked her head between her shoulders and watched Zoe eat. "Heard about Emily's sister being gone. Emily didn't like her sister much. Never wanted to see her."

Zoe leaned back and eyed Myrtle. "What's that mean, 'never wanted to see her'? They lived together for years."

Myrtle glanced around the empty restaurant. Her eyes, behind thick glasses, were magnified and wary. She leaned across the table. "I was in the hospital with her."

"What are you talking about?"

Myrtle made a face. "No choice. Like me. She was there. Long time after I got there. At first she acted like she wanted to be friends. Then she turned, like one of those snakes that rears back and strikes you. I just stepped out of her way, watched, and learned better than to trust her."

"When was this, Myrtle? When were you in the hospital together?"

She shrugged and kept her eye on the door. When people walked up or got out of their car at the curb, she would hunker down and set both hands on the table, as if preparing to get up and run. When the people walked on by, she visibly relaxed.

Myrtle shook her head. "Knew her, that's all. Played so sweet, but I remember once she got into big trouble. Ran away. Our nurse was so mad at her over stealing her car, she went out and brought her back herself. Nurse Proust. I liked Nurse Proust."

"Ran away?" Zoe looked doubtful.

Myrtle nodded. "Got out. Found her in town."

"What kind of hospital are you talking about?" Zoe narrowed her eyes as Myrtle felt in her pocket, pulled something out, and set it on the table just as the front door opened and a giggling group of teenaged girls walked in.

"Look at that." Myrtle nodded to the paper rocking slightly on the table between them, then got up and scurried back to the kitchen.

Zoe set her hand on top of the folded paper and transferred it to the pocket of her jacket.

"Do you know what hospital Myrtle's talking about?" Zoe asked Delaware when she was back, hovering over her.

"Huh? Myrtle's not sick."

Zoe shook her head. "She was saying she'd been in the hospital with . . . eh . . . somebody."

Delaware shrugged and glanced over at the table of teenagers poking each other and laughing.

"Myrtle was down in a mental hospital for a while. That's what Mom told me, but we don't talk about it. Sad story. Her brothers put her there 'cause their dad left this restaurant to her. The boys got mad about that. Can you imagine! Got some quack to sign off on her and she was there for . . . oh my God! Years and years."

"People can't do a thing like that." Zoe was appalled.

Delaware rolled her eyes. "That's what you think. Back then they could."

"Which hospital?"

"The state hospital at Traverse. Closed a while back. That's the only way Myrtle got out, you know. 'Cause it closed. She went after her brothers and got the restaurant from them. Myrtle's never going to leave this place. Even hates to go back to her house when we close at night. I'm sure glad my mom never had any boys."

The front door opened again, and a couple walked in. Delaware's head snapped around, her lips set and angry. "Geez, wouldn't you know it. Me and Larry wanted to go to the last show tonight, now I'll never get out of here."

She leaned back and gave the intruders the evilest eye she could come up with.

"Of all nights!" she muttered toward Zoe, then put on a big smile and told the newcomers to take any table they liked.

Before she left the restaurant, Zoe took the folded paper from her pocket and spread it free of wrinkles on the tabletop. It was an old photograph—more like a photo cut from a book or magazine. In the picture were two women standing in front of a brick-walled building. The women stood apart, arms behind their backs. One's head was down, her foot toeing the ground to the side of her. The other stared straight into the camera. She thought the staring girl was a much younger Myrtle Lambert, only with her hair cut very short and the clothes she wore more like a uniform.

The other woman's face wasn't clear enough to make out. Her hair was short, too, as if wherever they were staying had only one barber. Maybe only one haircut.

There was no knowing if Myrtle was telling the truth about being in the hospital with Lorna or not. Zoe couldn't be sure who the woman in the photo with Myrtle was—not by body size. This one was small and thin, a little like Emily, or maybe Emily's sister. But half the women in the world were small and thin. She folded the paper into a square and stuck it back in her pocket.

Chapter 19

Zoe wrapped her old sweater around her and walked out to her flowerbeds, kicking at the dying grass, then bending from time to time to remove a leaf from her shoe, until eventually she was on her knees, talking to small people about life and death and how sometimes she just wanted to pop a person in the nose for no reason whatsoever besides maybe making her keep secrets she didn't want to keep.

Soon the fairies would be moved to the potting shed, all of them: young and old, male and female, naughty and nice. Winter took too great a toll on pebble and wooden houses. The tiny theater's marquee could collapse under the weight of snow.

She would tuck everything away in the shed, the fairies facing each other in boxes so they could talk and complain and come up with petitions they would present to her in the spring.

Red car, she was thinking, because something else was bothering her, needing to come out of the shadows in her brain.

Alex had gone back to school, promising to return if they learned anything more about Lorna and her uncle. Zoe wasn't as easily convinced that Emily's secrets were the end of things. She still wanted to get a look at that car in Emily's shed. And she wanted to find out which hospital the Sutton girl had been sent to.

There were things that didn't smell right to her. And that thing in her head still nagged.

Not just the red car, but something else.

Thousands of red cars in Michigan, but still she thought about it. Only a fractured piece of nothing that fit nowhere, and how could she find out anything now that the three of them had promised to keep Emily's secret?

She was already missing Alex. Losing people made her sad. The girl was off to her own life. No reason to look back at Bear Falls, but still Zoe wished she could see her from time to time.

A word whispered through her head. Something she should remember, or think about.

She moved to the next fairy in line and found peace in conversation with this little bit of herself.

Here in her fairy garden, she was in charge of everything, and everything made sense. Here she was the constable, the magistrate, and psychiatrist. One fairy might be bored and need a change of scenery. Another could be claustrophobic. Another needed bigger quarters. Or one might be old and wanted to be near a child. One needed to be close to a friend. And on and on. Every excuse for moving around that real human beings came up with, fairies had them, too. Especially as winter neared, and they knew quarters would be tight inside the potting shed. Each of them flexed their elbows and demanded attention.

Dain, a tiny, shivering man standing behind the mill, asked to be moved inside for the winter sooner rather than later. He mentioned his rheumatism and said he was already having chills.

She promised.

Orin said the wind whipped through his house from end to end.

Marigold whispered that there wasn't enough light left for her to paint.

Little Nissa worried because her garden had died.

Eltri said that Zoe had put him too close to a goldenrod that made him sneeze.

Rodella, the peacemaker, said she would get them all together that evening at her house to air their grievances, draw up a petition, and formally present it to Zoe when they found the time.

Zoe laughed at her own imagination, then settled herself, put on a formal face, and said she would consider the petition as soon as her schedule permitted. But when Cosette, the ballerina, *en pointe*, said something that sounded mean in terse, clipped French—something about needing leg warmers—Zoe fixed the little fairy with an angry glare and whispered, under her breath, "Get them yourself, you little phony."

"Red" jumped into her head again as she sat back to survey her kingdom. *Red. Red. Red. Red. Red.*

She moved along the path, upright and too proud to kneel and be berated by people a hundred times smaller than she was. Until she got to Lilliana, when she heard a low rumble of thunder out over Lake Michigan. She swore Lilliana looked up and smiled a sympathetic smile.

Lilliana, who never disappointed, lived in the lovely ceramic house near the potting shed. She was the first of Zoe's fairies and still her favorite. Lilliana: the lily. Beautiful and stalwart. A friend, Lilliana was newly restored after having been broken when she'd been used as a weapon of death a few months before. Now she was back, in her magic crown and blue sculpted dress. A wand towered above her, held in her hand.

"How can people make such messes of their lives?" Zoe whispered toward the slim fairy princess.

Zoe thought the word she heard in return was *pride*, though Lilliana's painted face didn't change.

Zoe muttered to herself, not sure that was the right word or if she'd misheard. Something she would have to think about later.

She knew someone was behind her when a long shadow fell across the ground. She bounced to the next fairy, talking earnestly about the mill and why the wheel no longer turned, which was something to think about next spring. As she mumbled to herself, her hand went to her pocket. The photo Myrtle gave her was still in there. She'd looked at it many times. She could identify Myrtle, she was sure of that. It was the other woman, standing just apart from Myrtle, arms at her side, looking off to the side—Zoe didn't know who it really was. The picture was black and white so she couldn't tell the color of the hair. The face—oval. The eyes—were they as big Emily's? Could be a family resemblance.

At the sound of a throat clearing behind her, she turned her head then slowly looked way up to the colossus in a brown sweater and beige pants behind her.

Detective Minty smiled down. "Communing with Nature?" he asked and chuckled, which made Zoe's skin ripple as she stood, pushing herself up with both hands, ever so slowly. "Thought I'd come out to look into some things for myself."

"About the fire at the Suttons'?"

She didn't have the patience for games.

To cover his unease, he took a swipe at the cuffs of his pants, then straightened to look down at her. "Maybe we can go inside?" He indicated her house.

Zoe nodded and led him up the steps. Fida put on one of her impressive displays of snarling and barking but was waved away and shushed by Zoe.

The detective sat down at the table, not turning his back on the little dog with her one bright eye fixed on him.

Zoe offered tea, but he refused and pulled a notebook from his back pocket.

"I wanted to see Emily Sutton. After Ed called, I figured I'd better have a longer talk with her. Couldn't get here any sooner. Anyway, the medical examiner said no one's made any arrangements for the burial of Althea Sutton. I told him I'd see what I could find out while I was out here."

Zoe watched as he talked and talked.

He nodded a few times to fill in the blanks between sentences. "What I really wanted to tell her was that the body won't be released for another week or so. The ME has ordered more tests. Can't issue a death certificate until they're all in, so no funeral yet, but they'd like to know who to call when the time comes."

Zoe still said nothing.

"She didn't come to her door again."

"Won't answer her phone either, I'll bet."

"I've got to talk to her."

Zoe shrugged and spread her hands. "Nothing I can do about that."

"I left a note on her door. I asked her to call me. Think she will?"

Zoe had nothing to tell him. Who knew what Emily would do from day to day or minute to minute?

"I've been asking around town here about your poet."

"Not mine." Zoe threw her hands in the air. "Trust me. Not my poet."

He licked his lips and thought a minute. "I'm getting different stories about that fire."

"I didn't live here then."

"And I understand there's a sister. Do you know where she is? Think I could talk to her?"

Zoe shook her head. "What did Ed Warner tell you?"

"He didn't have a clue, but he called the man who'd been chief here before him. Seems the man saved the file on the fire."

"I've seen it."

"Possible arson."

Zoe took her time to shake her head. She had no right to break a semipromise to Emily. That was such an old, old story now. Nothing to do with Althea Sutton's murder.

He wrote in his notebook, then looked at her again, eyes half opened. "Is she an invalid, this poet? Didn't seem like one to me but I understand the cousin used to do her shopping for her, and now you're doing it. I figured if that's true, you're the best one to get me in there. Otherwise . . ." His face was deadly serious.

"I know." Zoe sighed. "She's a problem. But I don't think I can help you. She leaves me notes and money. I leave the groceries on her porch. That's as close as I get to her."

Detective Minty stared down at his hands. He wrote something, then snapped his notebook shut and stood.

"One more thing." He turned to put a finger in the air. "Ed Warner told me this girl, this Alex Shipley, who's staying with the Westons, was caught nosing around the Sutton house, and Emily called him. The girl was trespassing. You know anything about that?"

"She was looking for her uncle, Detective."

"She find him?"

Zoe shook her head too slowly. His eyebrows went up. "You'd better ask her," Zoe said.

"I will. Is she at the Westons' now?"

"She's goes to school at U of M. She went back there."

"I'll get in touch with her. Is there anything you all know that you're not telling me? Seems there's a lot of silence from over here all of a sudden."

Zoe didn't answer. She would respect the promise she shared with Dora, Jenny, and Alex until she couldn't anymore.

Detective Minty was headed to the Westons'. She walked over with him. A fine drizzle was falling. Zoe wished she could talk to the others first. Something really bothered her. This hospital stuff. Lorna gone. She kept telling herself that they shouldn't be pretending everything was fine. Alex didn't find her uncle. Nobody knew the truth about the mother's death—except their small group. The cousin was horribly murdered. Nothing was really fine. Every important fact they had came from Emily. They needed to look into the hospital story for themselves. They needed to search for Lorna. She felt as if a huge lie were growing inside her and beginning to hurt. She was going to choke on it. She had to talk to the others.

The lights were on in the Westons' kitchen because the day was getting dark fast. Clouds from over the lake were threatening another fall storm. Thunder rumbled way off.

Feeling formal and not deserving of a warm welcome since she was dragging a Trojan horse in behind her, Zoe knocked and waited.

When Dora opened the door, she smiled, then looked surprised that Zoe was knocking. She frowned when she caught sight of the man behind her, but asked them both in, talking about the rain and what the weatherman was saying on the TV.

Jenny, at the table, nodded to Minty.

"Expected you yesterday." She pointed to a chair, inviting him to sit.

"I've been busy."

Dora stood at the oven, waiting for the timer to go off so she could grab two sheets of chocolate chip cookies before they burned. She made a face behind Minty's back.

The timer rang. She pulled the cookies from the oven, slid them onto a waiting rack, then onto a dish she handed around the table.

"I found that book you were asking about." Dora smiled happily at Zoe.

Before Zoe could ask which book, having no clue what she was talking about, Dora urged more cookies on everyone.

Zoe said only "Thanks" and pretended to be happy about whatever it was Dora had found for her.

Minty asked Dora and Jenny the same questions he'd asked her. As they answered him the same way Zoe had, there was another knock at the door. Tony Ralenti walked in, nodding to everyone and looking hard at Minty until he was introduced before going over to Jenny and, in front of everyone, kissing her on the forehead.

Jenny's face colored but she pretended everything was normal. Soon Minty rose slowly, excused himself, and was gone.

There was silence around the table because of Tony. He wasn't in on the secrets Emily had told them.

"Does he have any idea yet who killed Althea?" Tony asked.

"He didn't tell me anything, only wanted to know about Alex and the fire. Then asked the same questions he asked you." Zoe looked from Dora to Jenny, both of whom looked stuffed with things they wanted to say but couldn't because Tony was there.

"What are we supposed to do now?" Dora shook her head, sounding close to tears.

"We'll talk later, Mom." Jenny reached over to squeeze her mother's hand. "Let's eat your cookies and be happy."

Tony's dark eyes slowly went from one of the women to the other. He glanced down at his hands, then back at each of them. "Not one of you can keep a secret, you know. What's going on here?"

They looked at each other and then each grabbed a cookie, taking bites in unison.

"Hey, I was a cop, remember? If you think that detective didn't catch on, you're crazy. He'll be back until one of you tells him what it is. Might as well tell me. Maybe I can help you figure what to do."

The women looked at each other.

"You told me," Dora said. "Might as well tell Tony."

Tony didn't say a word, only listened.

* * *

"So the sister killed their mother? That's what she said?" He thought a while. "This sister. This Lorna. Emily said she ran off with Alex's uncle. Why doesn't that story ring true, I wonder?"

"But that's Lorna's pattern. She takes away everything Emily loves," Dora said.

Tony nodded a couple of times. "Murders everyone, sounds more like it."

"Not Walter Shipley."

He shrugged. "And nobody knows where she is? That's really strange. People like that—killers—they like to stay close to home. You've got to call Minty and tell him this whole thing—the hospital, all of it. Maybe he can track Lorna Sutton down."

Dora got up and went into the living room. She came back with a book in her hands.

"This is what I was trying to tell you about, Zoe. When I said I had the book you were looking for."

She set it in the middle of the table so everyone could see and pointed to the title: *An Annotated History of the Traverse City State Hospital.*

They gathered around the book as Zoe told them what Myrtle had been saying—that she was in the hospital with Lorna.

They looked down at the cover photo of a huge stone Victorian building with strange cupolas sticking from the top. Small, blurred people were gathered on the grounds in front of the building.

"Looks like a prison," Zoe said under her breath as she took in the wall, the narrow windows, some with close-set bars over them. The building was stark and unlandscaped. It overpowered the photo—like too much sky.

"Traverse City State Hospital," Dora repeated. "That's where Myrtle's brothers sent her. We heard about it when Jim and I first moved to town. One of those whispered things: that the boys wanted the restaurant. And that's where Lorna went after she set the fire. I'll bet Emily blames herself for her mother's death. After all, that's what she came back to Bear Falls to prevent."

"So Lorna went back to that house when the hospital closed? That's thirty-seven years ago." Zoe shuddered at the thought. "And lived together all those years. Until Lorna left."

They turned page after page—photos of women in simple, identical dresses. Children—a lot of children.

Zoe pulled the folded picture from her pocket and smoothed it out on the table.

"Myrtle said Emily didn't like her sister much. Never came to see her."

Tony got up slowly, hands on the table. "I'll be back in the morning. I think what you've all got to do is decide if you're going to cover for Emily Sutton or call Detective Minty. You ask me, it's time to start looking for Lorna Sutton. She killed once, according to your poet. Who said she hasn't come back and is killing again?"

Chapter 20

With little left to say, Zoe made for the path between their houses. She was glad it was still raining. The weather fit her mood. More than anything, she wanted to shut her door behind her and hug Fida. She wanted to ask Fida how the devil she'd been dumb enough to get involved in this mess in the first place.

In the kitchen, Zoe pulled a juice drink from the bottom shelf of her refrigerator, where she kept most things she needed often. She got a glass from a cupboard, using a stool, and then sat at the table, pouring her drink slowly, thinking, then inviting Fida to sit with her, pushing a doggy treat across the table.

"Fida. I feel so bad for Emily. I've been horrible to her. I've been awful. Mainly because I don't think she likes me. I feel kind of bad about that. She's had a hard life."

She looked Fida straight in her good eye. "I'll bet you've run into circumstances like that, people who don't like small dogs. Who wouldn't take it personally? But I don't get her, and she doesn't get me. Anyway, I've decided to be nicer. And I'll help Abigail the best I can with Emily's big day. I will be a better human being."

Fida sneezed. As if bored, she looked at the floor, jumped down, and wandered off to her bed in the corner.

Zoe scowled at her faithful companion, thinking that with all the things she'd done for that dog, she should be able to expect a little of her time.

She checked her watch. Four thirty. Maybe a couple of hours to write. Alone, by herself, no talk of mad events or implosions by deluded writers. That's what she was herself, after all—a writer. Not a deluded one—yet. Not a famous one—yet. Not a mad one—at least, no more than all writers were mad, thinking what they slaved away at was as important to anyone as it was to them.

She left the kitchen, setting her glass on the counter and looking down at her snoring dog. Zoe thought maybe she would choose to come back in her next life as a West Highland White Terrier in a home with a single lady who doted on her. Not a bad life. One thing she knew—she would earn her keep by listening and not letting her eyes droop closed as her mistress talked. She would come when she was called, never pee on a rug, never poop when she got nervous. She would be the perfect companion. Unlike Fida, who snored at her now.

With a dismissive nod of her head, she left Fida to herself and went into her office to work on the *Two Emilys* book, beginning with the first of the Master letters to someone who sounded like a lover but probably was only directed to the whole of love—love as Dickinson imagined it might be.

There was something more than different about Emily Dickinson. Like no other earthbound poet she'd read, there was true imagination in that head. Lines constructed on paper that you could almost hold in your hand, lift the lines to look at the ideas this way and then that way, and always find yourself reflected somewhere.

Zoe leaned back to wonder if she would have liked Emily Dickinson as a person. Probably not, Zoe decided. Dickinson would annoy her—all that running from visitors and sitting at the top of the stairs to talk to company. Would Emily Dickinson know how to take a joke? Did she ever think a single swearword in her life? Zoe bet she had, if for nothing more than to try them out for sound and color.

It was after seven when she stopped writing, hating to pull herself away even then. She liked wandering, inside her head, through the Dickinson house in Amherst. Climbing the stairs to Emily Dickinson's bedroom, sitting at her desk and looking out her window, out over the Pelham hills.

But she was hungry and Fida was at her feet again, trying her best to look apologetic for whatever she'd done before so Zoe would feed her.

All she could find in her cupboard was a can of dog food for Fida and a box of crackers for herself. With a piece of gouda cheese from her refrigerator, she and Fida had a fine dinner and thought only happy thoughts—like dreams for Jenny and Tony. Whatever had gone wrong between them sure seemed taken care of. The kiss he'd planted on Jenny's forehead in front of everyone had been like a signal. And their eyes when they looked at each other. Something happened. It looked a lot like love to Zoe.

It was already getting late when she went to her office again and turned on her computer. She Googled "state hospital Traverse City." A list of websites popped up. Then new color photos of old Victorian buildings—imposing and institutional, with flat, creamy stone walls. Small windows. Pretty hallways with vaulted ceilings. Shop after shop. Restaurants. Displays of wine, jewelry, clothes. The gentrification of the asylum was ongoing.

Then came photos of the buildings as they used to be. She recognized some of the pictures from Dora's book. Vacant-eyed patients on the lawn, leaning away from each other, not touching. Photos of the hospital after it was closed, buildings fallen into ruin. One building, with a squat turret at the top, was especially sad.

There wasn't much on the patients who'd lived at the hospital in the early 1900s. A few names—mostly from relatives who didn't want them forgotten. One site mentioned patient lists, but the writer complained that he couldn't get his hands on them unless he was a relative of a patient. And there again was Myrtle's photo. Zoe looked close. She thought she recognized Myrtle again—this much younger Myrtle. The other woman was too blurred. It had to be Lorna, unless something was confused in Myrtle's mind Maybe because of the big event coming up and people in town talking of nothing but Emily. The height and shape was Emily's height and shape, or, again, what could be the height and shape of a million other women.

Zoe turned off the computer and sat back in her chair, drawing her robe around her.

Closed in 1989.

Lorna came back home. She was still there when Walter Shipley arrived. Now gone for three years. No word from either of them since the day they left together.

Nothing of what she looked at or read felt right to Zoe.

That night, in bed, a word whispered back into her head. Something from her garden, where she was always happiest. A word from Lilliana. Not one of the special words they shared at times like this, when life got overwhelming and she wanted to be a chipmunk—to pull back into a hole and hide. Sometimes words were all she had for beauty. The best word of all was tomorrow. Always *tomorrow*, when everything could change.

Psst—the word whistled right through her head, though she tried to catch it. It still sounded like *pride*. But that made no sense at all.

She woke up the next morning with a few things worked out.

First, there was that shed behind Emily's house where Alex saw a car. Somebody had to take a look and settle whose it was once and for all.

Second, for her own information, she wanted to get down to that hospital, walk around the grounds, imagine Lorna staying there and then coming home to the sister who had put her there.

Third, Walter and Lorna left together. They had to be somewhere. She'd call Detective Minty to see if he'd found out anything.

But before any of that, she would make a call to Christopher Morley. He was sending her a ticket to come to New York, and she wanted to thank him again. Maybe make him laugh. Maybe have it perk up her whole day before she went over to Emily's to get another of her interminable lists that seemed more about vanity now than food.

* * *

In the morning, Zoe went over to the Westons', but there was no one home. She went inside and called their names. No one answered. She called Jenny's cell from their kitchen to find that they were up in Charlevoix with Tony, taking photos of houses.

Zoe went home and worked. Even at five o'clock, there was no car in Dora's drive. She'd been thinking all day of how to sneak around the back of Emily's outbuildings and get a look in that garage. The idea seemed like a good one, but she didn't want to go alone.

She and Fida sat in the living room and listened to a Leonard Cohen CD. She sang "Hallelujah" over and over, until she was sick of her own voice and remembered she was supposed to have gone to Emily's for the latest list. Cursing herself for forgetting, probably on purpose, she dialed Emily's house to apologize. Emily, of course, didn't answer.

Nothing she could do about it now. She was hungry. She had nobody to talk to and had already screwed up badly enough for one day. What she wanted was to get out of the house, cat, and make herself feel better.

Demeter, Delaware's mother, was on duty at Myrtle's diner. She brought Zoe's meatloaf even faster than Delaware had. The chunk of meat, covered with canned beef gravy, and a side dish of peas and carrots, were like manna to Zoe. She dug into the mashed potatoes—real potatoes, whipped with plenty of butter. That was a good thing and Zoe wanted only to concentrate on good things at that moment.

The bread pudding was dry. Demeter shrugged and spread her hands when Zoe complained. Taller than her daughter, with dyed black hair puffed into a helmet around her head, she laughed at Zoe. "You been coming here for over a year. You think things are going to change?" She pulled the dish from under Zoe's spoon and took it to the kitchen.

"You want your bill," Demeter asked when she was back, "or you just going to sit and take root?"

"Is Myrtle back there?" Zoe motioned toward the kitchen.

"You ever know her not to be when the front door's open for business?" Demeter shook her head, dislodging the pencil stuck up there.

"Could I talk to her?"

Demeter laughed. "You want your nose bit off? Especially after I told her you said the bread pudding was too hard. I asked her if I could take it off your bill, and she said for me to charge you twice. Maybe now's not the best time to go back there."

Zoe sat awhile longer, hoping the restaurant would clear out and Myrtle would at least want to bawl her out about the bread pudding.

People left, but other people came in, some just for coffee. Zoe turned her water glass between her hands and waited.

Fifteen minutes passed.

Finally, Zoe got up when Demeter's back was turned. She toddled fast across the floor and through the swinging doors.

Myrtle turned from the deep sink with a butcher knife in her hand. "Get out of here, Zoe Zola," she hissed, setting the knife on end against the sink.

"I've got to talk to you," Zoe stood her ground. "It's about that hospital."

"What about it?" Myrtle turned to the sink, running hot water over a stack of stuck-on pans. When she turned back, she looked hard at Zoe. "You think I made up everything I told you. Right? Think I've got nothing better to do, working back here every day of my life except Christmas, than to make up stories."

Zoe shook her head. "I just need to know for sure."

Myrtle's face was set. She walked toward Zoe, drying her hands on her apron, rubber-soled shoes sticking to the tiles.

Myrtle stopped and spread her feet wide. "You know how your Emily was at that meeting Abigail had?" She finally asked. "Everybody in town knows about it. She went there half naked, like she'd make a big impression that way. Same thing back at the hospital. She had a hard time keeping her clothes on there, too. She said men liked her to do that." She shook her head. "They didn't."

"Wait a minute," Zoe put up a hand. "First of all, she's not 'my Emily.' Second, it wasn't Emily in the hospital with you. It was Lorna Sutton."

Myrtle shook her head. "You saw the picture. I never said it was the other one. That's me and Emily Sutton. Not the sister. Nose in the air, like she was better than the rest of us."

Zoe didn't dare argue.

"You want proof?" She poked deep into her apron pocket again. "Here, you talk to this lady. She was one of our nurses."

Zoe took the envelope Myrtle held out; it was the size of a Christmas card, with a candy cane–shaped stamp. It was addressed to "Myrtle Lambert, 221 Pine Street, Bear Falls, Michigan." The return address, written with a fine pen point, read "Constance Proust, 89 Fortune, Fife Lake, Michigan."

"Remember what I told you about her? She was always good to me. Nurse Proust. Didn't like Emily any better than I did. Call Nurse Proust. She'll tell you what kind of human being Emily Sutton is."

Chapter 21

Bear Falls was quiet—not many cars out yet. It was Friday, a day when people were usually shopping, but maybe it was still too early. Zoe had already dropped off Emily's groceries—quite a lot for one person, but you never knew about people—and she was leaving almost enough money now. Zoe suspected that maybe Emily was into stockpiling food like a lot of people in the north. Supplies for the apocalypse or when the big one dropped. Or, in Emily's case, when she ran out of people to shop for her.

Zoe left the bags on the porch and got out of there, no longer worried if the food would rot. Days were cooler now anyway. And the last thing she wanted to do was talk to Emily. The last few times had been about nothing but the opera house event: high drama and demands for things she would need—otherwise, of course, she couldn't possibly be there.

Zoe knew a blackmailer when she met one and was having trouble keeping a smile on her face around Emily Sutton.

Zoe wanted to check in with Ed Warner that morning. After that, she planned to go into Traverse City and drive by Althea's house again. Then maybe over to the old hospital. She was convinced Myrtle had it wrong about Emily. From everything Zoe had heard so far, it didn't seem possible Emily was the one who got put away, but she didn't want to open her mouth asking questions that would start more gossip.

At the station, the chief was happy to see her. He offered her a chair at the other side of his desk and asked how her writing was going, how plans for the opera house were proceeding, then ground to a halt and sat waiting for her to talk, hands folded across his stomach.

"I was wondering if you had any suspects yet."

"You mean Althea Sutton's murder, don't you?"

She nodded.

"Talked to Detective Minty just an hour ago. They got info on the blood samples from the garage. Two different blood types. Waiting on DNA. He's hoping for that. They've picked up a few guys with B&E records. Some drug dealers. A couple of alcoholics who can never find their own house when they've been drinking—over and over, those poor guys end up pounding on a neighbor's door, demanding to be let in. Officer Minty had the idea maybe one of them got in and scared her, then decided to ransack the place while he was there. Couple of homeless guys—looked at them, too. That's about all for now."

"I thought he said it had to be someone she knew?"

Ed shrugged. "You have to look at a lot of people, Miss Zola. We'll get him. We always do. Not many unsolved murders up here. Most are relatives, drunk and getting into a fight. Some are husbands killing their wives, and every-body knows why. Or wives killing their husbands—and everybody knows why. Sometimes it's a kid with a gun that should have been locked away. Not many killed the way Miss Sutton was killed though. We'll get him. Unless he was from down below. Like a hit man. Can't imagine that's the case up here, but you never know."

"Remember when you came over after you went through Chief Arnow's file on the Sutton house fire?"

He leaned back, sniffed, then nodded. "What about it?"

"You said you had questions the chief couldn't or wouldn't answer."

Ed nodded.

"If he thought the fire was arson, did he say who he thought did it?"

"Nobody was named in the file."

"Who do you think could have done it?"

"You're asking me to speculate about something going back a lot of years. Something I don't know anything about. Must've been about sixteen then."

"But if you had to take a guess. Would you say it was one of the girls?"

"You mean Emily or her sister?"

Zoe nodded.

"I'd say that's the craziest thing I ever heard."

"Didn't Lorna go away right after the fire?"

"If she did, I wasn't aware of it. Like I said, I was a kid then."

Zoe didn't like what she was feeling and didn't like that she was saying things behind Emily's back. She stood and told Ed she just remembered another place she had to be and hurried out of the station.

She called Jenny before heading for Traverse City.

"Sorry," was the first word out of Jenny's mouth. "I was just going to call you. Got time to grab lunch? Abigail called. She wants to make sure the two of us will supervise Emily the night of the opera house event. She's afraid her secretary doesn't have the backbone to stand up to her. Remember the committee meeting?"

"Does she mean dress her?"

"Something like that. At least not to let her out of the house without a bra. I'm to stick a small sized one in my purse in case Emily doesn't have any."

"Ooh. That's sounds like fun," Zoe said. "You hold her down, and I'll snap the thing around her."

"And she wants us to look over what she's going to read that night. If it's very, very bad, or even horrid, Abigail wants to make sure she reads only her old work."

"People were promised new poetry. That won't go over very well."

"What else can we do, Zoe? Abigail is having fits. She can't cancel and doesn't trust Emily as far as she can throw her. That's what she said."

They agreed that they were the only ones close enough to Emily to watch out for her.

"Will we be taking her to town?" Zoe asked.

"She didn't say. I think there's some arrangement that's already been made to pick her up."

"So, guess we're on for lunch then. I've got some things I have to tell somebody before I burst wide open. Makes me feel like a terrible gossip, but I don't know what's true and what's not true anymore. Remember that picture I showed you? The one Myrtle says is her while she was in the state hospital?"

"Her and Lorna Sutton. I remember. Why wouldn't I?"

"Well, now she's saying something else. I don't know if I believe her."

"Lunch is okay. But not the Brew."

"Yeah, the ghost of a past girlfriend might still be haunting the place."

"You stop it right now," Jenny laughed.

"Got it. But you two seem to have made up. I hope he had a good excuse for that ugly girl with him."

"She wasn't ugly. She was great looking."

"I know. Just wanted to cement our friendship. So you aren't going to tell me what happened?"

"Someday, Zoe. Right now it feels good to be happy."

"Just tell me if I guess right: long lost sister? Old kindergarten friend? A buddy from the police force in Detroit? A nurse from when he got shot. I'll bet that's who she was."

"Zoe! You cut it out. I'm happy with things the way they are."

"Sure thing, Jenny. Now, what about lunch?"

* * *

Since Zoe was driving, she decided they would start at the old hospital. She was curious to see the buildings for herself. She'd read all she could find on the Internet, but nothing took the place of being there.

From Division Street, she turned at the triangular fieldstone marker, following a line of cars that were turning before what was known as Building 50, an imposing structure lost among the trees.

Zoe drove slowly, looking at the buildings, many left as they were, windows empty though the grounds were well mowed. The buildings that were still abandoned, with windows broken in and paint peeling from the walls, looked sad, unoccupied, worn. Some of the windows were still covered with the old wire mesh.

"Imagine being confined here for years."

"I can't," Jenny said. "I can't imagine children being kept here."

"From what I found, it was because their families said they couldn't control them. Some were dyslexic, can you imagine? Epileptic, too."

"That's crazy. Inhumane."

"They didn't know what those things were back then." Zoe drove past a building with a squat dome on the top.

"Kids." Jenny said the word under her breath while looking at the institutional buildings they passed. She blinked her eyes and shook her head. She blinked and shook her head. "I can't imagine sending my kid to a place like this."

"Myrtle gave me the name of a nurse she liked when she was in there."

"Did you call her?"

"Not yet."

"Maybe we should. Just to check on what Emily told us. That's a serious charge, that Lorna set the fire on purpose and killed their mother."

"I know." Zoe was slow to bring out the rest. "But that's not even the worst of it."

"What now?"

"Myrtle swears the woman she was confined with wasn't Lorna Sutton at all."

"Well? What's all this about then?" Jenny waved her hand toward the hospital buildings. "Why are we here?"

"Myrtle swears it was Emily."

Jenny didn't say a word. She stared out the window, thinking hard.

She finally turned to Zoe. "Do you believe her?" Jenny asked.

Zoe shrugged. "I hate to think it. That would mean it was likely Emily who set that fire. And Emily's the only one who says Lorna and Walter ran away together. Emily's the only one who was still in touch with Althea."

"You can't blame Althea's death on her," Jenny said. "She doesn't drive. How would she have gotten to Traverse City and back?"

With too many things to think about, they stopped talking. After a while, Jenny offered to contact the nurse if that would take some of what was happening from Zoe's shoulders.

It was agreed. Zoe would keep on delivering groceries. Jenny would contact the nurse and ask her which Sutton woman had been confined with Myrtle Lambert.

After the hospital, they drove by Althea's house again. There was something, Zoe said, that she still wondered about. Back in front of the little ranch house, Zoe pulled to the curb. The grass was tall—the gardener wasn't getting paid anymore.

"You think anybody will buy it?" Jenny asked, looking at the ordinary little house. "I mean, with the history of murder?"

"Probably Emily owns it, if she's the only family left. Maybe she'll move here. You think?"

Jenny laughed at the hope in Zoe's voice. "And leave a musty old house at the edge of a swamp? Would you?"

Zoe's face fell. "I guess not."

Next door to the house, the same neighbor was out in her gardening hat and gloves. The woman stood with her back to them, watering her grass again.

"I'm going to ask her something," Jenny said.

Zoe pulled to the curb and Jenny was out of the car, heading toward the woman.

She stood talking to the woman for about five minutes before turning back to the car and hurrying across the lawn.

"What she'd say?" Zoe asked. "Anything new?"

Jenny shrugged, thinking. "I was wondering about that car she saw in Althea's drive. I never asked her what color it was."

"What'd she say?" Zoe knew something was coming. She could feel it right down to her toes.

"She said it was red."

"A Saturn?"

"That's all she knows: red."

"Did she tell Detective Minty?"

"Said she did." Jenny looked hard at Zoe. "Minty probably won't think anything of it."

Zoe nodded. "But we do, don't we? We know a lot of things."

"Maybe we should go home first," Jenny said. "Let's talk about it on the way. Then you go talk to Ed, and I'll call Myrtle's nurse."

"And then what?" Zoe was almost afraid to ask.

"Maybe we'll have to visit Abigail. She should be warned that the problems with Emily might be a lot worse than we thought."

"What about lunch?" Zoe groaned.

"Later," Jenny said.

"Too much later and I'll be dead."

Zoe wasn't happy.

Chapter 22

Ed Warner was just going inside the police station when Zoe pulled up for the second time that day. He stopped where he stood. He narrowed his eyes to see who was calling his name.

"Come on in, Miss Zola," he invited.

He called over to Edna Mark, the older woman manning the phones, who waved to Zoe as they went by her, back to Ed's office.

The first thing he asked was how everything was going with Abigail's event. "Town's sure buzzing. Hope it's a big success for Abigail. I'll tell you something, Miss Zola, that woman's been through a lot. I sure hope the town council agrees to take that statue of her old man down. She wants it bad, and if you ask me, she's got it coming to her. Everybody knows the history of that family. You don't keep that kind of meanness under a bushel for long." He shook his head. "Look what all that catting around and treating people like dirt did for Joshua Cane. Money doesn't change character, does it? I plan to be there, clapping the loudest when they bring old Joshua down. Now." He leaned back in his chair, head lolling off to the left. "What can I do for you?"

Zoe took a deep breath. "It's about Althea Sutton's murder. Ever since I found the poor woman I can't get her out of my mind."

"Understandable, considering the shape she was in."

"Is there anything new?"

Ed thought awhile, sitting up very straight in his chair. Finally, he said, "To be honest, Miss Zola. There isn't much."

"May I ask you something?"

"Sure. Go ahead. I'll do my best to answer."

"A neighbor of Althea's told us about a car parked in her drive a couple of times. I suppose it could be anything from an insurance agent to a friend of hers."

He nodded. "Detective Minty mentioned it, but with no make or model, no license plate, it's pretty hard to put out a BOLO. None of her friends from church had any idea who it could be. Not one of them. Her bird watching group never got together except out in the woods somewhere. Couldn't remember who drove what kind of car."

"Jenny and I stopped back to talk to that neighbor of Althea's. She remembered the color. Red."

He shrugged. "A lot of red cars in Michigan."

"Do you remember when Alex Shipley was picked up on Emily's property, looking in those out buildings?"

He nodded, waiting for more.

"Do you remember what she was looking for?"

"A car. Thought she found one in that old garage."

"Do you remember the color of the car she was looking for?"

He thought a while, then he smiled at Zoe. "Sure. Red."

"A red car. Her Uncle Walter's car. The car he loved. And he's been gone now three years. Along with his red car. A red Saturn."

Ed stared down at his desk, then shook his head. "Still, as I say, Miss Zola, a lot of red cars in Michigan. No knowing if the covered car in Emily Sutton's garage is the same one you're talking about."

"But what if it is? What if it's a red Saturn?"

"Nothing I can do about it. Without probable cause, no judge is going to give me a search warrant. And I'm not taking it on myself to go over there and get caught trespassing."

Zoe lowered her head, wondering how to go after this from another way.

"Remember what you told us about that fire?" she said.

"At the Sutton house?"

She nodded. "Were they sure it was Lorna who set it?"

"Lorna's the one went off to the mental hospital, far as the old chief knew."

"Myrtle was in that hospital at the same time. She says she was in there with Emily Sutton."

"Now, Miss Zola. She may be a lot of things, our lady poetess. I heard she was half naked over there at that meeting at the Cane's house. Everybody's just putting that down to poets being half cracked anyway." His face reddened. "Present company excepted, of course."

Zoe frowned hard at him. "I may be half cracked, but I'm not a poet."

"And," he went on, "you know how much we all like Myrtle. Salt of the earth. But I've got a feeling she came up with this new story after Emily Sutton got talked about so much. I wouldn't take what she says now too seriously. Fine woman. We all know her story. But . . ." He shook his head. "No sense adding to the fire with a lot of dead birch—if you know what I mean."

Zoe got up and walked to the door, where she turned, thought better of asking another question, and left.

* * *

"Connie's not home," a pleasant voice on the other end of the line said. "She'll be back in a few days. Up to Munising, visiting her aunt. Can I take a message?"

"Do you have another number for her?" Jenny asked.

The woman hesitated. "Does she know you?"

"No, ma'am. But I do need to talk to her as soon as possible."

"Well, since you don't know Connie, I'll bet you anything it can wait until she gets back. Are you with a credit card company? I can tell you right now, she's got a Sears card and won't have anything to do with any more of the things. Too much temptation, you know, having that card right in your pocket." The woman laughed.

"No. I really need to talk to her."

"May I ask about what?"

"It has to do with a patient of hers at the state hospital in Traverse City."

"Oh." The voice cooled. "That was a long time ago. Connie doesn't like to be reminded. Very hard work. A lot of tragedy up there in that place."

"If I leave my number, do you think she would call me back?"

"Of course she will. Connie's a good person. Least of all, she'll see what you want from her."

Number given, Jenny hung up as Zoe came in the back door.

"You get ahold of the nurse?" Zoe asked.

"Out of town. I left my number."

Zoe looked around the kitchen. "Where's Dora?"

"She's shopping and then going over to Abigail's house. Abigail's all worked up and worried about the event. Two weeks to go and Emily won't answer the phone nor come to the door. Abigail's afraid the whole thing's about to blow up in her face."

Zoe, barely listening, pulled herself up on a chair and made a face at Jenny. "I may be nuts."

Jenny shrugged. "Okay."

"Remember, that neighbor said it was a red car parked in Althea's drive?"

"Yes."

"A red car, Jenny. You know what that means."

"I've been thinking about that. If you're thinking ask yourself 'why?'"

"Maybe it's Lorna. Don't forget, she killed her mother."

Jenny thought a while. "You think Lorna's still around?"

"I don't know what to think any more. The whole thing's like trying to see through a dirty window. Be great if we had a magic mirror. 'Magic mirror on the wall, what the heck is going on . . .'"

"Doesn't rhyme."

"Who cares?"

"Let's wait and see what the nurse says. She should know the name of her patient. Then we'll go have a talk with Detective Minty. Maybe he's got more clout with the court and will be able to get in that garage."

Chapter 23

The weatherman on Channel 9&10 was talking about the possibility of thunderstorms and strong winds overnight. Power outages, he predicted. Trees down.

That could have been Walter Shipley at Althea's house,

Zoe opened the kitchen curtains and looked out at her yard. Everything had been so upside down that Zoe hadn't been paying attention to her garden, and now the fairies would be jostled and thrown about, their houses blown away. A much bigger calamity for them than for her. There was an hour of daylight left, enough time to get the last of the fairies tucked into the shed and wipe her hands of them until spring. For the first time, the idea of being free of work made her smile.

She wrapped her grandmother's moth-eaten green sweater around her body and went outside.

When her red wagon was loaded with fairies and houses, she hauled it over the brick path to the shed and set the houses carefully on the shelves, wrapping each of the fairies in brown paper and packing them away in boxes, wishing all of them a good sleep.

Lilliana was the last to get settled in because Zoe would miss her the most. Zoe would have considered taking Lilliana into the house with her but knew there would be jealousy if she did.

When she picked Lilliana up to kiss her gently on the top of her head and set her down in her own, very comfortable box, she was certain she heard the word again: *pride*. Or *proud*.

Or something else.

Proust.

Zoe was sure of it. Constance Proust. The nurse. That was the word scuttling around in her head. Some tiny part of her brain had been trying to get her attention.

Lilliana had helped. "Proust."

Lilliana had been trying to help out all along.

As she whispered the word to herself again and again, she heard someone call her name. Jenny was at the open back door of her house, yelling to Zoe to come on over.

"There's a storm coming," she called and waved. "Mom wants you and Fida to stay the night."

"Did you hear back from Myrtle's nurse?" She had to cup her hands around her mouth against the growing sound of the wind. Even then she had to repeat her question twice before Jenny shouted back, "No. Not yet. Come over when you can." Jenny pulled the door shut.

Wrapped in her dead grandmother's knitted arms, Zoe looked back at the house she'd never dreamed of owning. The wind pushed her hard, almost knocking her over. She saw the glass in the kitchen windows shake in the frames and prayed that her world would get through the night.

Inside, Zoe called Jenny.

"I'm going to stay home," she told her. "I'll be fine."

"Mom's worried about you," Jenny half-whispered. "She thinks all this Emily Sutton business is getting between you and your writing."

"Tell her that's why I'm staying home. I can work today."

"Okay. But if you hear anything coming get down in your basement."

"I don't have a basement. I'll sit in the bathtub."

"Don't play games, Zoe. We're worried about you."

"And I'll be worried about you, too. But we'll be fine."

"Did you just see that?" Jenny interrupted. "The lights flickered."

"I better get my candles and matches together. I'll make a fire in the fireplace," Zoe said and hung up.

It wasn't that she didn't want to go to Dora's; it was the thought of leaving her house alone. Not possible. The grandmother she never knew left it to her. Her grandmother had cut out all her other grandchildren, who then started legal battles to get the house away from Zoe. Zoe stood up to the unknown cousins as they battled her in court and yelled at her in the halls of the courthouse. The judge took one look at the group allied against Zoe and gave Zoe the house and all its "appurtenances," which left Zoe wondering which "appurtenances" he meant, and where she'd find them.

The walls moaned and shuddered in the wind. That didn't frighten her as much as when the wind stopped. Silence was worse, as if the wind had pulled away to gather strength and would soon roar back and blow her and her house and her friends and all her neighbors off to Oz.

Zoe curled up in a chair under a blanket, with her grandmother's arms pulled around her body. Fida burrowed under the blanket, her wet nose against Zoe's arm. The fire was lighted and soon glowing. Falling sticks crackled and fell as bright red-and-orange flames leaped.

She thought she heard her cell phone ringing again and again out in the kitchen, but she ignored it. The house was getting cold. She and Fida were safe where they were. She had no intention of getting up to answer a ringing phone and break the spell she'd wound round herself: safe in her grandmother's arms, safe with her dog, with her own fire, in her own house.

When she finally slept, it was only for an hour or two at a time. All night, she woke up hearing voices in the storm, and then the crash of falling trees. She thought of her fairies and was relieved that they were safe.

Chapter 24

Emily Sutton wasn't afraid of thunderstorms. She didn't mind the wild rain lashing at her walls. She welcomed it. With her hands in the air, she danced back and forth across the kitchen to static-filled music from the radio. The music was loud. It filled every corner of the kitchen and every room in the house. The house was alive again, the way she was alive again.

From time to time, she turned the radio down and called Zoe Zola, leaving a message when her voicemail picked up. She chided her that the delivery she'd been expecting hadn't arrived, telling Zoe that she hoped a little rain didn't bother her. Feeling expansive, and liking the sense of having someone to call, she left a lilting thank you to let her know there were no hard feelings.

She needed her delivery, of course. Makeup and hair dye. A brilliant red this time. A red that would keep her fans transfixed as she sat on that stage and read from her new work. Work like no other. Her own. Her very own. Poetry for the ages.

She danced and pumped her fists in the air, feeling joy down to her fingertips and toes. This had to be freedom, a loosening of life's constraints like nothing she could remember. Soon she would be traveling the world. She would be known. She would be applauded everywhere she went.

She stopped still when the naked light bulb above her head began swinging back and forth, flickering. Ah, soon there would be brighter lights around her. Soon she would walk out on to a stage dressed even more wondrously than she'd dressed for Abigail's tea. People would stand. They would applaud and applaud until the curtain was brought down to stop them.

She closed her eyes and pictured the outfit she planned: a sweeping skirt of sea-blue scarves. A bodice of sea blue wound over her bosom. A magenta scarf around her head. She'd found the perfect thing in the attic. Pure poetry as poetry should be—a frame for a true poet.

No interview on stage as Abigail Cane wanted. No one stealing her limelight.

If the audience had questions, she would answer them later, after she'd read her new work. Her own work. The best of her poetry. All wild and beautiful and deep. Like nothing Emily Sutton had ever written before.

She danced again, then fell into a chair to draw her notebook to her. Poems bubbled and lined up inside her brain. So many to write. Not two weeks left before the grand event.

She wrote:

I couldn't see him in the dark.
He wouldn't look at me.

I know that water closed his eyes
And drowning set him free.

Knocking came from upstairs and then a terrible clamor—hail beating against the house.

Nothing disturbed her. Not while she was caught in creation. Not when she had found the words that would finally release her from this place.

She curved her arm around the notebook, bending over it to write:

And then a bone, a skeleton, an eternal love—all mine.

The overhead light flickered. She sighed and got up to hunt for a candle in the pantry, in among the dusty cans and boxes. She chose a thick red candle for the table.

A candle to create wondrous poems by.

The wind blew hard enough to blow the house down. The lights went out. Nothing could stop her. She lit the candle. She stared into the flame for a long time before picking up her pen again. She was the candle, she told herself. She was the flame. She was the light. Soon everyone would follow.

Chapter 25

The next morning, chainsaws roared up and down Elderberry. When Jenny looked out her window, it was to a mess of branches and leaves everywhere. The old walnut tree leaned so close to the house, she could reach out and touch it. Tony, already working in the yard, was bent over a large limb he was cutting.

She heard Dora say something and Zoe answer. They were out there with him while she'd slept in, having spent a worrying and sleepless night, troubled by things Dora'd said in the dark. "Getting things off her chest," she called it. But painful for Jenny to hear.

She dressed in her oldest outfit and headed out to help. She was welcomed, when she pushed the back door open, by light that had never gotten through before, and masses of sticks and downed branches.

In the yard, Jenny tapped Tony on the back and mouthed "Thank you" when he looked up, dark eyes magnified by his safety glasses. He stopped long enough to put one gloved hand to his lips and blow her a kiss.

For most of the morning, Jenny helped Dora and Zoe drag broken limbs to the fire pit at the back of the yard. The three of them raked leaves into piles that would be used for mulch after the winter snows flattened them. With the work mostly done, she made lunch for everyone. She kissed each of them on the cheek, though Tony put an arm around her and pulled her close.

Because Zoe asked anxiously again and again about calling Myrtle's nurse, she assured her she would call that morning. And she did, after the electricity came back on. No answer. She left a message.

In the afternoon, Jenny was off to Trixie's House of Beauty. The shop was full.

This was her twice-yearly trim. Perfect time for it, with the opera house event coming up fast. She didn't mind the shop, always filled with town ladies, always with different things to talk about, though today she imagined it would be nothing but the storm and she welcomed it. What she didn't feel like hearing was anything about the Sutton event.

Dryers blew. Women laughed. Women said "Hi" and "Well, what do you know? If it isn't, Jenny Weston!" when she walked in. It was fun to sit down at Trixie's station, lean back to have her hair washed, and have women stop to make comments on the cut, offer suggestions, and share their own experiences: bad haircuts, bad color jobs, bad moods.

When someone did ask about the opera house and how Emily Sutton was doing, she walked around the question with a smile, a nod, and a single, "Fine. Just fine."

Cassandra Hatch wanted to know how Lisa was doing out in Montana and when she was coming home for a visit.

Louise Dyer smiled as she strolled past just as Trixie sat Jenny up straight in the chair. "And how's your carpenter boyfriend doing?" she asked.

There were hoots from the other stations.

"He's doing fine, Louise." Jenny looked out through the wet hair hanging down her forehead. "He was over all morning cutting the trees for Mom."

"Good thing." Louise grinned around at the women looking their way. "He'll have all the wood you can ask for, huh, Jenny?"

Laughter spread as Trixie turned Jenny to the mirror to face her own burning cheeks.

She should have been in a better mood when she got home with her hair so neat and curved around her face, black bangs straight across her forehead. The beauty shop women had been pleased, agreeing that she looked like Lady Mary from the TV show *Downton Abbey*.

She set her bag of shampoo, conditioner, and nail polish on the kitchen counter. She'd bought things she didn't need because everybody knew Trixie had a sick kid and could use the extra money.

Tony was gone. Dora wasn't home. A note on the table said she went shopping. At the bottom of the note were three *x*'s and the words "I won't be long. I have a surprise for you. And I'm sorry." Jenny smiled as she tucked the note into her pocket, wondering what the surprise would be. Maybe more chocolate chip cookies. Mom's surprises were beginning to make Jenny's jeans tight.

Zoe didn't seem to be around—her car wasn't in front of her house. Jenny checked her haircut in a small mirror over the sink and wished she felt better about everything. She was still disturbed by the night before and what Dora'd said to her, despite the "I'm sorry."

She didn't like to think that her mom had used the storm and the dark to get some things off her chest.

They'd stayed up a long time in the dark, talking by candlelight. Lightning flashed, the house shook, then Dora would say again how sorry she was to bring it all up.

"But I just don't want you hurt." She'd taken a deep breath.

Again and again she apologized, but went on anyway, saying things she must have had bottled inside for weeks.

"I didn't say a word when you got so serious about Johnny Arlen, Jenny. I didn't say a word and look what happened. Look what he did to you. All of it—none of it your fault. Then Ronald. I can't tell you how my heart hurt to see the way he treated you. I'm still sorry I never had the courage to open my mouth."

"You're talking about Tony now, aren't you?"

"Is he still married?"

"Oh, Mom. I didn't think you knew."

"I heard."

"He filed for a divorce."

"But he lied to you."

"I know, Mom. We've talked it out. Maybe it was a good thing. Now he knows what I won't tolerate."

"Oh, Jenny, the man you choose to marry has to be the right one for you. Women think love takes care of everything. It doesn't. Not after the kids come and the man's afraid he's getting old, or the woman decides she hasn't lived enough and takes off to find herself."

"Tony's a good man, Mom."

"It's not about good or bad."

Dora would stop talking when the whole house shook and they sat still, waiting for what came next. Then she'd go on. "He's already chosen one wrong woman. Maybe he needs to take time to be sure next time."

"I thought you liked him." Jenny heard a sad little girl's voice come out of her.

"I do. This isn't about liking him or not liking him. It's about you. I don't want you hurt again. Not in my lifetime. If I have to speak up to stop that from happening, then I will."

When neither one of them could find anything more to say, they went to bed, finding their way by candlelight, making the evening even stranger than it had been.

All night Jenny dealt with the emotions Dora had stirred. Maybe she should go back to Chicago after all. Get out of her mother's life. She'd made her worry plenty. Maybe when you're a thirty-six-year-old woman, you shouldn't make your mother as miserable as Jenny was making Dora. Next, Jenny would get angry. Then she'd question Dora's right to come down on her like that. Jenny was a grown woman. She would love whomever she wanted to love. And she wouldn't be told to watch what she was doing, to learn from her mistakes, to not jump into anything too fast.

Maybe that was part of what she felt was wrong here— her mother still thought of her as a child. Maybe the whole thing with Mom was her problem and not about Jenny at all.

Maybe Mom didn't want her marrying anybody. Maybe she didn't want her to leave Bear Falls. The thought hurt Jenny more than their late-night talk.

When she opened the door to her room, where she'd pulled the curtains across the windows to block out all that new light, the room was dark. She reached down for the chain to her old bedside lamp. It wasn't there, where she was used to grabbing it and pulling on the light before going into the room.

She pushed the door wider and saw a bouquet of asters on her dressing table. They were new colors: greens and yellows and bright magentas. Everything was new. She turned slowly to take in her quarters. Bright and grown-up.

The bear sheets and comforter were gone, replaced by very adult striped cream sheets and a thick flowered quilt. Bon Jovi was nowhere to be seen. Instead a framed photograph hung above the bed—a photograph of all of them: Mom, Dad, Lisa, and her. It was a photo taken on that last anniversary, the day Dad made the Little Library for Mom. They stood around the box grinning for the camera, Lisa hamming it up, pretending to stick her head in the box. Other photos hung on the other walls—all of them together as a family, and then of Jenny's graduation from high school, then from the University of Michigan. She'd just caught her cap after throwing it into the air. Her mouth was open. She was laughing. Her eyes were bright. She looked like a young woman ready to take on the world.

She heard Dora close the back door and, muttering to herself, walk across the kitchen floor. Jenny hesitated a minute, trying to come up with the right words to tell her mother how much she loved her.

Jenny didn't have to say a word when she went into the kitchen; Dora opened her arms and Jenny walked into them.

"I didn't say those things to trap you here, Jenny," Dora whispered to her daughter, holding her close. "I said them to set you free. You're a grown woman, not my child."

"I'll always be your child, Mom. And thank you so much for my big girl room."

"I wanted to give you something that would tell you—in my clumsy way—how proud I am of the woman you've become."

"I get it, Mom." Jenny looked into her mother's aging face. "You're teaching me what love is. You don't have to. I know. I think I really know this time."

"It isn't sex," Dora warned.

"Come on, Mom. That's a part of it, or men and women would never get together."

Dora blushed and thought before she nodded. "Well. I guess so." She thought a while longer, then broke into a smile. "Maybe the most fun part," she added, looking up merrily from the corner of her eyes. "But not the all of it, you know. No ma'am, not the all of it."

Chapter 26

When the knocking on her front door began, Emily waited before answering. That couldn't be Zoe Zola. She'd called to say she'd be by in an hour with the shopping. She always took Zoe's calls and found the little woman amusing: her rough voice, her frowns, then smiles. Really, a gentle creature, and one who served the purpose Emily had set for her.

The knocking came again. Louder. She looked down the hall from where she stood. It was that odious man. That detective who kept leaving his card stuck in her door. She'd outlasted him before and would again.

He knocked on one of the front windows and then was back to the front door.

This time he yelled something she couldn't hear but was certainly an order of some sort. As if the bothersome man could presume to tell her what to do in her own house.

He'd go away. They always did—eventually.

She tipped her head to listen to a sound coming from upstairs. Emily froze. Of all times to start things that shouldn't be set free. If she made her way back into the living room and across to the stairs to stop the noise, she took the chance that the man might be looking in and see her.

What might he do then? Break the glass and enter her home?

She had no idea if he could do that.

But if he heard a noise, or caught a glimpse of her, he would never leave.

She stuck her head out only far enough to see. There was a shadow on the porch but it looked as though his back was to her.

This was her chance. She hugged the wall and scurried toward the living room. As fast as the wind, she tiptoed around the chairs to the far wall, where she held still again. He didn't knock. She thought she heard his footsteps going down the front steps. Next she heard the motor of a car.

The noise from upstairs stopped.

For the next hour, Emily sat as straight and still as a human being could sit. She considered the implications of that policeman coming back again later. But it wouldn't be tonight. That wasn't his pattern. In a day or so, he would come back and knock at her door again.

She had to think. With her chest heaving, thinking wasn't easy. Maybe if she called and complained to Abigail Cane, she could stop the man from coming to her door. Certainly the woman was the most influential in town— Emily had seen it that day at the mansion. Women did her bidding. Followed her lead.

Emily felt her breathing slow. It seemed she had power, too, now. She could call Chief Warner, the policeman in town. Yes, she would call him and insist that her stalker be called off.

She had to be left in peace, at least until after her return to the world of literature. Then she would leave this place. She would go far away and begin a life filled with accolades and cheers. Filled with many swains, who would adore her and pledge to protect her from policemen like this Detective Minty.

Let the house fall into ruin. The thought made her laugh. Let the swamp take it, for all she cared. Maybe one day—a long time from now—she would return to see trees growing through the roof and branches hanging from the windows. Slime would crawl up the walls and snakes would slither across the water-covered floors.

The pictures in her head brought her peace.

When she went to the kitchen to make her lunch, she turned on the radio: Chopin. He matched her mood. Her heart beat normally again. She was in control. There was Zoe Zola's return to look forward to, with the makeup she'd put on her list, and the hair dye: the brightest Zoe could find. There was her red scarf to wind around her throat and hang among the many sea-blue scarves of the dress she would prepare. Scarves connecting her to her past and to her future. Something old and something new.

She was waiting behind a curtain when Zoe Zola's car pulled in to the curb. Emily pulled back a little to watch.

* * *

C o n s t a n c e   P r o u s t.

As Zoe parked in front of Emily's house, letters bounced in her head, forming nothing but a huge, empty circle.

What she wished for, as she went around to the back of her car, was a brain that snapped things together and held on to them. A Dickinson brain that worked everything into a pattern much faster than hers did. If she understood the pattern of what was happening, she could go to everyone involved and say, "See, this is why a woman's dead, why another woman's disappeared, why an uncle doesn't call his niece . . ." and on and on.

A puzzle such as Emily Dickinson would take and shake and solve in one cryptic poem.

Four bags to carry. All with handles, since Zoe had purchased eco-friendly shopping bags at Drapers. But still— too much for one trip. She started toward the house with two bags, opening the gate with difficulty and having it bounce into her rear end when she went through.

A curtain in the living room twitched. Emily was in there or a mouse was trying to escape. Zoe didn't know which possibility she preferred. She bristled at the idea of that able-bodied woman watching her lug groceries to the porch and not coming out to help.

At least she knew Emily wasn't in the swamp. She hoped Emily would get busy trying out the makeup she'd ordered: foundation, lipstick, powder, blush, eyeliner, mascara. Hair dye—the hottest Zoe could find. She wondered what might be the real color of that head of wild hair.

Zoe thought of her plan. Everything depended on Emily keeping busy with the groceries and then the makeup. There was the hair dye, but maybe not right now. Emily might wait until the day of the event, to get the full effect of the red dye.

Zoe figured she had at least a half hour to take care of what she had to take care of—to sneak around the back to the garage and settle the question once and for all: Red car, or no red car? If the car wasn't red, she would call Alex in Ann Arbor and confirm for her that the shed was another dead end.

The idea of what she was about to do made her queasy. She would leave and drive over from the other direction, leaving her car as far from the house as she could without wasting time. Then she would have to slip behind the rotting sheds, slide her flattened body over to the garage window, find something to stand on, reach the windowsill, and look inside.

She set the first two bags on the porch and went back for the last two.

Faint music came from inside the house. Zoe knew that Emily lurked on the other side of the door, laughing, waiting for Zoe to go so she could dive into the makeup.

Zoe looked toward the swamp not ten yards away. She leaned against a shaky railing to watch a single leaf shiver, though there was no wind to move it. She watched light and dark and tiny shafts of broken sunlight. She felt a chill pass through her but chased it away.

* * *

Inside the house, Emily saw the little person get out and go around to the back of her car. She pulled four bags, one at a time, from the trunk. She set the bags on the ground behind the car and picked up two. Emily watched as Zoe came through the gate, then snickered behind her hand when the gate hit Zoe and she turned to glare at it before continuing up the walk. On the porch, she dropped the two bags and went back to the car for the others.

When the small woman made her way a second time down the steps, hanging on tightly to the sagging railing, Emily waited.

She'd come to look forward to these days, when she got exactly the things she ordered, and had the fun of putting all of it away. Even the yogurt, which she never ate. And the cheddar cheese, which she couldn't tolerate. There was milk and a new type of cereal with chocolate in it. There were oranges and lettuce and tomatoes big enough to dwarf her hand when she held one up to examine it from all sides. The bounty of it made her mouth water. More than she could ever eat. Pure luxury, to throw food away. Wouldn't her mother be annoyed!

* * *

Zoe thought of the woman inside the house and hoped she was doing the right thing, betraying another writer, a poet who was not completely human, not completely animal, not completely sane, but born to create poetry, write poems no one else could write—lines of words with different shapes and meanings, put together as no one else could.

Zoe felt a twinge of jealousy, then shame, that maybe she had let her fear of the "other" turn into little angers and little disgusts, acting the way some people did toward her.

Zoe moved back carefully. She looked over the banister. She went down the steps to her car a last time.

In a way, Emily had made the choice for her. They were on opposite sides of whatever was happening. Zoe put her pity for the woman aside.

Proust. They had to find that nurse. Her head was filled with what the woman might know. She got in her car, pulled away, and turned in the direction of home.

* * *

Emily watched as the little woman climbed into her car and drove away without looking back. Emily rejoiced that she was gone and opened the door and pulled in her loot, her mind swimming in light. There was only joy inside her, the excitement of the new. She did a pirouette as, bag by bag, she carried her day's bounty to the kitchen.

It was best, she decided as she examined the four bags on the table, to delay delight by first putting away the butter, milk, yogurt, and meat.

Butter to the butter holder. Milk on the top shelf. Meat into a crisper, where her mother had always kept the meat—though there'd been little of it when that old woman was alive.

Then mixed greens and the tomatoes—how banal the world could get.

Cans of soup. A box of noodles.

Cheeses. Many cheeses because she loved to melt it, pour it over potatoes and noodles and vegetables and cereal because her mother had never allowed cheese in the house. Something against cheese, in the old woman's head. Not pure enough. They were to drink milk alone for dairy. And that only one time a day.

A box of crackers.

A magic life drawn in ordinary images like crackers. A cosmic joke—that her body had to be fed as ordinary bodies were fed.

And then, at last, the makeup. She pulled out each small box, taking time to enjoy the moment. To feel the heft of every one, the joy of pretty colors. There was something called "blush." She opened it and removed the small brush. She ran the soft bristles across her inner wrist, then ran the brush across the soft pink of the "blush," running it across the back of her hand until her skin bloomed.

There was mascara for her eyelashes. She saw the eyelashes on the package and imagined hers as long and lush. There was a bright-red lipstick and a dainty case of something gray and luminous. And needles and pins and thread.

She closed her eyes, picked up her treasures, and held them to her breast. She saw Emily Sutton on stage in the perfect outfit she'd created. Saw her painted the way an artist would paint her, so that when she turned one way in the light, she looked very young. But when she turned another way, she looked ancient. *Enigma*, came to mind. *Ineffable*. *Sacred*. Her name lost among the most powerful words of the ages.

She danced in circles, singing the words of a hymn she remembered. She dragged the words behind her like a silken train to the bathroom, where new words formed. She set her makeup on the vanity and ran back to the kitchen to find a pad of paper, then wrote as fast as her hand could go: "No pensive soul requires adornment / Or color past a perfect white / No poet needs to wear a mask / That doesn't suit her right."

Emily tore off the poem and held the sheet of paper up above her head as if to offer it to her gods. She was pleased at the monumental work she was turning out. Only a week before the huge event. The thought amazed her.

* * *

After she drove down the street toward her house for a ways, Zoe turned up a side street and headed back to Thimbleberry using the other route to get to Emily's house, by going through town.

She parked a block away, got out, and followed the road, where bushes grew to the edge of the swamp. She was half hidden where she finally stood, taking in the backs of the sheds and old garage. She couldn't see the house—the sheds stood between her and it. She stayed among the bushes, close to the edge of the swamp, until she made a dash to the sheds, then, crouching, she scuttled as best she could until her hands leaned on the back wall of one. There were three sheds—or maybe one was a chicken coop—between her and the garage.

She pushed flat against the wall behind her, then stuck her head out, looking up at the back of the house, waiting for a voice to scream at her and for Emily to come running.

Sunlight came from behind thick clouds and moved across the blackened back wall of the still house. On the wall, as if leading to nothing, there was a door with an *X* of wood nailed across it. No steps led up to the door. Across the back of the house, blackened timbers leaned where they had fallen. An old ladder stood among the timbers, as if someone had attempted to get their mother out.

That was where their mother died, in a fire started by one of her daughters. Zoe didn't know what to feel. As she stared at the wall, a curtain in an upstairs window moved to one side. A face looked out at Zoe, who scurried to hide behind the next shed, then held very still, breathing hard. She listened for Emily's voice, and when it didn't come, Zoe imagined she was on the phone with the police chief right then.

She had to be fast. There was no leaving without knowing.

She moved behind the next shed and then over to the old garage. The unpainted doors of the building hung crookedly, held closed by a large padlock. Zoe shook the lock. She shook the doors but they held fast. The small windows across the front were covered with cardboard.

Looking down, avoiding a mud puddle, Zoe noticed that the weeds here were beaten into two rows. Tire tracks. The beaten weeds were green, as if tires had passed over them not long ago.

Still keeping her eyes on the house, Zoe scurried around to the hidden side of the garage where there was another window. This one was cracked, but not covered. She wasn't tall enough to see in. She searched around her for a box, a crate, a log—anything she could stand on—and found a metal bucket, rusted and without a handle, but still sound.

She rolled the bucket over to the window and climbed on it, holding on as hard as she could to the side of the building.

* * *

From the corner of her eye Emily saw a shadow move across the back of the yard. She ran to see what was out there now, remembering that nosy girl she'd caught before. It could be a deer. Once a bear had come out of the swamp and got in their garbage can.

The figure moved into sunshine for a minute, then was lost, hidden behind a shed.

The figure had been small. It ran awkwardly. There was no question who was back there.

Zoe Zola hadn't left at all. She was snooping. Heading toward the garage, where that other awful girl had snooped.

It was time, Emily told herself, and pulled back from the window to think. It had to stop, once and for all. There was a new world ahead of her. Nothing else mattered. She put two fingers to her forehead and let her thoughts go deeper than she usually let them go.

A sound, a knocking, came from upstairs, disturbing her intense train of thought.

"*Not now,*" she shouted, hands covering her eyes. "*Not now. For Christ's sakes, can't you see I'm busy?*"

* * *

Looking in the window, Zoe had to wait for her eyes to adjust to the gloom before she could make out a large gray shape. Certainly a car, just as Alex said, with a tarp spread over it.

She pressed her hands to the broken glass, cupping her fingers around her eyes to keep out all competing light. Alex thought she saw a red edge—maybe part of a car door—at the bottom of the tarp.

She couldn't tell for sure. Couldn't see well enough. It might be her imagination. She blinked a few times then cupped her hands at the window and looked again.

Red. Only an inch or so showing under the tarp. But certainly red.

"Get away from there!"

Zoe fell off her stool, stumbling backward until she grabbed onto a small tree and pulled herself upright.

Emily stood at the corner of the garage, her body stiff, arms down at her sides, one hand holding onto a small board. Her face, eyes bulging, looked like something straight out of hell.

She took a step toward Zoe, raising the board ever so slightly.

Zoe stepped back. She looked quickly around, turned, and started to run. First she needed to get around to the other side of the garage. Maybe then she could slip back around the sheds and get to her car.

When she tried to double back, Emily stood there, between Zoe and what seemed to be the only way out. This time the piece of board was in both of her hands. She looked at Zoe, tipped her head, and smiled.

There was no way Zoe could run out toward the house or even to the street. Emily stood in her way. Zoe looked over her shoulder. There was a path behind her. At least it was an opening. It might lead to something. She took a few steps backward, then turned and ran up the path leading directly into the swamp.

The ground was slick, a little damp under foot at first. At least she could run, arms pumping, and feel she was headed somewhere where she could hide, even if it was deeper into the swamp. She could hide down between roots, or climb a tree. She was ahead of Emily Sutton. And she was smarter. She'd find a place. She looked over her shoulder and slowed to listen but heard nothing but her own breathing. The path underfoot got mushier, but continued straight ahead. She stopped to listen again, breathing harder. She heard nothing behind her.

She edged farther along the path, careful not to slip into the water on either edge as the path narrowed. With every step, a frog or lizard leaped or scurried ahead of her. Bulbous eyes stared up from the water through a scrim of pollen and floating algae.

She moved on, testing the ground at every step.

The air tasted green, almost furry, in her mouth. The sounds around her were unseen skitterings, then a splash. Bird calls. Nothing else. She was protected along this stretch of the path by thick cedar branches and dipping hemlock trees.

Another step.

Another.

The path curved, got mushier, water seeped into her footprints behind her. She walked carefully, in the very center of the path.

Gnats swarmed her face and head. They got in her open mouth so she had to stop to bend and spit. Like a miracle, the path got firm again and then opened into a wide plateau where Zoe stopped and bent, hands on her knees, to catch her breath.

She fell down to sit on a fallen log, then sat up to watch and listen, adjusting her bottom to the chinks and knobs of the dead tree.

She was alive. She'd stay here until it was safe. Until it was night. Until somebody came to get her.

Everything around her went quiet again. She wondered if she shouldn't go back. Emily must have given up the chase by now.

She could walk slowly, stopping to listen at every step.

Zoe gulped air and closed her eyes. When she opened them, she noticed that the grasses here, on this small island of land set above snaking black water, were bent as if pounded to the ground. Across from where she sat, she saw a ring of what looked like dead flowers. She got up to look closer. Dead roses. An entwined ring—brown and brittle. The dead flowers formed a wreath. At the center of the dead wreath, two long sticks formed a cross. She got down to crawl on her hands and knees to where the dead flowers lay. A grave came to mind. Maybe a beloved pet was buried here. Or maybe the animal had been lowered into the water and the wreath marked the spot. She moved, still on all fours, to the water's edge and looked over, at floating scum moving in waves. Something white beneath the scum swayed.

She stuck her hand down into the water and stirred the scum in circles until it pulled apart. Through the now-opened circle, she saw the white limbs of a tree, maybe petrified, not far beneath the surface.

She reached into the water and grabbed ahold of one of the white limbs to pull it up. If nothing else, it could be used as a weapon in case Emily waited back along the path. At least with a weapon, they would be equals.

The white limb broke the surface, tipping Zoe backward, so she lay at the center of the dead wreath. She looked up at what she held. A long white bone. At the end of the bone, a skeletal human hand hung above her head.

When she heard the scream behind her, she rolled away from the terrible noise, only to hang there, grabbing at nothing, before falling down, first through scum that choked her, then into dark, cool water. She stopped thrashing as she fell deeper, beyond where she could help herself.

Chapter 27

Inside her house, Dora peeked through the curtains and put a smile on her face when she saw Abigail Cane at her door in all her finery—and so early.

Abigail was dressed for fall in a brown pantsuit with gold chains over the jacket and a brown, green, and rust shawl draped across one shoulder. A leather bag hung from the other shoulder and, in the crook of one arm, she held a manila folder.

Dora knew what manila folders meant in the arms of a woman like Abigail. She was either taking names for contributions to one of her pet charities or she needed more help with the Emily Sutton event. Dora would have taken bets as to which it was.

Dora opened the door. She smiled and waved Abigail in. They kissed cheeks. Dora offered her a chair, then a cup of coffee.

"I have a twofold reason for coming this evening, Dora. And without calling first—I do abjectly apologize for that."

They sat across from each other in the living room, in the Queen Anne chairs. Abigail sat at the edge of her chair, as a proper lady would sit. Dora relaxed back and prepared to defend herself against whatever Abigail wanted this time.

"Are you here about Emily Sutton?" Dora broke through a stream of opening comments, cutting to the chase because she was weary of problems.

"Yes. For the most part. But also to bring good news."

Dora smiled a tired smile. "Good news first, please."

"The town council is in agreement with me. My father's statue will come down. To be replaced with something of my choosing. It won't be for a few weeks yet, and I want to plan a party for all of Bear Falls. I wish it could be closer to Emily's event. Two birds with one stone, you understand. But it can't be."

"I'm happy for you," Dora said and meant it, knowing the full story of what Joshua Cane did to Abigail's siblings, two of them dead now because of the terrible man.

"I've found as many of his other children as I can find. And talked to each of the women who mothered a child of his. The mothers of children he refused to claim. Women he lied to, cheated, and left bereft. They want to come to our little ceremony in the park. I hope the cheers raised fly to the heavens. Or in the other direction, if that's where Joshua Cane was rightly sent."

"So now. What else brings you here?"

For the first time since Dora had known Abigail, she looked flummoxed.

"It's Emily Sutton." Abigail took a deep breath. "I spoke to her this morning. I refused to leave her porch and knocked steadily until she opened the door. I've tried being patient but Emily Sutton would try the patience of Job. She's come out of her shell with a vengeance. You should have seen her this morning. Hair as wild as a savage. Face livid. I told her I've been trying for days to get a hold of her. There are so many details to work out." Abigail half-rolled her eyes. "Between us, Dora, the greatest detail is what the woman chooses to wear."

Dora smiled and relaxed. Zoe and Jenny already agreed to see to her wardrobe and go over her poetry. She assured Abigail that her girls would take care of everything.

"But that's not all. I had everything planned. I would interview her and then she would read her work. She went so far as to stomp her foot at me. No interview, she demanded. Nobody on stage but her. No podium. She wants a high-backed chair where she can sit and read. The chair is to be covered with red velvet. There is to be a table beside her—with a huge bowl of white and pink water lilies. Now, where do you imagine I'm to get water lilies at this time of the year?"

Dora thought. "That's a tough one. You'd better negotiate with her. Maybe urns with fall leaves would be more practical."

"Negotiate? Emily Sutton doesn't negotiate. She gives orders." Abigail closed her eyes a minute, either resting or too aggravated to talk. "I know Jenny and Zola plan to see to her clothes, but I went ahead and purchased a lovely dress for her."

Dora felt trouble coming.

"I left it on her porch yesterday afternoon. Of course she hates it. She said she simply wouldn't appear dressed as a drab old lady."

"Goodness! What now?"

"She's making her own dress—heaven help us! I've done everything I can humanly do to tame that woman." Abigail looked around. "Is Jenny home by any chance? I called Zoe Zola but she didn't answer."

"Jenny's not home." Her face flushed as she tried to come up with a good reason Jenny hadn't been home all night, that she'd called from Tony's house to say she'd be home in the morning.

Abigail didn't press the matter; she was too distracted for ordinary curiosity.

"I need your help in the morning, Dora. I hope you're free. We're having a run-through at the opera house. I have to find that chair she wants. The table. The flowers. If you will help, I will be deeply grateful. We'll check on tickets and the seating chart. So many details. Minnie's been a tremendous help but she doesn't seem to be a detail person. Once I'd thought I would be doing these things with Emily. Obviously we will be lucky if she shows up and reads her damned poetry."

"I wouldn't worry. From what I've seen of Emily, she's really excited."

"Oh? Really? Anyway, would you ask Jenny and Zoe to call? We need to talk."

* * *

The next morning Dora didn't ask Jenny a thing when she walked in the house, only if she'd had breakfast. Remembering Tony's pancakes with Northwoods maple syrup made Jenny smile as she assured Dora that she'd eaten.

The first thing Jenny wanted to do was call that nurse again. She and Tony had talked about Myrtle and how she thought it was Emily who'd been in the hospital with her. They agreed that the nurse was crucial. If for nothing else, then to rule out the wild idea that Emily had killed her mother.

She called Zoe first but got no answer. Zoe had her hands full already with a deadline and her upcoming trip to New York. She was nervous about it. Nervous about meeting with people from PBS, and nervous about something else she'd been worrying about.

"What if Christopher proposes?" Zoe had asked Jenny the night before last.

"Proposes what?"

"You know very well what I mean."

"You've never even been out with him."

"That's not always how things work, Jenny." Zoe pursed her lips.

"Did he say anything?"

"Lots of things. This could be very big for all of us."

"Say anything about proposing?"

"Don't be silly. Why would he?"

"Then why are you worried?"

Zoe had looked away and changed the subject.

Jenny called Zoe again just before noon and left another message. She called the number she had for Constance Proust, got the answering machine, and asked again that Constance call her as soon as possible.

Dora was dressed and hunting for her new fall shoes to wear to Traverse City. Jenny followed along behind her, feeling at loose ends and thinking maybe she would take a ride to Fife Lake and find Constance herself.

"Did you look in the front closet?" Jenny asked.

"You're probably right." Dora hurried back to the living room, glancing out the window to see Abigail's black Cadillac pulling up the drive.

"For goodness sakes. Here she is. Help me, Jenny. Look in the back of the closet, will you? I don't want to kneel down in these slacks."

Jenny pulled the shoebox from the closet just as Abigail came through the front door, huffing from climbing the steps.

She greeted Jenny but turned quickly to Dora. "I think I've forgotten my list of things to see to. All those orders from Emily. Who would have thought she'd get so high-handed? Now of all times for me to get absent-minded. Well, I'm glad to see at least you're ready."

Shoes on, Dora picked up her purse and stood smiling in the open doorway, waiting now for Abigail.

Abigail turned to Jenny. "I stopped at your neighbor's house this morning, then called and left a message for her to call me back. I haven't heard a word. Do you know where she is?"

Jenny looked at her mother, then shook her head. "I haven't seen her. But she's been busy."

"Isn't she supposed to go to New York soon?" Dora asked. "Something with PBS?"

"Not before our event, I hope." Abigail's face was alarmed.

"Oh, no. Of course not. Anyway, she would have asked us to watch Fida if she had to leave," Jenny assured her.

"Maybe she went for a drive." Dora hurried to calm Abigail.

"I certainly hope so." Abigail was through the door. "We know how flaky poets can be."

"Zoe's not a poet." Dora wasn't happy.

"Well, then writers. They're all cut from the same crazy quilt."

* * *

Jenny heard nothing from anyone all day. Toward evening, when Dora and Abigail weren't back and there were no lights in Zoe's windows, she wondered if she should be getting worried.

Dora came home after eight. "That woman could wear out an elephant," she said as she kicked off her shoes, dropped her purse to the floor, and made her way down the hall to her bedroom with no mention of dinner.

Jenny made a last call to the Proust home and left yet another message. She called Zoe's cell, expecting to hear her voice. It rang and rang.

Later, in her own room, Jenny heard a distant barking and got up to listen.

The barking stopped. It sounded as if it came from somewhere down the street.

She slept, but not peacefully. Odd things kept running through her head. The worst being Zoe's pretty face.

Chapter 28

There was no light and there was no dark. Wherever she was when she awoke, it wasn't her house. She was not in her bedroom—the way she expected to be when she opened her eyes. And she wasn't anywhere else she could think of.

Not New York. It wasn't time to go there yet. There'd been no call from Christopher Morley that she could remember. But that was one of her problems at the moment. She couldn't seem to remember much of anything.

And even if this was New York, she wouldn't be in this kind of place—wherever this place was.

She blinked hard to see if it was her eyes—strained from too much work. But no, nothing changed when she opened them.

Because I could not stop for death . . .

A line from Emily Dickinson was in her head. An omen. An explanation.

She wondered if this was what it was—death—then touched her own clammy, but still living, skin.

She moved from where she lay on a bare wood floor to sit up against a wall of nothing but studs. Everything hurt—her head especially. Her whole body. Her clothes were damp and clinging to her skin. She had no idea how she'd gotten here nor any idea where she'd been.

Light was almost nonexistent except for a very weak glow coming in from what seemed to be a vent, high on one of the walls. There was no window. She could make out the faint outline of a door.

What happened? She reached up to touch her face and hair. Her hair was damp, too. Her arms hurt, as if someone had been pulling them. She began to shiver uncontrollably. When she could, she patted her hands along the floor around her. She hoped for a blanket, some old clothes—anything to wrap herself in. There was nothing but the dust and grit she wiped from her fingers. It was a little hard to breathe; the air was thick and stale.

The boards under her felt like raw wood. She touched the studs behind her. An unfinished room.

She sat still to think, until she began to shiver and had to rub her arms with her hands. She'd gone to Emily's to drop off the groceries and other things she'd bought her. Oh! She sat straight up. She'd seen a car in that garage. That much she could remember. She rubbed at her forehead. And then being chased into Pewee Swamp.

All of it came back too fast. She felt her hands, one rubbing the other, and remembered what they'd pulled from the water.

She curled into a ball and hugged herself as tightly as she could. She remembered holding those bones above her head.

A few deep breaths helped to calm her. She remembered falling into the water, or being pushed. She put a hand to her head and felt a lump on the left side.

Emily had to have attacked her. She was the only one around, the only one who didn't want people looking in her garage. Now she had a fact to hold on to. Zoe pushed herself up to think of other rational things. She was probably somewhere in the Sutton house now. How Emily could have gotten her here, she couldn't imagine. There had been a wheelbarrow behind one of the sheds. And she was small. No wonder her arms hurt, she must have been pulled and pummeled.

She listened to the noises in the house. A faint hum coming from somewhere. It could be music. Or just a sound the house made.

She didn't think she was on the first floor—this space was more like an attic.

When she moved her hands over the bare boards under her, a sliver went into her finger, hurting. She pulled the splinter out with her teeth and spit it away. There seemed to be nothing there, at the end of the room where she sat. She crawled to the other end and came across a single wide-mouthed jar. A wide-mouthed, empty jar.

When she stood, her hair brushed the ceiling on one side where the ceiling sloped. The door at the end of the room was full height, and locked.

She knocked and waited. She knocked harder. She threw her body at the door. It didn't give and her shoulder hurt more than it had already.

She put her ear to the wood. There was no sound beyond the hum that came from everywhere. She listened harder. She listened with all her being and heard the faint-est sound, though not of a voice. It was music. What she heard was a sonata. Chopin.

She knocked louder, pounded, and then yelled until her lungs hurt and the yelling brought on pain, so she had to stop, swallow hard, and sit with her back to the door, tears finally rolling down her face as she remembered sinking into black water, remembered vines twining around her legs. And she remembered a snake, at least something long and undulating, brushing past her face.

Then a branch had poked at her. She remembered grab-bing on and seeming to fly out of the water to lie again in that circle of dead flowers, until something hit her hard on the back of her head.

* * *

"Have you tried calling Zoe?" Dora asked the next morn-ing. "Why won't she answer? She'd have her phone with her, no matter where she's gone."

"Maybe it's dead. She might have forgotten to charge it, that's what makes me think she's somewhere where she's too busy for phone calls. Probably New York, after all."

"And took Fida with her?"

"People do take dogs on trips with them."

"On an airplane?" Dora shook her head.

"Her car's gone, remember? She drove."

"I don't believe she'd go away without telling us," Dora said, yawning. "I'm going to lie down for a while. That woman pulled me everywhere yesterday—one place and then another. She's going to be the death of me yet. I wish Zoe were here."

"Emily's making her own dress. She ordered needles and pins and thread last time Zoe went shopping for her. Don't let Abigail talk you into anything."

Dora turned in the doorway. "But Lord save us from a repeat of her hoochie-coochie dress."

By afternoon, Jenny was on her way to the post office. The last alimony check was late, and she wanted to put a trace on it. If it happened one more time, she swore, she would get a hold of Ronald herself and demand he pay on time or she was going to petition the court to have her check sent to them and they would send it to her. That would do it. Ronald was afraid of anything with muscle behind it.

She had enough money in her account to go shopping. She wanted something new for Emily's reading.

It was at the bank that her phone rang, and she grabbed it out of her purse and hit the button.

"Where the heck have you been?" she demanded before checking caller ID.

* * *

Zoe stopped caring about time. She was hungry, and she was thirsty, and she couldn't tell which one was worse. She slept a lot. Like Fida, she told herself, who always slept if nothing exciting was going on.

Now Zoe was sleeping for the same reason.

The only thing of any use in the slope-ceilinged room was the wide-mouth jar. At least she wasn't peeing on the floor, but that probably wouldn't be a problem. With nothing going into her body, nothing was coming out. At least peeing gave her something to think about—how to squat properly. She smelled bad already. She could hardly stand her own stink.

When she was awake, she worked on the Emily Dickinson book in her head, editing and writing the ending, then committing it all to memory. And she hummed to herself. She sang every song she could remember: a lot of the Beatles. "Eleanor Rigby" got stuck up there for a couple of hours. Then she'd sing as many hymns as she could remember from childhood church on Sundays, then marched around her space, bent over, to "Onward, Christian Soldiers."

Once in a while, the sound of the radio came through the floorboards again. When the music went off later, she figured it must be night. When the music came back on it had to be morning. In that way, she figured out she'd been there two full days.

Her head wasn't hurting the way it had at first, but from time to time shooting pains went across her forehead. Her stomach had stopped rumbling. She thought about all the people across the world who were on cleanses and starvation diets. If they could make it, so could she.

Her main concern was: Make it for how long?

She ran her hands along the walls and thought maybe she was in a box room, where Victorians kept their trunks and suitcases for long ocean voyages. Or maybe—since this had been a farm family—just an unfinished space in the attic.

There wasn't the smell of mold around her. Dust— plenty of dust, which made her sneeze from time to time. But at least it wasn't a basement room, which Zoe shuddered to think about in this old house.

The worst thing about her situation was not knowing how long Emily would hold her. And why she had been put here to begin with. That was her biggest worry.

And the thirst. That was getting so bad she tried licking her arm to see if she had spit left.

She sank into the boredom of silence, tapping rhythmically with one finger: one and two and three . . .

Seconds ticked by. Then, after what she thought was an hour, she'd picture the number of the hour in her head and try to hold on to it. But after she fell asleep she had to start all over when she woke up—leading nowhere and to nothing.

When she thought of food now, the thought made her sick. The thought of water made her sad.

When she was awake, she tapped.

At one point she crawled back to the door. She was going to become a nuisance. Even if it cost her everything.

She tapped a simple *tap tap tap* then stopped to listen. Maybe Emily had forgotten she was up here. In all the scrambling toward her grand occasion, only a few days away if Zoe figured right, maybe it had slipped her mind that Zoe was in her attic.

The thought made Zoe happy. Only a slip of the mind. She liked the sound of the word—*slipped*. If she kept tapping, Emily would hear and come running to let her out.

She tapped and tapped until she made up a song to go with the taps. She tapped and sang until she fell back to sleep.

Later, when she wasn't certain if she was awake or asleep, the tapping still went on, though her own hands were buried beneath her head, where she lay on the floor.

It was in the room with her. Could be she was going crazy. There'd been nothing there before. No sound but hers.

She listened hard. She held her breath and went on listening.

"Are you there?" said a soft voice that came from everywhere.

"Yes," Zoe answered, then scurried around the walls, saying "yes" again and again.

"I'm at the inside wall. Not the wall under the sloped ceiling, but the long wall." The voice was a whisper.

Zoe laid both hands on the inner wall, trying to feel what could be beyond there. Not only "what," but "who."

"Feel down near the bottom. Run your hand along the base of the wall slowly. I have something for you."

Zoe did as she was told. Carefully, she ran her fingers along the floor, where it met the wall, until her fingers touched something that hadn't been there before. A cup. She stuck her finger in the cup. It came out wet.

Someone had pushed a cup of water through a hole in the wall.

"Emily?" Zoe said the name softly.

"Yes," the whisperer answered. "Yes, it's me."

Zoe drank and wondered if she really held a cup in her hands or if this was a grotesque dream. Maybe a dying dream. She finished drinking and wiped the cup with her finger to get the last of the water. The cup in her hands was real. She held it, felt it, and then settled down to hold the cup delicately in her lap for hours.

* * *

"Zoe? Zoe? Is this you?" Jenny hung on to the phone, wishing hard.

"I'm sorry? Is this Jenny Weston?" The voice on the line was hesitant.

Jenny realized she'd made a mistake. The woman's voice sounded nothing like Zoe's.

"Yes, I'm Jenny Weston. I thought you were someone else." She hurried out of the bank to her car.

"I'm Constance Proust. It seems you've been leaving me a message every half hour or so." Her voice was cool.

"Oh, Miss Proust. I'm so happy to hear from you. I've been calling about . . . well, about the time you worked at the Traverse City State Hospital."

"Really?" There was almost humor in her voice. "I suppose you're a writer. A historian. And you want me to give you a lot of salacious detail about my time there."

"No, it . . ."

"I'll tell you right now, I'm not interested. Those people there were my friends. When they closed the hospital, I worried about many of them. It wasn't an easy life, you know. Some still needed some form of structure, but the state abandoned them. That's all I can tell you. Abandoned them."

"You don't understand. I need to talk to you about Myrtle Lambert. She says she was a patient there."

Constance Proust said nothing for a while. "Myrtle's one of the patients I'm proudest of. She's got her own restaurant in Bear Falls. Very successful. You won't be getting a bad word out of me about her."

"That's not it." Jenny was afraid she was losing her, and fast. "Please call Myrtle, if you don't believe me, but she's the one who gave me your name. I live in Bear Falls. We have a problem here and . . ."

"I'll call Myrtle. If she says I can talk to you, I'll call you back. If you don't hear from me, please don't call this number again."

Jenny heard Constance hang up and felt as if she was slipping off the edge of a cliff. Who else was there to turn to for the information? No public records. No one else she knew that had been in the hospital with Myrtle and Lorna. And if she could find someone, she wouldn't contact them. She could only imagine how anyone would feel, being asked about another patient after all these years, when maybe they'd put the hospital behind them.

Oh, where was Zoe when she needed her? Jenny moaned as she drove home.

Jenny didn't leave the house all day. She waited for Constance Proust to call back.

She sneaked in another call to Zoe, but the phone rang and rang.

She got the sinking suspicion that Myrtle had said no, that Jenny had no right calling anybody about her.

It was almost six o'clock. Dora came in with a bag of groceries, set the bag on the table, and declared that she was still worn out and dinner would be canned soup.

"Zoe call?" she asked, then shook her head when Jenny said no. "I think we'd better get over there and at least leave a note on her door. This isn't like her. She's not the kind to make people worry. At least not her friends."

Jenny was about to agree when her phone rang.

"Jenny Weston?" the woman's voice demanded. "This is Constance Proust. I spoke to Myrtle. She says you're as good as anybody to talk to."

"Yes," Jenny hurried to nail her down. "It's about Emily—or maybe Lorna—Sutton, a patient Myrtle says she knew."

"I won't talk to you over the phone about anything having to do with a patient. I don't know if you are recording this or not."

"Believe me . . ."

"Well, I won't," Constance said. "I will meet you at the hospital tomorrow. I have to go to Traverse in the afternoon. Two o'clock would be fine."

She went on to describe where they should meet, in the building where she used to work, and how to get to there. And then she lowered her voice and asked what kind of car Jenny drove.

"Please park in front of the building I described. We'll talk there. And Jenny," she said before hanging up, "if the woman that you want to know about is the one I remember . . . I can tell you plenty."

Chapter 29

"I'll knock," Jenny said, going up the front steps of Zoe's house.

"Yes, you do that, dear. I'll look in the window, see what I can see."

Jenny pushed the bell.

The response inside the house was immediate. A high, hysterical barking. Jenny's mouth dropped. Dora's eyes grew wide. They ran to the window, cupping their eyes to see into the living room. At first they only heard Fida, and then her panicked face was on the other side of the glass. She stood on the back of Zoe's sofa, running back and forth, then reaching out with her paws to touch the window, falling off the sofa, only to climb back up and bark frantically at the familiar faces.

They called Ed Warner. He was there in three minutes. He had the door open and stood out of the way as Fida raced out to jump on Dora, then Jenny, then Dora, then Jenny, and then even on Ed. Her happiness was unbound.

Jenny gathered her into her arms and endured face licking and ear biting while Ed Warner went inside to look around.

"Better stay out there," he turned to warn Dora, who was on his heels. "The dog's been in here a while. It stinks."

His smile, when he came back to the porch, was priceless.

"Nothing," he said. "She's not in there. But man oh man, that little dog's left her mark."

Ed called one of his deputies to get right over there.

Someone told someone they'd seen two police cars at the Zola house, and the word spread fast through town. Abigail was the first to arrive, offering any help she could give. Minnie Moon was there. Neighbors gathered on the sidewalk to watch and ask worried questions about their friend, Zoe Zola.

Tony Ralenti pulled his truck in front of the house, then ran up the grass, only to be turned away by Deputy Nash. He stepped back and yelled out Jenny's name.

She went running down the front steps to hold on to him, then tell him that Zoe was gone. Just gone.

"She'd never leave Fida alone." Jenny talked fast. "I've got to get back inside. They're checking fingerprints and want me and Mom to point out anything that looks wrong."

"I'll wait in my truck."

"Mom's in the house now calling Christopher Morley. We found the number in Zoe's office."

"That's her agent, right?"

She nodded. "He invited her to go to New York. Paid for the tickets. But it wasn't for a week or so, I thought."

By the time Jenny got back inside Zoe's house, Dora was hitting the button on her cell, hanging up.

She looked from Jenny to Ed and shook her head. "Christopher said the trip isn't until the week after next. She's not in New York, as far as he knows."

Jenny looked down into Fida's worried face.

"I told him Zoe's missing. He's very upset. Wants to get on the next plane and come out here to help search for her."

"Not yet," Ed broke in. "There'll be plenty of us out looking. Hope you told him to wait until he heard from us."

Dora nodded. "I did, but I'm not sure that alone will keep the man away."

The crowd, gathering out on the lawn, grew. Cassandra heard and rushed over, as did the other cashiers from Draper's. Demeter and Delaware came over for a moment, but Delaware was on her way to the restaurant, and Demeter had to go shopping for Myrtle, who was out of vanilla extract and distressed about it.

People from the stores along Oak Street showed up. Everyone postulated places Zoe might have gone. They talked about her poor dog. They mentioned strangers they'd seen in the neighborhood and guessed where she might have been taken.

Ed called Detective Minty and waited fifteen minutes for Minty to call back. Minty thought nobody should push the panic button, not yet. "Maybe she went off to think. Don't writers do that?" he asked.

"Not without her dog," Ed said.

"Her car is gone. Let's get neighboring departments to start checking the roadsides."

Ed gave him the make, model, and color to look for and hung up. Minty would get the license plate number.

Abigail raised a hand to put in her two cents. "Isn't Zoe still shopping for Emily? If you ask me, Emily might have been one of the last people to see her."

Tony offered to go to Emily's and ask when she'd last seen Zoe.

Ed said he'd send a deputy, then remembered Deputy Swenson was over at the high school. There'd been a fight at an early football practice.

"Go," he said to Tony and Jenny. "See if she'll answer her door. It's pretty late. If she does, just ask if she's seen Zoe. Don't enter the house or go anywhere else on the grounds. If you think there's cause for worry—that Zoe might be there, or might have wandered out in the swamp—I'll take it from there. As a citizen, you know you can't force your way in anywhere."

"Let's go." Jenny reached for Tony's arm.

* * *

The jar in the room was full, which gave Zoe something to worry about. It was almost a relief to have something to obsess over. Thinking about nothing but dying in this place was getting dull.

She sat with her back to the wall, picking at her finger-nails and waiting for Emily to come back to the other side of the wall. Back to that place where food and water were being pushed through to her. A rat hole between the rooms; a half circle chiseled through the drywall from the other side.

It was a ritual now, to wait for the knock. She would crawl to the hole. If it was daylight, and sunny outside, there'd be enough light through the hole to guide her so she didn't have to feel along the wall.

When Zoe sat in front of the hole, her hands out to take the food and water, she would say, "I'm here," and a cup of water and a sandwich or a pack of vegetables would come through, and Zoe would grab them both up and drink and eat as fast as she could.

From time to time, she tried talking to Emily. She told her she should be getting home soon. Fida was alone. She tried to laugh. "You know how dogs can be. She's going to be pooping everywhere. And she's probably hungry . . ."

That's as far as Zoe got. The thought of Fida alone and waiting broke her heart. If there were only a way to get a message out to somebody.

How long had she been in here already? Three days?

"Emily?" she bent down, trying to get one eye to the hole. Dark on the other side, too. But she could make out outlines of things. A pair of feet in slippers stood close to the wall.

"Yes." The word was whispered from the other side.

"I was wondering when you were going to let me out of here. I've got a lot of things to do in my garden."

"I'm sorry to hear that," the wispy voice came back.

"Can you tell me?"

"I wish I could . . ."

There was the sound of footsteps, and the slippers were gone.

"Emily?" Zoe called with her mouth directly at the hole. "Emily?"

She moved to the opposite wall and sat down to be very still, as if in stillness there were thoughts enough to get her out of there, some magic she hadn't come on yet. If she thought and thought, she'd think of something. There had to be a line of *Alice's* that would work. Maybe a poem in her head from Emily Dickinson. Didn't she, after all, close herself up in the family home for years, too?

She searched and searched, trying line after line, then crawled back to the wall and whispered, in case she might be in there, "Emily? Emily? Did you know a lot of your poetry approaches what Emily Dickinson wrote about?"

There was shuffling on the other side and then the quiet voice said, "Not any more. I wouldn't dare."

* * *

Neither Jenny nor Tony said a word as they drove toward Thimbleberry Street.

Once Tony asked, "Ed check the hospitals?"

"First thing," she said.

"Accidents?"

"His deputy checked."

"How about relatives?"

"None that she would visit."

He pulled to the curb in front of Emily's house and shut off the motor. They sat looking at the dark house for a minute.

He helped Jenny out of the truck. She was exhausted, mostly from worry. She held his arm as they went through the gate and up the steps.

Tony knocked but no one answered.

He knocked again and again, harder each time, hoping to anger Emily into opening the door, threatening to call the police. Anything was better than leaving with the hole Zoe'd dropped into still yawning around them.

They went back down the steps and around one side of the house. They rapped at the windows, then went around to the back of the house, where there were no windows and the door—leading to nowhere—was boarded over.

"You hear music?" Jenny asked, her head tipped.

He nodded. "She's got the radio on."

"She's in there," Jenny said, looking around the yard at an abandoned chicken coop, two dilapidated sheds, and one old garage. "She's ignoring us."

"Could be she's just not home."

"I don't believe it," Jenny said. "This gets worse and worse." She moaned. "Another one gone missing."

They headed out to Tony's truck.

"She'd better answer in the morning." Jenny gritted her teeth as she climbed in beside Tony.

"She will. Ed'll get her to open that door."

Jenny shivered and rubbed her arms. She looked over her shoulder at the house and shivered again.

* * *

After the terrible knocking stopped, there was the squeak of furniture being dragged across the floor. Zoe held still, analyzing the sound as she did every sound that came from the other room.

Emily was dragging something. She wondered what the sound could mean. Zoe listened hard. It was a sound she couldn't place. She felt like a blind person must feel, she thought, then listened again. This time for a sound that meant the rat hole was being closed and she'd be left to starve.

"Emily?" She put one eye down to the hole, trying to see what was going on in there. There was yellow light, as if from a lamp. She put her lips closer to the hole to call softly, not wanting to frighten Emily away. "Are you there?"

"Yes." The whispering voice came back at her.

Zoe saw the outline of a slipper.

"What are you doing? I heard something."

"I'm moving my table closer to the window. The days have been so dark."

"What are you writing?"

"Poems, of course. I need three more for the reading."

"I'm sorry you're in that little room," she went on. "It's very small. My mother used to keep canning jars and crocks in there."

"It's dark, too. And I have no place left to go to the bathroom."

"Terrible. I'll see what I can do."

"Could I go home? I'm assisting at the reading. Remember?"

"I . . . I don't know . . . I'm so sorry. It seems such a terrible way to treat the woman who brought me that wonderful poetry. Poems in code. I've read it again and again."

"Yes, that was me. You remember! Good."

There was a noise, a low grunt, and Emily was gone.

* * *

Jenny drove the curving streets leading to the state hospital.

Cars were parked everywhere. It was Saturday; people gathered for the farmer's market and the shops. They hurried in and out of the buildings. Cars moved slowly ahead and behind her.

The building where Nurse Constance said to meet her had not been renovated. It sat in a field of cut grass. The walls were blank and peeling. There were broken windows. A squat turret sat at the top—not a pretty building. More utilitarian. Ugly.

Jenny was early, hers the only car parked in front of the unused building. She got out and walked up on the porch and looked through the window. An empty room. Fallen plaster littered the floor. There were scribbles on the walls that she couldn't read from where she stood, but could imagine. The room was painted to match the outside of the building, a pale shade of cream, paint peeling in long streamers from the walls.

There was no color anywhere but the institutional cream. The room she looked in on might have been antiseptic if it had been clean. Pipes ran up the walls. Rust drew lines from an open transom above the door.

She ran her hands up and down her arms, imagining being confined in such a place. Confined the way Myrtle was, her brothers scheming to get the restaurant by having her committed. A few lies to a doctor. A bonus to a friendly lawyer.

But not Emily. Myrtle had to be wrong.

"Miss Weston?" She jumped at the voice behind her.

She turned to a very tall woman, flat chested, square bodied, in brown slacks and a brown blouse. Her short brown hair showed gray at the temples. She stood with her hands in front of her, closed over the handle of a square brown purse. Her feet were spread to hold her steady in the damp grass. She wore low-heeled pumps. The fact that the shoes were brown instead of white did nothing to diminish her authority and power: The nurse to whom all requests were made, all messages passed. The nurse with the quieting medications if a person was in too much misery.

Jenny nodded.

"Nurse Proust," the woman said. She didn't hold her hand out. It was a statement. "I wanted to get a look at you before we talked."

"Did I pass?"

"Evidently," Constance said. "I'm here."

The woman flustered Jenny. Jenny went through the ritual of offering to buy coffee, suggesting they go to Java Joe's so they could sit and talk.

"We'll talk right here." Constance indicated the place where they stood. "Myrtle said to tell you everything I know about the woman." She paused. "Stole my car, you know." She nodded. Her hair didn't move. "I had to go myself to find her and bring her back."

"Are we talking about the same person?"

"Emily. Yes. A troubled woman." She narrowed her eyes and nodded. "Always one scheme or the other. And she liked the men, if I remember right. Had to keep her locked in her room at night or she'd wander the halls." The nurse cleared her throat. "May I ask what this is about? Was Emily a relative of yours?"

Jenny shook her head. "A poet."

Constance threw her head back and laughed. "Not our Emily. So what else can I help you with?"

"There've been some problems lately."

"Nothing to do with the poor soul found murdered here in Traverse City, I hope. A friend told me about it."

"I'm not sure if there's a connection."

"Then?" Constance Proust began to look annoyed. "You said it was important."

"I know. I appreciate your meeting me. I need to know more about Emily. I'm not sure she's the one . . . I don't want to cause trouble over nothing." Jenny took a deep breath. "Did she have red hair?"

"No. Brown. Plain brown."

Jenny nodded, feeling at least she'd come up with this much.

"But you realize, Miss Weston, I haven't seen her in twenty-seven years."

Jenny reached into her pocket and brought out a copy of Zoe's folded picture, one she'd copied from the state hospital book. She handed it to Constance.

She looked at the blurred photo, frowned, then smiled and handed it back. "That's Myrtle and Emily."

"Emily Sutton?"

"I don't remember last names. You realize we had many patients."

"You know Myrtle's."

She made a face. "Myrtle and I are friends. We stay in touch. Sorry. I have to go now." Constance stepped away. "I hope I've told you enough to help."

Jenny thanked her for her time and walked back to her car while Constance Proust headed off in the other direction. Myrtle was wrong. She hadn't been in this place with one of the Suttons at all. Emily with brown hair. It was an Emily distinctly different from Emily Sutton. That part of the mystery could be cut out. Myrtle's Emily Sutton was back to being strange, but probably harmless.

Jenny got in her car and rolled down the windows. She was about to leave when she heard her name called, and Constance Proust hurried back across the lawn toward her.

When she got to Jenny's open car window, she put a hand to her chest, fighting to catch her breath. "You got me thinking about the Emily in the hospital. Maybe this will help. I remembered something—maybe why that Emily was so hard to deal with. This should clinch it for you. She wasn't an 'Emily' at all. Not even on her charts. The odd thing was, you see, she wouldn't answer to anything but Emily. Even the doctors called her that—they wrote 'Emily' on her charts so we'd know who they meant. Call that one anything else and she would go straight into hysterics."

"Then she definitely wasn't Emily Sutton?"

The nurse thought hard "Oh, the Sutton part could have been right. I don't remember what her real name was. It's been years. All I know is, that person was only Emily in her own head. She stayed determined about that until the day she left." She smiled. "There, you've got your answer."

* * *

As if she'd done something right, a sandwich and a cookie were passed through the rat hole to Zoe that evening.

She nibbled at the chocolate chip cookie, making every bite last.

During the previous night—or what she imagined was night—the door had been unlocked and opened.

An empty jar was pushed through, as she'd asked, and the old jar pulled out. Zoe scurried on her hands and knees, reaching for the door, grabbing at the edge. She was too slow, or Emily was too fast. The door came within an inch of slamming shut on her fingers. She moved back and heard the lock turn.

Zoe closed her eyes. If yesterday had been Sunday, that meant today was Monday, and tonight was Emily's big night. No wonder she'd been writing as fast as she could in that other room, preparing work for her comeback. Zoe thought of the awful poem she'd read at Abigail's and prayed all of them would be that bad. She prayed that Emily would be exposed as a fraud. No talent. Maybe that was what brought her back to this house to begin with. Maybe she'd realized the spark she'd treasured was gone. Then it took twenty-five years for her to convince herself that she'd been wrong and begin to write again.

Zoe couldn't imagine why she'd been brought to this room. For finding the tarp-covered car? No, no, no . . . there had been bones. There'd been a shrine.

She would never leave this place. The secret in Pewee Swamp was too deep and terrible to come out. The car in the garage. That was probably Walter Shipley's car.

"My uncle loved that red car . . ."

The red car in Althea's driveway.

"He wouldn't go anywhere without that car."

Zoe let the random pieces in her brain fly, then form the only pattern the pieces could possibly form.

The bone she'd brought out of the water came back in another huge flash—a hand hanging above her head. She'd fallen into a grave, an important grave, marked with a circle of flowers and a wooden cross. She'd fallen into something so sacred, she had to die for knowing about it.

Now that she knew where Walter Shipley, and probably Lorna, were, she would never leave this place.

"Zoe?" Her name was called through the wall. And then again. "Zoe? May I read something to you?"

She lay still, exhausted from thinking.

She was going to die here and the woman wanted her to critique her work!

She crawled to lie down on her stomach and look through the rat hole. "Is it a poem? I'm not in the mood."

"Just tell me if it's bad enough. Could you do that for me? Sometimes I'm not the best judge of my own work. And it must be bad. Very, very bad."

Emily was serious. Something new was going on. Zoe closed her eyes and said a prayer. Maybe, in this new-sounding Emily, there would be an emotion she could plead with.

Emily cleared her throat. "I caught a toady in the grass. / It jumped and jumped at me. / I thought I'd squish him with my foot, / but pained by death, I set him free."

It was quiet in the other room. Then Emily asked, "Well, what do you think?"

"It's fine," Zoe said when she could spit the lie out of her mouth.

"Dear me. It shouldn't be fine. Listen to this next one: This house has rooms at the very top, / Rooms that lock with keys. / When I am closed inside a room, / I'm a specter no one sees."

Zoe could almost hear Emily waiting for a reaction.

"Well? What do you think?" The voice was stern, demanding an answer. "Wait, here's another one: Jealousy snares me in its claws. / Soon the one is two. / Together with my cloistered friend, / I await a taste of dew."

"Fine. Just fine," Zoe said, trying to recapture the words she'd barely listened to. *Cloistered friend! Is she writing about me?* Zoe asked herself.

"Do you think anyone will understand?"

"Oh, I'm certain of it. They are fine. Truly fine. Are you talking about me? Am I your friend? That's very nice."

"Fine! Fine! You have no taste at all, Zoe Zola. No taste at all."

Zoe had done the thing she feared the most. She'd given Emily Sutton a wrong answer. And like giving the wrong answer to the Queen of Hearts, there was only one possible outcome:

Off with her head.

Chapter 30

"I'm beginning to think she disappeared to spite me." Abigail stood in Dora's kitchen, talking to Jenny. "She knew I needed her help. Here we are, the event is tonight."

Abigail was beyond exasperation. There were dark circles under her eyes, as if she hadn't slept. Her clothes were wrinkled. She might have pulled them from the back of a chair and put them on. Her hair stood on end.

Jenny hurried to reassure her that she would handle Emily herself. That she'd get over there in the afternoon and see to Emily's dress and ask to take a look at what she planned to read.

"It begins at seven. I would get to her house at least by three o'clock. Elizabeth will pick her up and have her to the opera house by six-thirty. Is your friend, the Italian man, able to help? We have things to transport. Emily's come up with props she'd like on the stage." Abigail sighed. "I'm sorry, Jenny. I sound as if Zoe isn't the most important person we should be considering. I wish I'd never started with that woman. Emily Sutton doesn't deserve our concern. I pray she doesn't read what she calls her new poetry. I pray time will pass fast and all of this will be over. Most of all, that Zoe will be home safe and sound." Abigail closed her eyes and held on to the back of a chair. "In a few weeks, they're pulling my father's statue down. I promised a party for the town. I won't go back on that promise no matter what happens tonight."

"I understand." Jenny did understand how much Abigail wanted the whole thing over with. "I'll ask Tony if he can help," she said as Abigail got up to leave. "He's been out looking for Zoe these last few days, along with everybody else."

Abigail turned, her face drawn even more. "Then don't bother him. Please. Let's keep our minds on the important things. Emily Sutton and Joshua Cane aren't among them."

Dora, her arms filled with bags, walked past Abigail, who reached out to take her arm, stopping her in place. "Don't let me ever do a thing like this again, Dora. I'm worn to a frazzle. I'm nothing if not a glutton for punishment. First we have to get this Emily thing over with, and then I have to plan a party."

Dora wasn't happy. "If we don't find Zoe, Abigail, I don't think anyone will have the stomach for a party."

"Don't even say that. I have perfect faith she'll be home soon." She blew worry away with a flick of her hand. "She needed a few days to herself, no doubt. I completely understand the feeling."

And then she was in motion, turning to hurry through the house and out the front door.

* * *

Jenny would have been on time to pick up Emily but for Tony.

It was early in the afternoon when he came pounding up the front walk.

"Freddy from Freddy's Bait Shop just called Ed Warner. Ed called me. Freddy found Zoe's car not a hundred yards from his store, he said. Driven nose down into the swamp, hidden by underbrush, and half submerged in the water. I just came from there." Tony hit his chest to catch his breath.

"Was she in it?" Jenny asked but didn't want to hear his answer.

He shook his head. "No sign of her."

A relief. But what was next?

"Five days! I don't understand." Dora, holding Fida in her arms, patted her as fast as her hand would move. "Where would she have gone?"

"Ed Warner's thinking maybe she was dazed from the crash and wandered into the swamp."

"Oh no. Not five days in there," Jenny moaned.

Tony was about to say something, then snapped his mouth shut, letting the thought that it wasn't likely that Zoe was still alive hang in the air between them.

"What's the chief doing?" Jenny didn't dare take time to feel anything.

"He's got a wrecker there now. They're winching the car out of the water. I've been calling as many men as I can find, telling them to spread the word to meet up at Freddy's. We've got to form a search party and start looking."

"What can I do? I don't want to leave town." Dora shook her head.

"You've both got your hands full with the Emily Sutton thing. You go do what you have to do, and I'll call as soon as we find her."

"I want to help search." Jenny meant it.

"You promised Abigail." Dora's voice broke. "As long as Tony calls us . . ."

Tony put a hand on Jenny's arm. He leaned down to look into her eyes. "You can't go into that swamp anyway. Next thing we know, we'd be looking for you."

"Zoe did."

"Listen, trust me, if Zoe's in there, we'll get her out. And I'll call you as soon as we do."

Jenny nodded. Good sense wasn't attractive right then, but it was still good sense.

"I'm late now," she said, looking at her watch. "I'd better get to Emily's before she throws a fit."

She grabbed Tony's arm as he turned to hurry out.

"Call me. One way or the other. I mean it. I'll be going crazy until I hear."

Nobody asked what Jenny meant by "one way or the other." Everyone in the room seemed to know.

Jenny hurried back to her room and changed into the first dress she found in her closet. It wasn't the new dress. Not fancy. More summer than fall, but it didn't matter.

Speed mattered. Getting this thing over with mattered. Zoe mattered.

Minnie Moon stopped by to pick up Dora. She knew about Zoe's car and the men out searching in the swamp.

"Never saw anything like it," Minnie said, her wide eyes looking very scared. "Can't get that little person out of my mind. Wish we weren't going to this thing tonight."

Jenny delayed leaving the house for another half an hour, hoping Tony would call. He didn't. She put Fida into a bathroom with her food and water and with plenty of newspapers on the floor. She kissed the dog's head again and again, looked in her one good eye, and promised what she knew she had no right to promise: "We'll find her. Don't you worry. Zoe'll come home soon."

* * *

The shortest route to Emily's house was cordoned off by police cars with flashing lights. A few of the cars were Traverse City police cars. Jenny felt slightly better knowing that other departments had been called in. Maybe it wouldn't take any time at all. She could picture Zoe clinging to the top of a tree or sitting on a hillock of grass. Pictured her and prayed, then couldn't stop the tears, even as she laughed at the image of Zoe on a hillock.

She had to back up and turn around to take the other way, through town, over to Emily's house.

Jenny sprinted across Thimbleberry, being careful of a particular crack in the pavement where her heels could catch. She was up the sunken walk and standing on the porch, knocking, before she realized she'd expected more, here at the house. She'd got it into her head that the house would be brighter, the door might be open. Maybe the sun would shine through the windows and puddle on the carpets inside because the heavy curtains would be gone. She'd had a vision of reformation and deliverance. This was Emily's triumphant day. Something should be different. It was a disappointment that it was all the same.

She knocked again, then thought she heard an echoing tap from inside the house. But when she listened harder, she didn't hear it.

Jenny knew she should be getting angry. Even today Emily was being difficult and would come to the door whenever she pleased. But anger wasn't what she felt. It didn't matter to her how Emily indulged herself. No matter what she pulled, Jenny was going to wait.

She gripped the railings around the porch until her knuckles were white. She stared into the swamp. If anything, the underbrush was thicker now. The water was darker. For a minute she tried listening for a voice, then called out: "Zoe! Zoe!"

She listened with all her might. She'd been so sure she'd get an answer.

She called again and held still, trying to convince herself she heard an answering voice.

She heard birds. She heard leaves rattling.

She knocked at the door again then sat on the top step, though the back of her dress would probably get dirty and she'd walk around all evening with a smudged behind.

She waited.

A half hour went by. Thirty slow minutes. Jenny decided either there would be no reading tonight or Emily had gone ahead with someone else, afraid Jenny wasn't coming.

Which meant no supervising her outfit and no prereading of the work. She'd let Abigail down.

Jenny clamped her teeth together. "*Shit*," she whispered, reaching for her phone. She had to call Abigail and tell her Emily was loose, on her own. She had to call Dora. Maybe there was no reason for her to go to town at all. She'd failed at every job she'd promised to do.

"She's probably on her way now. My secretary was supposed to pick her up, but not this early." Abigail sounded neither hopeful nor too upset. Evidently she was willing to take anything that happened in stride.

"I'm not coming then," Jenny said. "There's nothing more I can do. I'm going to Freddy's to wait . . ."

"Please come into town, Jenny Weston. We need a ticket taker."

* * *

It was a long, slow drive to Traverse City, waiting all the while for her phone to ring. Jenny found a parking place down Union Street.

"Emily's here." Abigail ran to Jenny at the theater door, grabbing her by the arm.

"Have you seen her? What's she wearing?"

Abigail shook her head. "She's locked herself in the backstage bathroom. She says she will come out when she hears applause from the audience."

"But that's still an hour." Jenny checked her watch. "And who brought her?"

Abigail shrugged and hurried off.

Dora was next, running up to take Jenny's hand and pull her around to the front hall of the opera house to take tickets. "You've got the first half hour. Cassandra will take the next half hour."

"Who brought Emily, Mom? Do you know?"

Dora shook her head, then hurried off.

Jenny waited as a crowd gathered on the sidewalk in front of the building. An older woman she didn't know came down to join her. "It'll be a madhouse when they open the doors," the woman said, then leaned close to Jenny. "Have you heard the stories going around about her? Just awful. You'd never believe what people are saying. All these years of not writing and now—and I have this from a reliable source—her new work is terrible."

Jenny wanted to groan. All the worrying and time spent trying to make this one night a special time for Emily and she'd blown it herself. Or the gossips had blown it for her.

If she didn't have so much on her mind, she could be almost sympathetic.

When the doors opened at six thirty, people pushed in, swamping the ticket takers at the bottom of the stairs. When Jenny was relieved at the end of a half an hour, she headed up to the theater, then backstage.

Abigail stood outside the bathroom, looking off into space.

"Have you seen her?" Jenny demanded.

Abigail nodded absently, as if she wasn't there.

"Is she showing body parts?"

Abigail focused with difficulty. She nodded. "I don't really know if those are body parts sticking out here and there or if she's got a costume on under her flapping scarves. She's wrapped herself in blue with a red scarf around her head. Her makeup is . . . I would call it artistic, but I'm not feeling kind at the moment."

"Oh, no. Don't worry. People are here for the spectacle. She won't disappoint them."

"She's clutching sheets of her poetry in her hands. She won't let me see them."

"Where is she now?"

"She's on stage, supervising. She demanded that velvet chair—I got a shop in town to bring one over. Now she says her feet don't reach the floor. Dora's hunting for a footstool. She wants a floor lamp. Can you imagine? Now! The floor lamp must have fringe around the shade. Dora called around and found one. It's coming. If this night doesn't end soon, I'm going to choke the woman."

Chapter 31

Jenny walked through the double doors into the darkened auditorium, just in time to witness the thunderous applause and a standing ovation from the main floor to the balcony.

She stood at the back, inside the closed doors, as the small woman, only a dark shadow with gauzy scarves waving around her, came onstage. She walked quickly, in mincing Geisha steps, to the front of the stage where a spotlight caught her. Her head of blazing red hair, wrapped in an even brighter red scarf, was bowed. Her hands were clasped in front of her, as if in prayer. When she reached center stage, she stood very still, highlighted in that single spotlight. The crowd roared, then stood again to clap and whistle.

Jenny could see it on Emily's plain face. She sensed that she was a sensation; her return to life was being celebrated.

After a long dramatic pause, she lifted her face to the audience, then threw her arms in the air and bowed deeply.

The applause went on and on. Emily Sutton soaked it in.

It wasn't until the applause was dying and Emily wasn't moving that Abigail Cane came onstage and gently led her to the waiting chair. People noisily took their seats.

Before Emily was settled in her large red chair with a red footstool, a stagehand came out to clip a mic to her dress, or whatever it was she was wearing. The kid looked at her right shoulder, and then the left, mostly covered by veils. He opted for someplace in the middle, gathering a handful of chiffon and sticking the mic there.

Emily sat, now only lighted by the fringed floor lamp. She cleared her throat—which echoed out to every corner of the theater. She reached for the crystal glass filled with water. She drank, looked over the glass of water at her audience, flirted with them, then laughed as she set the glass back on the table.

"Thank you so much for the wondrous greeting. It's been a very long time since I sat on a stage like this." Her voice, at first, was weak. It seemed to come from a place as far away as Emily had been for so long.

She smiled to every corner of the audience and up into the balcony, though, even with no stage lights, Jenny doubted she could see anyone.

Emily settled herself, looked up, and smiled around again, then reached into the veils and chiffon. Out came—as if by magic—a handful of papers. It took some time for her to get settled, to get into a comfortable position, and finally she open her mouth and begin to read in sonorous, melodramatic tones:

Echoes in the house
Predict the universe.

Simple sounds that
Only death can know.

She finished reading to another standing ovation.

And on and on she read, until people clapped after each poem, but no longer stood.

She read awhile, then stopped to take a drink and smile. When she began each poem, she lowered her head to read in what soon became a monotone.

There was a thing in the whispering then raised voice that felt hypnotic to Jenny.

She stopped listening to watch the few faces in the audience she could see, those lit by wall lights. The rest was a sea of silhouetted heads. So many there for the poetry. Some, Jenny imagined, for the spectacle. She never would have thought a poet would draw such a crowd. But, though the poems were decades old, they resonated. Sometimes it was by a cluster of words, or with a string of sounds. Sometimes it was an image drawn far beyond the image's true existence. She read her death poem series, then her life poems. Jenny listened as the poems lodged themselves inside her head. She enjoyed herself more than she'd expected to.

In a few minutes, she checked her cell phone. She hadn't dared turn it off, but it was on vibrate.

She shifted from one foot to the other.

Eight fifteen and no call from Tony. One hour of Emily reading poem after poem. It was going beyond Jenny's attention span.

She wasn't alone. There were the growing sounds of moving chairs and coughing.

And then Emily stopped reading. Abruptly. Just like that. She put up both her hands at the clapping, stood and bowed, then bowed again. When the applause stopped, Emily went back to her chair and sat down.

"For the second part of my presentation . . ."

Her voice lilted over the words, as if playing with the people in the room.

"I will read new work. Some of these I wrote only today, especially for all of you who have gathered here to honor me."

There was an unenthusiastic smattering of applause, and Emily began again, a new batch of papers in her hands.

"I caught a toady in the grass. / It jumped and jumped at me. / I thought I'd squish him with my foot, / but pained by death, I set him free."

Emily looked up and smiled. The applause was tepid. Jenny figured people's hands were hurting by now, or the audience was half asleep, or they felt as she did: the poem was awful.

Emily was on to her next poem. Another bad poem.

Chairs moved and squeaked in places around the auditorium. A few people, bent almost double to escape, hurried from the darkened theater, sneaking by Jenny to go out through the doors.

Emily started another poem without waiting for applause, as if she had a mission to fulfill and would fulfill it no matter what happened.

She read faster, as more people headed for the doors, the glare from the outer hall flashing light into the darkened theater again and again.

Emily didn't stop reading. She didn't lift her head. She heard only her work, cocking her head to one side, enjoying herself.

Jenny was beginning to pity her. She wished she could start applauding loud enough to stop her—to get what was left of the audience to join in.

This house has rooms at the very top.
Rooms that lock with keys.
When I am closed inside a room,
I'm a specter no one sees.

Jenny listened with her eyes closed—imagining the place, the locked rooms. Odd. Why did it sound familiar, as if there was a message buried in the words? Nonsense, Jenny told herself. She was beyond the point of true response. She wanted to go home. She wanted Tony to call.

Emily read another.

Jealousy snares me in its claw.
A slurred pewee makes a call.
Soon the one of us are two.
Cloistered friends, we're held in thrall.

The new words circled inside Jenny's head. She saw a spinning wheel. *Where do you or it begin?* They'd brought Hannah Weiner's *Code Poems* to Emily, a gift from Amy at Horizon Books. And poems in shapes and Morse code. New ideas for Emily Sutton.

"*Soon the one of us are two—Cloistered friends . . . A slurred pewee makes a call.*"

Jenny pictured the house on Pewee Swamp. She'd heard the sounds. She'd watched as a curtain was pulled aside.

After waiting only another minute, she pushed through the doors to the lobby, rushing to find Dora and Abigail.

Abigail, wringing her hands, saw Jenny first. "She just ran off the stage," Abigail moaned. "Between poems she looked up and saw that the theater was empty. Poor soul. I don't know what to do. We don't know who brought her. How will she get home? Please help me find her."

They looked first behind the curtains at the back of the stage to see if she'd hidden herself. The stage manager said Emily Sutton had run out the stage door.

Outside the theater, on Front Street, the last of the parked cars were pulling away from the curb.

"We'll go out the back way. She could be there," Jenny said and drew Dora after her as Minnie Moon pulled up in her Jeep and rolled down a window. "You see Emily in that red car? Almost clipped me, pulling out like a bat out of hell."

Abigail waved her on. "We're looking for her now."

"Long gone, you ask me," Minnie said and drove off.

The theater lights went out. The building was dark and soon locked up tight. The three of them stood there, not knowing what to do.

"Minnie was mistaken," Abigail, exhausted, said. "It couldn't have been Emily leaving."

Dora's face was stricken. "Then where is she?"

Abigail looked up and down Front Street as the sidewalks emptied.

"Did you hear those poems?" Jenny turned to her mom. Dore nodded. "Strange."

"Remember Zoe and I bought her a book called *Code Poems*?"

Dora nodded.

"Emily read about the one being two. She mentioned the slur of the pewee. Cloistered friends. I'm thinking . . ."

Dora put a hand on her arm. "Do we know where Emily's gone? And where she's put Zoe?" Dora's eyes grew large.

Jenny nodded. "I think so."

There was no time to explain to Abigail, only time to say they had to get back to Bear Falls. Only time to get into Jenny's car and head north.

* * *

The drive home was endless. Lights along the side of the road barely moved, though Jenny was doing seventy. Dora made call after call, trying to get a hold of someone in Bear Falls to warn them. No one answered. Even the police station seemed to be closed. Myrtle's, which should still be open, didn't answer.

Dora called neighbors. After the third call she didn't bother any more. She settled back and watched the growing dark out the window and reminded herself to breathe.

At the turn from the highway, a roaring fire truck came up behind them, siren blaring, red lights strobing. Between the road and a ditch, there was little room to pull over. It took Jenny a minute too long to slow and pull off the road. The car bounced. The truck sped past.

She was back up on the road.

In town, she turned on Oak Street only to be forced over again as an Elk Rapids fire truck screamed past them.

311

People from the shops along Oak were out on the sidewalk, talking in knots and pointing. Some ran to their cars and followed behind the fire truck, forcing Jenny to slow and join the line behind the others.

"What's that?" Dora pointed ahead.

A faint glow lighted the horizon from time to time, as if from far off fireworks.

The cars ahead pulled off the road, parking on the verge next to the swamp, as close as they could get to where the fire trucks were pulled in at all angles. People ran along beside the road.

Jenny drove ahead toward the fire, slowly now so as not to hit one of the people cutting back and forth across the road. Ed Warner, directing traffic with a flashlight, waved Jenny back, then seeing who was in the car, pointed her to a place between the trucks.

The scene was chaos. Red lights flashed all along Thimbleberry Street. Men and women ran with hoses. Everyone yelled at once, arms flailing as men directed trucks and hoses and personnel toward the old Sutton house.

A fire chief yelled for help as Jenny and Dora got out of the car to stand beside it, taking in the wild scene. The fire chief was screaming out for men to hurry over to where he stood at the front gate. He pointed to the red car blocking the way in through the crooked gate. Men ran to push the car out of the way while other men took axes and hacked the picket fence to pieces.

"Where the hell's the tanker?" The chief, his eyes mirroring fire in the windows, yelled while waving to men with hoses over their shoulders to take up positions around the old stone house.

Jenny and Dora stood off to the side, hands covering their mouths, eyes wide as they saw curtains at the front windows of the living room go up in flames.

"There are women in there!" Jenny yelled to the fire chief, who nodded.

"That's what we figured." He gestured toward the red car. "You know where? Front or back?"

"I don't know." Jenny hollered at the man, whose face was red and perspiring.

He nodded as he waved a tanker into place near the swamp side of the house. He ran around to warn the men as their hoses were hooked up. Water streamed at the house from all angles. Hoses were refilled. The tanker pumped water from the Pewee. Firemen made it through the front door and inside the house.

Chapter 32

"Do you smell the smoke?" the nervous voice came through the rat hole.

Zoe was on her hands and knees. How could she not smell it? Her cubbyhole was beginning to fill with smoke.

"She's doing it again. She's had her gas cans hidden for years. She didn't know I knew."

"Knew what? Who started the fire?"

"Lorna."

"Lorna's back?"

"She never left. Except for those seven years."

"It's getting bad in here," Zoe said, coughing. "Is there any way to get out?"

There was a light laugh. "Of course. We aren't victims, are we, Zoe?"

"No, Emily. We aren't victims. I'll stand at the door. Please open it, now."

"I don't have the key."

"Please, Emily. We'll be burned alive."

Zoe moaned at what was going to happen. No way out. *Poor Fida!*

A pounding started on the other side of the wall. Emily ordered her to stand back.

Zoe heard the cracking of the drywall between the studs. Plaster showered her, so she had to cover her head with her arms and scurry away as chunks of the wall came down.

"Pound on your side," the order came through a widening hole in the wall. "I have a knife I'm cutting into the stud. I hope you're not too big, Zoe."

"You know what size I am." Zoe hit the wall angrily with her fists, then kicked near the bottom. The plaster cracked. But she wasn't strong enough to pull bigger pieces away.

Her throat burned. She inhaled the smoke edging into her prison from around the door.

Her eyes burned, made worse by the sweat running into them.

She pounded with both fists. She kicked with both feet.

She heard the sound of sawing from the other side, a steady back and forth rasp.

When the plasterboard broke into large pieces, she pushed them out until three studs were cleared. She could see the woman on the other side, squatting at her work; auburn hair swinging around her face as she sawed. She didn't stop, not even as she glanced up at Zoe.

It wasn't Emily Sutton. No bright-red hair. No large, dark eyes.

It wasn't Emily Sutton.

"My, you are a little one," the woman said and took Zoe's hand. "How lucky for you. We should have no trouble getting you out."

She pulled Zoe through the opening in the wall and across the room to the window, where the glass was broken out already. "I've signaled to the fire men. There's a ladder against the wall."

A voice from near the door surprised both of them. When they turned, the woman Zoe had thought was Emily stood there, a gas can in her hands.

"As if I'd let either one of you get away now." This Emily stood outlined in the doorway, the scarves she wore etched in golden light from the fire along the stairway behind her. Her hair was wild. Her eyes wide open. She smiled as she set the gas can to the floor.

"We'll wait together. It shouldn't be long."

She stepped daintily into the room, clasped her arms across her chest, challenging them.

"Stop it, Lorna," the woman beside Zoe ordered, then took a step toward her, only stopping when Lorna moved back and picked up the gas can.

"Oh, no, dear Emily. I'm through with you and all your poetry—nonsense in your head. I've always been the smarter one. The most talented. But you, a witch, you turned people against me as you built yourself into a star. Then you locked me away so the world would never discover my talent."

"I write poetry, Lorna. I never tried to outshine you."

"Well, you did outshine me. But look at us now. Which one will burn the brighter, do you think? Which one of us is the brighter star?" Lorna took a few more steps into the room with her neck stuck out, head in front of her body. Her lips were tight, straining open. "You. You. You. All about you. She never gave a thought to me, who I was, how I was far more talented than you. The best day of my life was when they found her bones."

She looked from her sister to Zoe. "This will be the second best day of my life."

Zoe looked around for something to use as a weapon in case Lorna ran at them. She might as well die fighting rather than waiting to burn to death.

"You're dying, too," Zoe yelled at Lorna.

"Shut up!" Lorna screamed. "You wouldn't be here if you hadn't found Walter in the swamp."

"Let her go, Lorna," Emily pleaded. "She didn't know about any of the things you've done."

"She does now."

"Why Althea?" Emily edged in front of Zoe, pushing her closer to the window.

"She heard you up here one day. She wanted to know if that was you and then accused me of lying because I told her you ran away with Walter Shipley. She heard you and knew the truth. I shut her up with a story, but she called and gave me three days to produce you or she was going to the police. Three days! Can you imagine! She threatened me! Well, I fixed that one. No more threats. She didn't think I'd do anything about it. But I did." She smiled. "People have no idea how powerful I am."

"You've kept me here . . ." Emily began as she pushed Zoe to the edge of the window and motioned, with a hand behind her back, for Zoe to climb out to where the ladder rested. "I was the only one who knew what you did to Walter. I've paid. I'll die with you. We'll die here together. Just the two of us. Then everything will be over. And no one will know what you did to Walter because he didn't love you. And to Althea because she cared."

"She knows." Lorna pointed a shaking finger toward Zoe. "She'll tell everybody and . . ."

Lorna stopped. The staircase behind her fell away from the wall in a shower of sparks. A roaring wind swept into the room, and flames danced just beyond the door.

Emily fell back against Zoe, who was now climbing out over the windowsill.

Lorna picked up the gas can at her feet.

Zoe heard the sound of a man's voice from below, yelling for them to come out.

Emily's eyes focused on her sister as Lorna poured the gas out from the can. Gas trickled down Lorna's skirt of scarves. The scarves exploded into flames that ran up around her chest and then to the red scarf wound around her red hair. She was a whirl of flames and sparks and screams. Lorna Sutton became a torch, lighting the way for Emily as she pushed Zoe out on to the ledge, helping her hook one short leg around to get a foot on the ladder. Zoe held on to the ladder with everything she had. She took a step down, then another, while above her, the real Emily Sutton stepped out to the sill, to the ladder, out to safety as a man on the ladder grabbed first Zoe and then Emily and got them to the ground. The stunned and injured women were met with cheers.

Strong arms, and then many hands, grabbed on to Zoe and carried her away from the burning house. She was laid carefully on a stretcher. Someone slid an oxygen mask over her face. She breathed in the oxygen, then lifted the mask to cough. Her eyes were on the house. Flames licked through the roof.

"Zoe." Dora wound her arms around her and held on until Zoe groaned, pain crawling over her skin.

The voices of the men around them were louder now, calling to the firemen inside to come out.

The roof fell in. There were explosions from leaking gas.

The center of the house fell down into rubble. Empty windows framed dancing flames. The stone walls stood, but the interior of the house disappeared. Inside, a woman was already dead.

* * *

Zoe felt the painful jolt as the stretcher she was lying on rolled into the back of the ambulance.

She felt a cuff go around her arm and a needle prick her skin.

Once the ambulance was moving, Zoe let her head turn to the stretcher beside her. The woman, her plain face shining with tears, auburn hair loose and caught behind her head, was, like Zoe, swathed in white sheets.

Emily Sutton opened her eyes and turned her head. Above her mask, her eyes widened. Her hand moved. She wiggled her fingers, then reached across the narrow space between their stretchers, around an EMT, and took Zoe's hand.

Exhausted, Zoe held the hand offered her and fell asleep.

Chapter 33

They were both in the hospital for almost a week. Their hands were burned. For some reason, half of Zoe's hair was gone, though wiry fuzz was already growing back.

When they were released, still in pain at times, still stiff with healing skin, Emily came to stay at Dora's house, and the flow of visitors began—staunched at times when Jenny or Dora saw that their patients were tired.

"You look a lot skinnier." Minnie Moon bent down to stare closely at Zoe, propped on pillows in Dora's living room. Then at Emily, who lay on the sofa, covered with a white comforter. "Guess being locked up like that can do some good."

"I wasn't stuck in there that long," Zoe shot back. On her lap, Fida snapped out of a deep sleep to sit up, blink, and show her teeth, in case lethal force was needed.

"And anyway, Emily gave me half her food. I got on the scale this morning. Didn't lose a pound."

"That's too bad," Minnie cocked her head to one side. "Seems a waste if you can't even get that much out of an ordeal like you two have been through."

Minnie smiled shyly over at Emily and got up to leave, promising to come back the next day with one of her famous dump cakes.

Seven days since the fire. Lisa was on her way from Montana. Alex Shipley had been there from the night of the fire, sleeping in a hospital waiting room to stay close. For hours of every day, she sat beside Emily's bed, talking to her, though Emily, locked into a dark place, hardly responded. Until one afternoon on the fourth day, when Emily reached out and touched Alex's face.

"He talked about you," she said, and smiled.

They cried together and, over the next few days, shared stories about the man they both had loved. Alex made arrangements for Walter Shipley's burial. The two of them planned for when Emily was well, and strong. They were going to Maine together, to bury Walter in the place he loved.

She got up close in Emily's face, stepped back and, in a disappointed voice, said only, "That's not Emily."

Tony was there every evening, bringing CDs of old Italian ballads to soothe the injured women, and one night a dish of lasagna he'd made, he said, with a dose of Italian healing power inside.

Christopher Morley came from New York. He stayed over for two days while he sat beside Zoe, assuring her again and again that PBS was happy to change their meeting date, their only concern being Zoe's health.

"And my only concern, too." Christopher gave Zoe a gentlemanly bow and, once, a kiss on the forehead.

When he left, he promised to come back for Abigail's party in the park, with Abigail assuring him that he'd find the trip well worth his time.

* * *

Both women's burns healed slowly. They still coughed from smoke in their lungs. Zoe, with little hair on one side of her head, looked lopsided. Those were the obvious wounds. Jenny thought it was hard to know how much Emily had suffered. She was thin and lifeless at first. Three years of being imprisoned. Three years of solitary confinement—until, like a miracle, she said, she heard Zoe in the room next to her and knew she had to get them both out of there.

As the next days passed, Emily talked more and more: a woman finding her voice.

"I didn't know who she was, nor why she was there," Emily began one evening. "But having someone to talk to made me happy. One time though, Lorna slipped and called her Zoe. I remembered hearing Lorna say the name at the front door. When I'd asked, Lorna, always whispering so Zoe couldn't hear, said it was the same person who'd brought us books of poetry."

"What happened to .her?" Dora's voice was gentle. "Lorna?"

Emily looked off, away from the faces around her. "She wanted to be me. My mother warned me it was getting worse. Lorna's jealousy was out of control. That's why I came home. To watch her. To protect my mother. I failed.

"I called an attorney after the fire. I knew how it had started. I'd seen Lorna's gas cans hidden in the garage and thought nothing of it until the fire. I looked for those cans afterward but they were gone. The attorney promised to keep everything quiet—about the fire, about my mother. We didn't see any reason to tell the police, not if we could have Lorna put away where she wouldn't hurt anyone else. A judge signed Lorna's commitment papers. I had seven years of peace. Except for once, when she stole a car at the hospital and came home. I found her at the kitchen table, listening to the radio. A nurse came to get her.

"Thank you so much again, for the *Code Poems*." She turned, with an almost happy smile, from Zoe to Jenny.

"The poems you wrote saved your life. And Zoe's, too," Jenny said from where she sat on the floor next to Zoe's chair, Fida in her lap. "No one would have known you two were in those upstairs rooms if it hadn't been for the lines you wrote."

"Bad poetry, as bad as I could write, hoping people would know it wasn't mine. I had hopes for the 'slurred pewee' line. Maybe the 'upstairs room,' or the 'two of us.'"

Dora watched from the doorway, her arm around Lisa's shoulders. "I hope you make something beautiful out of this, Emily," she said.

"I've begun," Emily nodded. "My head's filling with words. First I have to polish them, then shape them, then march them into lines. I have to understand the story of Lorna and who she couldn't help but be." She narrowed her eyes. "I want to hunt for beauty, Dora. Maybe forgiveness—after a while. But mostly beauty. That's what I'd always wished for Lorna."

Epilogue

On Saturday, the fifteenth of October, Abigail Cane threw her party in Cane Park. The day was glorious: warm, with a deep-blue sky. All she could have asked for.

A recent rain made the falls at the edge of the park thunder through the rapids on their way out to Lake Michigan. In the park, the grass was still green. Park benches dotted the wide lawns. Tables were set up off to the side, away from the falls. Food was being spread along the tables. Myrtle, in a new green hat, along with Demeter and Delaware, set covered platters of sandwiches down the length of one table. On another, they set up salads—picnic fare, to Myrtle's way of thinking—potato salad, macaroni salad, and Jell-O salad, all lined up: one, two, three, red, yellow, and green.

One table was left open for desserts. Bear Falls women brought their specialties. There were upside-down cakes and chocolate cakes and cakes with fancy icings. There were two dump cakes. Apple pies. Peach pies. Rhubarb pies. Apple and peach crumbles. All fresh. Most just one step from the orchard. It was everything people expected on such a grand occasion.

Tony, Ed Warner, and two deputies set up chairs from the funeral home around the brick-paved circle that surrounded Abigail Cane's replacement gift, covered in a blue silk cloth, waiting to be unveiled.

Christopher Morley, back as he'd promised, walked Zoe and Jenny formally into the park, then settled them in chairs and offered refreshments from the bar set up not far from Joshua's statue, where two men were tying ropes around the head, the torso, and the legs.

Fida sat decorously next to Zoe and watched the townspeople gather.

Emily Sutton drove over with Alex, bringing Dora and Lisa with them. Lisa took up a place at the entrance to the park, handing out flyers announcing her new documentary coming to the Falls theater at Christmas.

Minnie Moon came with Deanna and Candace. Both were dressed as if for a tea party on the White House lawn. Dora leaned close to Minnie and remarked on how pretty her girls looked. Minnie beamed at Dora's remark and looked proudly after her two girls, who were headed toward the food table where the boys had gathered.

The crowd swelled. Women and men came up to Abigail and introduced themselves—her half brothers and half sisters, whom she'd never met before. A few women said they were the mothers of Joshua Cane's children, most with the worn look of women who'd led sad lives. None of them seemed to have much in common with the others. They stood off by themselves, as if not certain why they'd come at all.

"The moment," Abigail raised her hands, "has arrived. Every one of us is gathered here today because Joshua Cane is coming down. He is falling in my name and in the names of my two dead brothers, Aaron and Adam. And in the name of you, his other children, whom Joshua never claimed. And in the name of the women he tricked. For the people of the town he harmed in any way—ways that, after today, I never want to know about."

She raised her arms, stepped back, and signaled to the three men who lifted their ropes and pulled until the ropes were taut. Joshua Cane rocked on his pedestal. The men pulled harder. The statue fell. Joshua Cane's head snapped off and rolled into a ditch. His arms twisted off as his body hit the ground. The crowd watched. There were no cheers. There was no loud clapping. They all stood still, looking away from each other. Everyone turned when Abigail beckoned them to follow her to the other side of the park, where the chairs had been set up.

Chief Warner rang a bell and called out, "Let the older people sit in the chairs, kids."

He stopped boys from running to grab seats ahead of anyone too slow to beat them. Teenagers hung way at the back, pretending they didn't know a single adult there.

The time had come for the unveiling of Abigail's first gift to the town—before the restroom signs and cannonballs. She took Emily Sutton's hand and brought her to the center of the circle to stand with her beside whatever sat beneath the blue silk cloth.

"I want the Cane name associated with all that's best in our dear town," she called out, hushing everyone. "First, that will be a one hundred thousand dollar donation toward a new recreation center for our children. And second . . . this." She put her hand out toward the covered object in front of her. She put a blue silk cord into Emily's hand and told her to pull.

Emily pulled and the covering came away in billows. Beneath it was a fluted marble column. Atop the column was a large marble book held in marble hands.

"Please." Abigail waved Emily to stand in front of the book and read what was etched there.

Tony came up behind Jenny and held her close. Christopher Morley helped Zoe to stand on her chair so she could see and hear. Dora, Lisa, and Alex smiled at each other and moved to stand among the others as the crowd pulled in closer.

Emily Sutton put a hand on either side of marble book and read her poem to Bear Falls:

This Place We Live

Our mysteries are many.
Our flaws, unbidden, glare.
A child is never told her lot,
Nor her future time laid bare.

But we, the lucky, give our love,
Claiming only some in kind.
And beg that our unluckier kin
Be better blessed in time.

Let the neighbors in this place
Forgive, forget that hatred flared.

Let the fires die, the wounds be healed.
Let childlike awe be shared.

This time the deafening applause made Fida hug Christopher Morley's ankles, the only ankles she could reach. Zoe held on to Christopher's arm and beamed around at all the new people in her life. Jenny leaned back against Tony's chest and felt his arms around her, his head down next to hers. Dora and Lisa were at the marble column, reading the poem again as Abigail, arm in arm with Emily, led her from group to group, introducing her to her neighbors and new friends.